THE NAMES WE TAKE

TRACE KERR

OOLIGAN PRESS | PORTLAND, OREGON

The Names We Take
© 2020 Trace Kerr

ISBN13: 978-1-947845-16-9

Ooligan Press
Portland State University
Post Office Box 751, Portland, Oregon 97207
503.725.9748
ooligan@ooliganpress.pdx.edu
www.ooliganpress.pdx.edu

Library of Congress Cataloging-in-Publication Data
Names: Kerr, Trace, 1973- author.
Title: The names we take / Trace Kerr.
Description: Portland, Oregon : Ooligan Press, [2020]
Identifiers: LCCN 2019051785 (print) | LCCN 2019051786 (ebook) | ISBN 9781947845169 (paperback) | ISBN 9781947845176 (ebook)
Subjects: CYAC: Survival--Fiction. | Gender identity--Fiction. | Sexual orientation--Fiction. | Spokane (Wash.)--Fiction.
Classification: LCC PZ7.1.K50973 Nam 2020 (print) | LCC PZ7.1.K50973 (ebook) | DDC [Fic]--dc23 LC record available at https://lccn.loc.gov/2019051785
LC ebook record available at https://lccn.loc.gov/2019051786
Cover design – Des Hewson | Interior design – Chris Leal
References to website URLs were accurate at the time of writing. Neither the author nor Ooligan Press is responsible for URLs that have changed. Printed in the United States of America

For Dane.
Without you this story would be nothing
but a jumble of lost words.

CHAPTER 1

Purple gondolas hung above the river like a cluster of grapes at the end of the growing season. Just downstream, a froth of mist boiled from rapids cascading under the concrete span of the Monroe Street Bridge. Even the second floor of the library vibrated with the water's thunder. Pip rested against a bookshelf and admired the ferocity. She could remember swinging over the falls in a gondola when she was little, laughing at the idea of danger.

Now she knew better.

Danger was the feeling of hunger eating you from the inside out: a tickle in the back of your throat, a virus racking your body with coughs. She cringed at the memory of people hacking their lives away in overfilled hospital rooms.

It was quiet as death in the library, and Pip relaxed into the silence with a sigh.

Quiet meant safety.

She tucked a thick book into her backpack and cinched the top. It had been a year since One Mile Cough slaughtered her old life. One year since she'd read anything other than instructions: how to use a camp stove, how to reheat a pack of freeze-dried food, how to clean a wound. Her hands trembled at the thought of reading an honest-to-God book.

Now her pack was full of them. A belated present to herself. Her March birthday had been lost in the last bite of winter. She'd turned seventeen and missed it. Pip flopped her pack onto the floor and used it like a pillow. Pressing her ear against a hardback book inside the pack, she looked over the city of Spokane. Rising above basalt columns of rock lining the shore, a pall of black smoke dropped the ashes of the houses that burned onto those that hadn't. Ash filled the air with black flecks; they floated like birds in the windy up-currents over the river.

The Spokane River split the downtown right in half. Six bridges spanned the rush of meltwater. Trees blooming with the first flush of spring edged paths that wound through a vast riverfront park where Pip used to hide and sleep at night. A large mall and swanky shops competed for space on the same side of the city as the library. They hugged tight to the riverfront.

Going north or south from downtown meant heading uphill. The expensive homes of the South Hill neighborhoods—built in the 1800s—watched over this side of the river. On the other side, older businesses and rougher neighborhoods crawled down to the water. But One Mile Cough hadn't been thwarted by geography. Both rich and poor alike had died, piled together in mass graves.

Pip glanced back at the water.

Keep your eye on the river, she thought. *Pretend it's just an ordinary day. A regular day of living on the streets and coming into the library to sit in a comfy chair and read. Not the nightmare of surviving One Mile Cough.*

Metal rattled against stone. Pip sat up. It sounded like someone was on the first floor.

Footsteps echoed up a long set of stairs, and she instantly regretted agreeing to Whistler's idea "to do something fun for once." Crawling to the end of a curved bookshelf, she dragged her pack along the floor and peered around the corner.

Too many shelves in the way.

She also regretted putting herself in a space with only one way out.

An out-of-tune-wind-chime crash of metal against metal set her pulse racing. Someone was climbing through the ragged hole sawed through the security gate. A chopped-away section of the gate hung loose, dangling low enough to clatter against the floor. The hollow clunks of metal banging against the tile entryway got lost in the sound of a rude laugh.

"You're too fat for the hole," a woman chuckled.

"Shut it, Navvy," a deep voice grunted.

A chorus of mean laughter bounced around the open spaces of the second floor, snapping at Pip like little dogs. She used the noise to cover the rustle of her backpack straps slipping over her shoulders. Palms sweating, she moved along the line of shelves and chanced a look. A sickly-pale white woman and two white men carried plastic milk crates into the how-to section.

Literary fiction took up most of the right side of the library. How-to was farthest from the entrance, all the way in the back. She counted herself lucky as they disappeared into the stacks. The young adult area where she'd hidden herself was filled with a maze of chest-high bookshelves used to enclose a reading nook. It made for tons of places to hide. And the newcomers were noisy.

She slipped between two close-together shelves and moved at a steady creep, hunched over to keep her pack from peeking over the stacks. What she wouldn't give for the protection of Whistler's automatic rifle, *But no,* she thought, massaging a cramp forming in her calf, *today just had to be his day to start an art project.*

Another laugh came from the how-to stacks, and Pip belly crawled to the end of the last shelf for a clearer view. Between her and the ragged hole in the security gate was a stretch of open floor past the checkout desk. The crash of a milk crate full of books hitting the floor almost sent her bursting into a run, flushed like a hunted bird.

She gasped, covering her mouth with a hand that smelled like the dusty calm of books. She inhaled long and slow.

"How many of these do you want?" the young guy who'd dropped the overfilled crate shouted.

Indistinct mumbles answered his question. The bigger man, the brunt of the fat joke, set his half-filled crate down and shuffled some books from the other crate, evening the load.

"Damn it, Curtis. If it shifts in the truck and makes a mess, Navvy'll beat your ass."

The big guy wore a greasy camouflage jacket unzipped over a rounded gut. Even though his clothes were dirty, he looked cleaner than most. Like he'd bathed recently. Pip's nose wrinkled in disgust. The camo guy was probably a trader, someone with resources and access to soap. Which meant he wasn't a good guy. After the devastation of One Mile Cough, anybody with anything worth having probably took it from someone else. They were here to take and wouldn't care who got hurt.

She had to assume at least one of the three was armed. Most people carried weapons, or they didn't survive long. And her metal bat couldn't compete with a gun. The distance to the exit suddenly felt a lot farther. She settled into the floor and hoped for invisibility.

"This is stupid. Who'd want to learn about bees?" Curtis's voice had a nasal quality, probably from the giant kink in his nose. It took a hard right on his face. Somebody'd punched him and really put some effort into it.

"We're grabbing anything people might want to trade." Camo guy waved a book about gardening in Curtis's face. "If you think you're going to leave the Skins and start working for me, you'd best learn to start using your brain."

Pip gave Curtis a once-over. The Skins were a group of ragged boys running wild through Spokane, terrorizing everyone who crossed their path. Curtis even wore their signature haircut. He'd buzzed his hair so the pink of his sunburnt scalp gleamed through blond stubble.

Curtis hocked and spit on the library carpet. "The house wasn't my fault."

The teasing smile melted off Camo's face. "Setting the fire was stupid." He waved toward the wall of windows behind Pip. "Half the town's burnt up."

"We got three girls—"

"You ladies done with your tea?" The pale woman who'd followed them into the library poked her head out of the stacks. She was much closer than Pip would've liked. "Hurry up, this place gives me the creeps."

"Watch out, Navvy, the books, they're comin' for ya," Camo taunted.

She flipped him off.

Pip rose to her knees, preparing to run. She couldn't risk being seen. It would be three against one. Who knew what they'd have in mind?

Curtis tripped over his feet and Navvy shoulder-checked him. Pip closed her eyes, gathering courage while books tumbled off shelves.

"Better shape up, Curtis," Navvy said. "I might send you along."

"To where?"

"Wouldn't you like to know?"

"Nav," Camo muttered.

She crossed her arms, sticking a bony hip out to the side. "Thistle Hill wants mostly women and kids. Only a *few* men." She sized up Curtis. "Men. Know what they are?"

Camo snorted and slapped Curtis on the chest, knocking him against the metal shelves a second time. "Tell the Skins we need a few more before we leave. You do that and you can join up."

What are they talking about? Are they stealing people?

Adrenaline buzzed along Pip's nerves. The sour tang of fear coated her mouth. Twitching muscles screamed for her to run. On the verge of breaking, she forced herself to wait until all three of them turned their backs.

Now or never. She stood and sprinted to the gate. Grabbing the edges of the hole, she tore through the gap. A strap on her pack caught on the uneven cuts of metal. She yanked her pack out of the ragged tear in the security gate and raced for the stairs, catching the railing with one hand, sliding onto the first step.

She was so busy watching her footing, she didn't see the man standing openmouthed with shock at the avalanche of girl coming down the stairs. They hit the floor in a tangle. Her pack hit him square in the chest; the stink of him blew across her face. Pip left him gasping like a fish as she dove through the broken glass of the library's front door.

Where she'd left an empty street, a yellow moving truck and a motorcycle now waited at the curb. She cautiously jogged around the truck and sprinted all out toward the river, sliding to a stop behind a statue of Abraham Lincoln. The statue rose above the ground on a wide concrete pillar, standing watch over the Monroe Street Bridge from across an intersection.

Pip looked up at the vague smile on Abe's metal face. The remains of a knit scarf hung around his neck. Knitting. That's what had gotten her into this mess: Whistler and his stupid urge to scavenge through the yarn store a few blocks north of their home.

Wind tossed her short hair and lifted the faded tassels of Abe's scarf. The tassels waved like flags, the ends snarled from months of snapping in the wind. A ratcheting sound, unfamiliar and almost forgotten in a year of mostly quiet streets, caught her ear. There was another clank, and then the stuttery lawn-mower rattle of an engine barking to life. The buzz of cylinders increased in tempo as the motorcycle's engine burned more gas.

"Shit."

The guy she'd clobbered coming out of the library raced past on the motorcycle. Shifting gears, he accelerated into a left turn away from the river and tore down the next block with a roar. Pip exhaled relief. He hadn't seen her.

She studied the bridge crossing the Spokane River as she unloaded a few handfuls of books from the pack to lighten the load. The bridge stood four lanes wide, its stone and concrete aged to a soft gray. Upstream, waterfalls threw off a haze of fog, blending into the smoke from the burning houses.

Buckling her pack into place, Pip took a wary step out of cover, onto the open road. Her stomach clenched as she moved to the hip-high railing bordering the bridge's pedestrian path. She was exposed, a vulnerable target. The traders from the library could be anywhere. She broke into a jog, ducking low behind the railing.

Two prominent concrete alcoves separated the bridge's span into thirds, standing like sentinels on guard against the river's spray. Each alcove was a concrete enclosure the size of a small bedroom. They arched over the pedestrian walkway to hide people inside from view. She was determined to keep moving until she reached the shelter of the first alcove. Braving this much exposure in broad daylight had all her nerves on high alert. Her back muscles jerked as she ran, anticipating the piercing slap of a bullet.

Inside the protection of the first alcove, she slid to a stop next to a concrete bench built into the wall and crouched there, body vibrating with adrenaline. She forced herself to hold still and check her surroundings, hoping she hadn't been discovered.

This close to the waterfall, she couldn't hear the rev of a nearby engine. She'd have to make a dash for it anyway. Trusting the way was clear, she burst from the other side and raced over the middle span of the bridge.

The pavement was waterfall-spray slick, but Pip didn't hesitate. Her feet flew over damp gravel and trash as she cast a frantic look behind her. Up ahead was the second alcove. Pip slid to a stop inside it, hissing in pain as the books shifted in her pack. She huddled as close to the concrete wall as she could get and scooted forward to peer out the front.

Sweat prickled along her scalp. She scrubbed at the itch and inhaled a deep, smoky breath that felt gritty in her lungs. To her left were the newest apartments in town, completed right before the virus's outbreak. Now they were ruled by the people who once lived in tent camps on the banks of the river. Their number was small, maybe thirty people, but the residents of Kendall Yards wouldn't bother with her when she stepped off the bridge. They kept to themselves. Even the Skins seemed to avoid the swanky apartments with their artsy sculptures and stunning views.

To the right, on the other side of the road, a YMCA and a funeral home were the biggest buildings on the hill. That same hill led her to the music store, where she lived with Whistler. It was just a matter of getting across the bridge and leaving the motorcyclist and the traders far behind. Only a little over a mile up the road to safety.

After she reamed out Whist for his stupid idea to take a day off, they'd celebrate another day of not dying with cans of soup and pie filling. Energized by the thought, she took one last look behind and choked on a startled scream. A kid's dirt-smudged face stared out from a greasy pile of blankets on the bench. Pip lurched away from the mummy-blanket kid and tripped over her own feet, landing in a heap on the bridge path.

"Wait!" a high-pitched voice croaked.

Pip whirled around for a second look. The kid's face was covered with red welts and a thick layer of soot.

Mind reeling with surprise, Pip almost shouted. "What are you doing here?"

The kid cringed.

"It isn't safe. There's a guy out there on a motorcycle trying to catch me."

The kid stared back, their pupils dilated wide into giant circles of terror. Reaching for any excuse to look away, Pip peeked over the low guardrail. She swore as the roar of an oncoming motorcycle pierced the thunderous torrent of the falls. The sound was too close.

"Time to move." She grabbed a handful of blanket and tugged. "Can you run?"

The kid's only response was a blink. Pip knew they must be paralyzed with fear. Hating herself, she delivered a quick slap to the kid's cheek. Their brimming eyes only stared. Tears tracked through the soot on their face, making rivers of clean on blackened cheeks.

"Can. You. Run?" Pip asked again. She leaned close, speaking through clenched teeth. "If you won't, they'll take you."

The kid nodded. Pip seized a double handful of blanket and dragged the kid off the bench. They tumbled off in a heap of fabric. Pip wasted no time pushing them against the wall of the alcove to rip the stinking blankets away. The kid's clothes reeked of campfire. Pip dumped the blankets onto the bench and pulled the kid to the far end of the alcove, away from the approaching motorcycle.

"Stay down," Pip instructed.

Roaring onto the bridge, the man swung his bike in a tight circle midway over the span, spraying trash over the side. He revved the engine—the sound rang in Pip's ears like a warning. She crossed her fingers that he wouldn't notice them as he looked around. The bridge's curve hid her and the kid, but it was almost two blocks of open space to cover. If they bolted, he'd be sure to run them down.

She grabbed the kid's shirt between their bony shoulder blades, clenching her fist tight on the slippery fabric. With her free hand she drew an aluminum bat from a pocket on the outside of her backpack.

"When I say 'go,' you're gonna run. Understand?"

Tears wound their way down the kid's face as they nodded.

The man popped the kickstand and launched off his bike. Pip held her breath while he walked to the guardrail on the far side of the bridge. He looked back the way he'd come before hopping over the rail. He walked toward the first alcove and vanished inside.

"Shit," Pip groaned.

He was checking the bridge. She grimaced and did a quick calculation. At this rate, he'd find her in no time. He was at least a hundred feet from his bike and out of sight.

Now or never, she decided. *Time to run for it.*

CHAPTER 2

She jerked the kid to their feet and shifted into a sprint, strides lengthening. The kid stumbled—Pip's hold on their shirt dragged them off balance. They moved so fast, the kid's feet only touched the ground every other step.

Pip started to hope. If the man didn't turn around, they might stand a chance.

The sudden roar of the motorcycle's engine flip-flopped her already-racing heart. Her legs straining with the effort, she scooped up the kid and tossed them inside a building's shattered doorway. Pip spun on her heels to face the vicious growl of the accelerating bike.

Life fast-forwarded in uneven blinks: the kid curled on yellowed linoleum, the motorcycle dodging around a crashed car, someone yelling incoherently. The kid's mouth sagged open as they stared up at Pip, reminding her of that painting with the screaming man.

Another blink: the motorcycle was close. The man riding it hollered over the noise of the engine for her to drop the bat. Pip took a running shuffle in front of the bike and it almost crashed as he swerved. She glimpsed his shocked face streaking past; then he peeled up the street to turn around.

Time to finish things before his trader friends heard the commotion and came running like wolves smelling blood. Shrugging off her backpack, Pip heaved its bulk into the bike's path and gripped the bat tight in her fists. The motorcycle skidded, tires squealing. The man yelled for her to stop and raised a gun, aiming it right at her. He fired an instant before Pip swung.

Her ears rang with the boom of the shot. Agony blazed along her side, folding her in half. She barely noticed the pain of the bat yanking out of her hands. The man flipped backward off the motorcycle and crashed to the pavement in a cloud of dust. His bike sputtered, coasting down the hill before it crashed into a wall on the other side of the bridge.

The man sprawled on the pavement, arms and legs twisted, like a broken doll. He'd landed on his side with his neck bent at a grotesque angle. A wave of nausea threatened to drag Pip under as she understood the damage she'd done. He was dead. Of that she was sure.

Grabbing her pack and slinging it on, she ran into the building and muscled the skinny kid off the ground. Pip moved with frightened speed, her heart thundering as she staggered through debris on her way back out. The kid's sharp chin jammed into Pip's throat when she hid their face from the sight of the man in the street. Loaded down with the extra weight of the kid, Pip scurried past the man's feet and into an alley.

After a block, the alley dead-ended on a street that paralleled Monroe. If she headed south, she'd be trapped against the river and farther away from home. North would take her into a de-molished neighborhood. If they went straight ahead and cut through the burning houses, she'd add a few miles onto her route to the music store and be sure that she didn't lead anyone back to Whistler. She wasn't thrilled with skirting so close to the fires, but maybe the library traders would feel the same way and let them go.

Smoke drifted lazily from nearby houses, filling the air with the rank scent of burning trash. There was no telling if the fire might turn with the wind and burn them as they ran. Pip stamped her foot, unable to decide. A clock was ticking; she didn't have the luxury of time.

"Go with your gut," she muttered.

Relaxing her grip on the kid, Pip set them down and flexed her fingers. She grabbed their hand and announced, "We're going straight."

They'd only taken a few steps when the kid transformed into a wild animal. Pip fought to hold on as they struggled to run the other way.

"What—" Pip said, protecting her face from their small, flailing hands.

"Can't go that way! CAN'T go that way!" they screeched and kicked.

Pip caught the front of their shirt. "Enough!" she roared.

Stunned into silence, the kid gaped at her, openmouthed.

"If you do that again—" Pip searched for something that would scare the kid into complying. "I'll knock you out and leave you. Understand?"

"...yes."

Pip surveyed the neighborhood. Maybe they could go another way. To the north, the homes were mostly burnt, and she *did* know the route better. Pip gave the kid a once-over, then warily let them go. Black hair stuck out from the kid's head like a million whiskers. Their face was flushed, but all the running had cleaned off some of the soot. The slight child was older than she'd originally thought. Something about the angles of their face made Pip think they were probably ten to twelve years old.

"What's your name?" Pip asked.

"Iris."

Pip studied the soot-streaked purple unicorn shirt and the soft brown eyes lost in the dirt of their face. Changing tack, Pip asked, "So you're...a girl?"

They rolled their eyes. "Yeah."

"Okay. I'm Pip. Let's go."

"Are *you* a girl?"

Pip froze and looked over her shoulder. It'd been so long since anyone had challenged who she was. Iris's words felt like a slap to the face.

"It's just...you don't look like one. But you sound like one."

"A girl can have short hair and wear cargo pants and combat boots." Pip knew she sounded defensive. "Look, I'm a girl, okay?"

"Fine."

At the mouth of the alley, they minced around several skeletons moldering inside the remains of cardboard-box homes.

"We're gonna hug this wall like mice, staying in the cracks and moving quiet. No getting caught by the cat today."

Iris didn't acknowledge Pip's words. She was transfixed by the skeletons. Iris's inattention might put them both in danger. In that moment, Pip considered leaving her.

Pip adjusted the dog collar at her throat, feeling the burden of the promise she'd made when she had buckled it around her neck. It'd been an easy pledge to make at the time, but harder to fulfill in the moment: never leave someone behind. The conviction to do right by Iris pressed hard against her, abrading the hard shell she'd built to protect herself.

Pip caught Iris scrutinizing the dog collar and tucked it inside her shirt. Tapping on her front teeth in thought, Pip stared at the zigzag of two cars crashed in the middle of the street. A partial skeleton lay in the gutter not far from the cars. Empty sockets watched her decide.

She'd never forgive herself if she left the kid on her own. "Ready to go?"

Iris nodded. Pip gave Iris's fingers a reassuring squeeze, disconcerted by the unexpected comfort of holding someone's hand.

They speed walked past several blocks of crumbling brick buildings scorched from the heat of old fires. Moving into the neighborhood with purpose, they halted frequently to listen and watch for pursuit. When the trader's yellow moving truck rumbled past a few streets over, Pip pulled Iris off the street, into the remains of a daylight-basement entrance.

Piles of newspapers and bedding filled the basement's concrete stairway. Broken glass crunched under their shoes as they hunkered on the stairs. Iris slipped on the forgotten bed and tripped down the stairs, kicking up the stale reek of urine and unwashed bodies.

"You okay?" Pip whispered.

Iris looked up at her with frightened eyes and nodded.

The sound of the truck faded. Pip exhaled and nudged weathered newspapers out from under her feet.

After a long moment, Iris spoke. "Are they following us?"

"Let's give it a minute." Pip brushed her grimy fingers over the newspaper's stark headlines.

One Mile Cough had jumped from Asian fruit bats to farmed pigs to people, striking everywhere around the globe without mercy. It spread through saliva, starting like a bad flu with high fevers that caused convulsions. If you managed to survive the infection, brain damage and seizures were your reward.

It took only fourteen days before the first outbreak exploded in Spokane. By the third week, hundreds of pyres burned all across the city. Nonstop fires threw death into the sky as people succumbed to One Mile Cough. The remembered taste of ash was acid in Pip's mouth as she reread the executive order mandating all citizens quarantine in their homes or in one of Spokane's many hospitals.

Before her phone's batteries died, she'd bided time by the Spokane River, watching bodies float in the murky water as she listened to a static-filled broadcast of a coughing vice president praying for them all. He'd called the virus "One Mile Cough." For the coughs that went on and on until you died.

Pip picked up the front page of one of the last newspapers she remembered reading. Words of warning and fear surrounded photographs of bodies laid out by the thousands in abandoned football fields. Printed in a terrifying crimson ink was a warning: "Wear your mask! People have succumbed to the virus in just three to four days." She flipped over the paper and read the story headline under the fold: 300,000 dead.

Ninety-five percent of every living soul in Spokane and the Spokane Valley gone in less than a month. Everything collapsed. As the lights went out one by one, the ailing overwhelmed those able to help.

Iris took the paper out of her hands and mashed it into a ball.

The destruction and decimation had spread everywhere. The world burned itself out.

Pip tried to offer Iris a reassuring smile, but it soured and blew away with the breeze. Iris tossed the crumpled newspaper down the stairs with a resigned shrug. Pip took notice of Iris's resilience with a huge helping of respect. So much for those helicopter parents who wrapped their children in layers of comfort and protection. The kids who survived the virus went feral, making their way alone. They were savvy enough to keep swimming when everyone else sank to the bottom and died.

"Do you have a home?" Pip asked.

Iris crossed her arms protectively. "It's gone."

Pip made a mental inventory of the supplies she and Whist had managed to scrounge. There wasn't a lot, but it might be enough. She considered the weight of her promise versus the responsibility of taking on a stray and sighed.

"If you want to come with me, I have food and water."

Iris nodded.

"I have a friend there too. He's kinda twitchy—"

"One Mile Cough." It was a statement of fact. Some of those who survived the Cough ended up acting a little strange.

"Yeah. But Whistler's a good guy. We'll put you two together real careful to keep from setting him off."

Iris nodded again.

A few more blocks and they were deep in a run-down neighborhood nearly a mile from the Monroe Street Bridge. Taking a chance, Pip turned west and took a side street back to Monroe. A flock of turkeys crossed the street half a block ahead of them. The big tom stopped on the centerline and fluffed out his tail, using the broad fan of brown-and-black-striped feathers to warn them away from his ladies. He spooked as Iris and Pip moved closer, gobbling in defiance. Wary of being attacked by the main course of a Thanksgiving dinner, Pip stopped walking until he finished crossing the street. Iris picked up a loose feather from the pavement, twirling it between her fingers while they walked the rest of the way to Monroe Street. Pip signaled for Iris to pause near the intersection.

The stillness rang heavy in Pip's ears. Even after a year, the silence unnerved her. No cars, no airplanes, no people talking at the nearby bus stop. Listening hard to the quiet, she hoped the yellow moving truck wasn't idling up the block, waiting for them to break cover. She glanced back at the bridge and the blurry shape of the man she'd killed in the street. From this angle she couldn't see his motorcycle. Hopefully the trader's truck was long gone.

Pip stepped around a pile of bones wearing the scraps of winter clothes, moving past the vandalized funeral parlor. Every window in the building was broken, and the doors gaped like loose teeth. Shoals of ash settled on empty windowsills like dirty snow. Pip forced herself to check every dusky opening for signs of danger. They were safer now, but still several long blocks south of the music store. Fearful their luck would run out, she pushed them into a jog. Iris barely kept pace but didn't complain. When the store came into view, Pip's knees shook with relief. They were almost there.

On the corner of two formerly busy streets, Myers Music was a bunker of an off-white building painted with a mural of black musical notes and silhouettes of musicians playing their instruments. Iris froze and pointed to her ear. The urgent sound of running feet ricocheted off the brick buildings surrounding them. Heart pounding, Pip grabbed Iris and dodged into the Myers parking lot. Scrambling for cover, they dove behind a car.

A petite black cat ran around the corner ahead of a scrawny, sunburnt old man with an automatic weapon strapped across his chest. He looked and moved like an action hero, except for his whistling. The tune was an exuberant march, his notes rising and falling with the cadence of his footsteps.

His beat-up army jacket was lined with pockets bursting with tangles of colorful yarn. A red string of it trailed behind him, and the small cat made a dash around his feet, trying to snag the loose end. Whistler paused to take a breath and yanked the string out of reach, shaking a scolding finger at the cat.

CHAPTER 3

"Whistler," Pip breathed. She motioned for Iris to stay low. Even on a good day, it was safer to get his attention from a distance—give him time to figure out who was talking.

"It's me." Pip stood up, stepping out from behind the car with her hands raised.

The rifle came up faster than she would have thought possible. He might have brain damage, but Whistler sure knew how to handle a gun.

"Get down! Right the hell down!" Whistler's body shook with tension. He closed the gap between them at a jog, the barrel of the gun never wavering. The glass eyes in the flattened head of the fox fur he'd stitched to the shoulders of his jacket winked in the sunlight.

Pip dropped to her knees to present a smaller target. "It's Pip. Remember? The good Pip who helped you when Kitty was lost? I climbed the big tree, and you tossed me the cat food..."

Whistler lowered his gun, not all the way, but enough to make her less concerned about being accidentally shot. She was getting through to him.

"We should get inside," she said. "I killed a man on the Monroe Street Bridge."

"Not safe." Whistler lowered the gun another fraction.

"No. Not safe for Pip. Not safe for you...or Kitty." Pip waited.

"Pip!" Whistler said in surprise. He dropped the gun, letting it swing away from his hands to hang from a strap around his chest. "I didn't see you there."

She took her time getting up, not wanting to startle him. Whistler laughed as she came closer and clapped him on the shoulder. He reached out and brushed the dog collar she wore with his thumb.

"Dog tags," Whistler said.

Pip tucked the collar inside her shirt. She still hadn't told him about Utah. She hadn't told *anyone* about Utah. She wasn't ready yet.

"Where's your grocery cart?" Pip asked.

Whistler cut his eyes at her and looked away. It was a goldfish-quick flash under murky water. Most people would have missed it. For a moment, Whistler looked scared. He shrugged.

"Forgot it."

"Bull."

Whistler never went anywhere without his metal shopping cart. Kitty rode in it like a queen, pushed down the street with the wind in her ears. He always used it to collect supplies. It made a god-awful racket that attracted far too much attention. Whistler never worried. His gun protected him from anyone who might want to help themselves to what he had.

He scratched his tangled hair. "Yeah. I might've killed somebody too."

"They took your cart?"

"There might have been a few of them."

"Whist," Pip sighed. So much for his idea of a fun day out. Out of habit, she checked the street. "The traders I ran into had a yellow moving truck and a motorcycle."

"I thought I heard engines. That was you?"

"They were in the library."

Whistler huffed and scrubbed the stubble on his face. "Time to move on?"

"I think it might be." The skin on the back of Pip's neck prickled. Someone could be watching them right now. Better hurry up and introduce him to Iris.

"I found a stray."

His eyes, washed of their blue from years of living outside, searched the parking lot. "Oh?"

Taking the chance that he'd be okay with a new person, Pip gestured for Iris to come out of hiding. Whistler took a quick inventory of how unthreatening Iris was. Pip could recite the checklist he'd taught her by heart: *Young, unarmed, alone. Safe.*

Whistler grinned. "Hey, kid."

"Hi."

"Whistler, Iris. Iris, Whistler." Pip introduced them while at the same time drawing Iris closer to the music store's front door.

Whistler snapped his fingers. "And this is Kitty."

The lithe cat sprang off the ground, clawing her way up his body. She ended up on his fur-covered shoulder. The golden-eyed animal perched there like a pirate's parrot, keeping balance with needle-sharp claws sunk deep into the dead fox's rust-colored fur.

Pip pointed at the cat. "Nobody touches Kitty except Whistler."

Iris squinted, considering.

"She's as mean as she is pretty." Pip crossed her arms over the white slashes of old scars along one forearm. She'd learned the hard way when she'd gone up a tree to rescue the damn cat for Whistler.

After breaking quarantine—in a mad dash to save herself from the virus running rampant through the hospital—Pip had wound up on the South Hill living in a shelter she'd built under a park's aging bandstand. She'd waited there for the virus to kill her too. But she never got sick.

She'd huddled in a pile of blankets in the dim half-light of the bandstand, and the sound of random gunshots and screams had kept her company as people panicked and died. She'd stayed hidden until her water ran out, hungrily waiting out the chaos as the city sank into the quiet of death. One crisp morning—not long after the silence descended—she'd woken to the tearful sound of a man's voice pleading for someone to come back.

His unending sobs racked her nerves to the point of breaking and overwhelmed her caution. She'd crawled out from under the bandstand and found the man she would come to call Whistler kneeling under an oak tree with an unopened can of cat food. High up in the branches was a midnight-black cat refusing to climb down.

Offering to help, Pip scaled the tree and neatly caught the can when Whistler tossed it. Attracted by the hiss of the pull top opening, Kitty jumped off the high, thin branches and ate with surgical precision, licking her whiskers after every mouthful. Pip was enchanted.

When Kitty stopped eating, Pip reached to pick her up and the black cat zipped away, claws slashing. Surprised by the bright stabs of pain all along her right arm, Pip fumbled the can and nearly fell out of the tree. Kitty raced after the food.

Whistler hugged his black-furred demon with relief and thanked Pip by taking her into his care. The three of them had been together ever since.

Almost a year, and yet Kitty's golden eyes still squinted with malice as she hissed at Pip from Whistler's shoulder. Kitty was a bitch, but Pip had to admit that the furry monster seemed to love the old man. He ignored his angry shoulder-cat and rustled in his pockets for the music store keys.

Since the building's glass double doors were shattered, they used six heavy-duty bike locks to fasten the metal security gate over the main entrance. Pip pulled a keychain from around her neck and crouched by the door.

"I've got it," she said.

She slid each U-shaped lock onto her arm after unlatching it. Their solid weight rested in the crook of her elbow while she raised the security gate. When the gap was a few feet wide, Kitty leapt off her man perch and disappeared into the dim building. Whistler picked up his gun, keeping a lookout while Iris and Pip crawled inside. Once through, Pip scanned the road, watching Whistler's back. He dropped the gun, slid under, and pulled the gate down behind him.

Lying on their stomachs watching the street, Pip and Whistler made a strange pair. Tall and short, young and decidedly late middle aged, they'd saved each other's asses so many times that she'd lost count.

Pip hooked the six locks through the door's metal bars, setting each in place with a thick snap. She tucked the keys inside her shirt next to Utah's collar.

"That'll keep 'em out," Whistler said.

He rose to his feet, clicking the safety off his gun. He began his sweep of the building's entrance. Reconnaissance was his routine no matter where they went, and his habit had saved their lives more than once. The quiet squeak of his leather shoes as he took confident steps into the shadowy building never wavered. Pip sighed as waves of tension washed away, leaving her limp and tired. The only time she felt safe anymore was with a twitchy man who carried a gun.

"It's dark in there," Iris whispered.

Iris stood on the edge of a beam of sunlight and traced the burgeoning gloom with a toe. The entrance was daylight bright. The rest of the grocery store–sized building didn't have a single window and was nightmare-fueling black. A ramp from the entrance to the lower main floor disappeared into the dark.

Stand where you can't be seen from the street." Pip pulled Iris a few steps down the ramp, then dug in her bag for a flashlight. "I'm gonna follow Whistler and double-check that no one's broken into the rear entrance."

Pip clicked on the flashlight. "I'll come back for you."

"No." Iris made a panicky grab at Pip's sleeve. "Don't leave me."

Iris's words trembled with fear. The longing in her voice made Pip's heart lurch in her chest, pulling her up short. Taking on a stray was more complicated than she'd thought. She studied Iris's earnest face and felt a grain of feeling rub at the hard core of her heart.

Pip yanked the dog tags from under her shirt collar and unwrapped them.

"I'm not going to leave you. I'll be right back. Listen for the tags. That way you'll know where I am." She jingled the collar, offering a reassuring smile. "When I go into the big room in the rear of the store, you might not be able to hear me—there are walls in the way. I promise I won't be gone long. Watch for my flashlight. Okay?"

"Okay," Iris said with quiet fear.

"Whistler!" Pip called. "I'm coming in."

Most of the instruments in the showroom had been stolen. A few guitars were smashed to pieces, their strings bent and curled like grass after a heavy wind. Pip took stock of the debris, checking for anything out of place. She made her way down the short ramp to the main floor. Crossing the room, she stepped on several synthesizers' worth of broken piano keys. The black-and-white plastic rectangles made hollow seashell clinks with each step.

Before they'd found the bike locks, they'd left the main room a complete mess in the hope that anyone who did get inside would see the destruction and decide the music store wasn't worth the trip. Once they'd secured the doors, the plastic piano keys were left as a last line of defense. They'd hear an attack if it came. So far, they'd been lucky. Though the store was darker than inside the belly of a cow, having only two entrances and no windows made the building a perfect place to make camp.

A cavernous doorway on her left passed into a room once used to hold acoustic guitars and ukuleles. All the two-pronged hooks lining the walls were empty except for three that held scrounged aluminum bats. She'd raided a high school gym and taken the lot. Bats were easier to care for than a rifle or gun; they didn't need ammunition. Pip gave one of the bats an affectionate pat.

She flashed her light at the girl. Iris waved half-heartedly, blinking as the light bounced over her.

"Be right back." Pip hoped Iris wouldn't panic when the bright spot of light faded.

After they'd found the store unoccupied and decided to stay, Pip spent several days muscling pyramid-shaped display racks into the doorway between the second and third rooms. A mountain range of eight-foot music stands slowed anyone's passage and kept the room from view. Clamping her teeth into the spongy handle of the flashlight, Pip stepped onto the nearest stand and used both hands to climb the triangle-shaped rack.

Whistler's voice came from the rear of the store. "Clear!"

"Clear," Pip repeated. She felt stupid saying it, like she was playing pretend, but shouting "clear" let Whistler know where she was and made him happy.

Easing her head over the top, she checked the other side. The third and largest room in Myers was where they'd stored classical instruments and heavy racks of sheet music. Brass trumpets on the walls winked in the wavering light of a lantern, flickering with a golden glow that reminded Pip of a welcoming fire.

Even with Whistler's all clear, their habit was for her to inspect whatever building they entered as thoroughly as he had. She wiped spit off the flashlight handle and made a slow study of the room's nooks and crannies. Smaller rooms for repairing instruments lined the walls—each had a glass front and were almost completely untouched by whoever had destroyed the rest of the store. Satisfied nothing was amiss, Pip climbed over the barricade and made her way to the back door.

Whistler was already cleaning his gun in a lantern's dim light. He looked up as Pip walked by.

"Clear?" he asked.

"Not quite." Pip trained her light on the back door. "Probably a huge fire hazard," she muttered, gesturing to the useless glass emergency box next to the back door.

Completely stuffed with junk, the back door was blocked by the store's safe, music stands, and every instrument case Whistler had found in the storage area. The hard-sided containers were wedged together like a 3-D puzzle. The tangle they'd created was nearly impossible to shift. She clicked off the light. "Clear."

Whistler grunted. "Gonna get the kid?"

"Iris," Pip reminded him.

She dumped her pack of books onto the floor with a relieved sigh. The gunshot wound in her side was really starting to ache. Kitty wandered into the light, casting long cat shadows on the walls. The diffused light made the empty room even creepier. Pip shrugged off the unsettling feeling of being judged by the cat and headed to the front of the store.

Pip was throwing her leg over the top of the barricade when she fumbled the flashlight. It clattered down the other side, bouncing off shelves. It landed with a thud on a pile of sheet music and shone on the doorway to the front room.

"Damn it." Pip straddled the top. "I'm coming back, Iris."

A subtle rustle came from somewhere nearby.

"Iris?"

Dirty fingers reached into the light and wrapped around the door frame.

CHAPTER 4

Pip nearly had a heart attack when Iris walked around the corner.

"Jesus! You scared the crap out of me."

Iris shaded her eyes from the flashlight's glare and picked it up. "You were taking too long."

"How'd you get over here?" Pip looked to the entrance's faint glow.

"I tripped a lot."

Pip laughed—a long chuckle that gained strength as she imagined a determined Iris bumbling her way through the dark.

"It's not funny." Iris put her hands on her hips.

Gales of hysterical laughter cramped Pip's injured side as tears rolled down her face. It hurt to laugh, but it felt so good. She waved at Iris to climb and helped her over the top. The sight of Iris's dirt-smeared butt hovering at the top of the music rack set Pip braying.

"Stop!" Iris's disembodied voice carried over Pip's gasping laughter.

Snorting out a last chuckle, she joined Iris on the other side.

"I've got to pee," Pip said as she jumped off the music rack. "How 'bout you?"

Iris nodded eagerly.

"Come on." She gestured for Iris to follow.

They walked to one of the glass-fronted rooms. Pip drew back a tarp curtain to reveal shoved-aside worktables making room for a five-gallon bucket with a toilet seat–type lid. A large bag of cedar shavings, the kind used to line hamster cages, sat next to the bucket.

"Welcome to the portable privy," Pip announced.

"Huh?"

She nudged the bucket with her toe. "You know, portable, 'cause you can carry it and privy, 'cause that's where you poo."

Iris made a face. "Gross."

"It's safer to do your business in here than to go outside every time."

Iris looked surprised.

"What?"

"We always went outside."

Pip flashed back to her life on the streets, before the outbreak. "That gets messy if there's a lot of you."

"It kinda did," Iris said in a whisper.

Not knowing what to say, Pip tossed a handful of fragrant shavings into the bag lining the bucket. "When you're done, toss in another handful. Keeps the smell down."

When Iris finished, Pip took a turn and washed up with a squirt of hand sanitizer. She grabbed another lantern and limped to the real bathroom to examine the wound in her side.

Dirt and blood caked her short hair into uneven spikes, and her shirt was a crusty ruin. She felt like a low-budget zombie and looked like one of those androgynous mannequins they used in clothing stores. Straight up and down, flat chest, no hips, and a square jaw. It wasn't any wonder that Iris had asked if she was a girl, but she was more than just what people saw on the outside. Pip turned to study her profile, trying to catch what Iris had seen, and grimaced as a cramping pain flared along her side.

The gunshot wound was on fire. She rolled her shirt out of the way, gasping when fabric peeled out of the scab. A shallow graze tracked diagonally up her torso in the direction of her armpit. The edges were torn and jagged like flames on the side of a hot rod.

Her side screamed as she shrugged out of her canvas jacket. Trying to catch her breath, she leaned on the sink and wished for a cool shower. Even five minutes of pounding water spraying over her body would go a long way toward helping her feel human again. Instead, she pulled a baby wipe out of the package on the counter and rubbed spattered blood off her arms and face. Tossing the rust-colored wipe into the trash can by the sink, Pip scuffed a hand through her spiky hair and gave her hollow cheeks a once-over in the mirror.

Under the thin fabric of her ripped shirt, her ribs stood out like posts on a picket fence. A lopsided hole cut through the fabric where the bullet hit and skipped across her skin. It was a bad angle and pure luck that had saved her from broken ribs, or worse. Drawing the shirt out of the way, Pip studied the shallow gash a second time, poking gingerly around the wound. It wasn't deep enough to warrant stitches, but she'd definitely need a bandage.

"That was close," she muttered, then rolled down her shirt with a pained hiss.

The wound rode high up on her side; she'd need help cleaning it. She considered calling Whistler, then grimaced at her reflection in the mirror. They'd been through a lot together, but that didn't mean she wanted him accidentally seeing anything he shouldn't.

She returned to the storage room and hefted a giant first aid kit off one of the shelves. Whistler raised his eyebrows as Pip crooked a finger at Iris. "I'm gonna need your help."

Iris looked up from a violin laid crosswise on her lap and plucked the strings. Out-of-tune notes twanged into silence.

"Where'd you find that?" Pip asked.

"It was in a cupboard under the cash register," Whistler said while scratching Kitty under the chin. "We never thought to look there."

"Huh. You play?"

Iris white-knuckled the neck of the instrument. Her upper lip formed a defensive curl. "Fiddle. Sometimes."

Pip exchanged a look with Whistler. There was a history there. *Best leave it for now,* Pip decided.

"You any good?" Whistler asked.

Iris's victorious smile said it all. But the moment passed, and she deflated. Her gaze retreated inward, and the smile slipped from her face. Unsettled by the abrupt change, Pip snagged a cleanish shirt out of a pile, grabbed the overloaded first aid kit, and gave Iris an encouraging nod to follow. Iris trailed her to the bathroom, catching her own reflection in the mirror. Iris paused at the sight of herself, touching the burns on her face with a look of surprise. Pip gave Iris a moment to collect herself and gingerly changed into her new shirt while standing behind the bathroom door for privacy. Kicking her ruined shirt toward the useless toilet, Pip set the first aid kit on a small counter next to an electric coffeepot.

Finding the first aid kit had been a stroke of luck. Not long after she'd moved in with Whistler, she'd found a wrecked ambulance partially wrapped around a power pole. The driver inside was very dead. Somehow he'd wrecked the ambulance in a back alley. The high fever of One Mile Cough had probably made him lose control, ramming through a fence and smashing into a merciful end.

The vehicle was partially buried in a pile of trash and compost behind a house. Pip had used her bat to bash in the cracked passenger-side window and climbed between the seats into the back. She'd grabbed a red emergency box the paramedics used on house calls and stuffed it full of all the drugs and medical supplies it would hold.

She was out of the ambulance and searching in a nearby building when the Skins approached the ambulance pack-of-dogs style, spread out and looking hungry. There had been seven of them sniffing around the wreck, but she'd given them the slip. The risk had been more than worth it. She'd found enough supplies to last for a while, and more than enough to patch a bullet graze. Pip flicked open the latch and lifted the inner rack of the box to check the little shelves inside. Three whole tubes of antibiotic ointment were still left.

Iris hovered nervously in the doorway. Pip held out a tube of ointment along with a sterile cotton swab on a stick and rolled up her shirt so Iris could see the gunshot wound. "Put some of that gunk on the swab and dab it all over the graze."

"Will it hurt?"

"Most definitely. But I promise not to scream...much."

Iris tucked the tube into her pants and ripped the paper wrapping off the swab. She held out the swab for Pip to hold, then squirted some of the ointment onto the cotton. Iris's hand shook with nerves, but that didn't stop her from bending to wipe the wound. Pip growled deep in her throat when the swab caught on a raw edge. Lips held in a grim line, Iris shot Pip an anxious look and hesitated.

"Hurts like a bitch. Why stop now?" Pip tried to laugh and ended up panting.

Iris tossed the swab into the trash and selected a large gauze pad from the first aid kit. Her nimble fingers gently held the gauze in place while Pip ripped pieces of tape with her teeth to secure it. Together they wrapped a stretchy bandage around her middle to keep everything in place. Pip admired the first aid job in the mirror, then ruffled Iris's hair.

Iris dodged. "Don't. I hate that."

Pip closed her outstretched hand into an apologetic fist. "Sorry."

"It's okay."

"I won't do it again."

Iris finger-combed her thick, shoulder-length hair into place. Pip watched her in the mirror and admired Iris's grit as the awkward moment passed. Never in a million years would she have stood up for herself like that when she was younger. Maybe if she'd done it more often, her family wouldn't have thrown her out when she'd finally spoken up.

"None of the burns on your face look too bad, but they'd benefit from some magic goo," Pip waved the tube of ointment invitingly.

"It doesn't hurt."

Iris nodded. In the bluish light of the lantern, the mostly dime-sized welts were purplish blotches. The dabbed-on goo made the burns look worse. Iris said they felt better, cooler. Pip put the first aid kit away and dragged her backpack over to her bedroll to unload the books into neat stacks against the wall. Iris stayed by the bathroom, watching as Pip worked. After a while, she cautiously skirted Whistler and moved a little closer.

"Books?" Iris asked.

Pip sat on her heels. Now that she had them, she didn't feel much like reading. The four stacks of books had been paid for with blood. "Yeah. It seemed like a good idea this morning."

Whistler snorted. His sleeping bag was covered with a mountain of tangled yarn. "Taking a day off to do something fun wasn't the best idea I've ever had."

"Worse than the raccoon jerky?"

Iris made a face while Whistler considered. "It's a close second."

Pip's stomach growled at the thought of food. "Come on, I'll show ya the storage room."

The last practice room, the one closest to the back door, was where they stored food and water. A couple of foil-wrapped pouches and twenty cans of miscellaneous food on the shelves were all that stood between them and starvation. They were living on the thinnest edge, picking away at the scraps of scraps. The mostly empty shelves were another vote for leaving the music store and moving on.

"We've got chicken noodle, bean and bacon, cherry filling, three cans of peaches, and stewed tomatoes. Or"—she pointed at a few out-of-date pouches of freeze-dried food—"what's left from the camping store down the street."

On impulse, Pip tossed a small package she'd been saving to Iris and grinned at the joy that bloomed on the girl's face.

"Ice cream?" she asked. "Is this *really* ice cream?"

"Hope you like strawberry, chocolate, and vanilla."

Iris tore open the package with her teeth and inspected the contents. "It's all dry. Is this a joke?"

Pip reached in and snapped off a chunk of freeze-dried strawberry ice cream. She popped the chalky pink bit into her mouth. Flavor exploded on her tongue. She nudged the hard lump of ice cream into a cheek and smiled.

"No joke."

Iris broke off a microscopic piece and gave it a lick. Her eyes widened in pleasure.

"Right?" Pip grinned. "And two days ago Whistler found a cache of white gas for the camp stove, so it's a hot dinner for a change."

The stove wasn't even lit before Iris let out a satisfied sigh. She licked one finger and dipped it into the bottom of the empty bag.

Dinner was a shared can of cherry pie filling eaten while soup heated on a dented camp stove. The combined scent of chicken noodle and bean and bacon was discordant and better than it had any right to be. Noodles and beans danced in the bubbles when the soup began to boil.

"You didn't have to mix them," Pip muttered.

Whistler stirred the soup and shrugged. "It's all the same on the way down."

"Ugh." Pip considered Iris. She'd curled herself around the violin again, rubbing its dusty sides to a caramel gleam with a soft cloth. "Mixed bacon and chicken soup—gross, right?"

"I'm a vegetarian. Or...I was," Iris said. "My whole family was against eating meat. I'd never had it until after..."

"Ah." Pip tapped her front tooth with a finger. "I could open the tomatoes?"

"It doesn't matter anymore."

Dinner was quiet. Pip burned with guilt every time she chewed a piece of canned meat, but it didn't stop her from licking her spoon clean when she finished her portion. She watched Iris out of the corner of her eye. The girl was an island unto herself, eating her soup in messy slurps while checking on her new violin.

Satisfied that Iris seemed to be settling in, Pip turned her attention to Whistler and poked him with a toe. He stirred his almost empty can of soup while Pip dug another cherry out of the gooey pie filling and popped it into her mouth.

"Find anything good besides the yarn?"

Whistler picked thoughtfully at a scabby hangnail on the end of a finger, making it bleed. His hands looked painful, all of his fingers chapped, knuckles swollen. Pip wondered, not for the first time, just how much damage One Mile Cough had done to his brain. As an ex-member of the military, he'd weathered the virus outbreak on the air force base not far from downtown Spokane.

A group of veterans and enlisted soldiers had created a community of sorts on what was left of the base by hoarding and trading treated fuel. Whistler was with them until he was ordered to shoot an outsider begging for food. He slipped off base in the night and never looked back.

Even in his more lucid moments, Whistler suffered a variety of seizures as a side effect of survival. One Mile Cough hadn't managed to kill him, but his mind was broken, weakened by the plague that had taken so many. Pip watched him study his sore fingers and thanked her lucky stars she'd never caught the virus.

He sniffed. "Just the yarn."

When she'd left the music store before sunrise, the library had been her ultimate destination. But she'd taken a detour into the grocery store to scrounge a gift for Whistler. What little gifts she could find were the only way she could think of to thank him for helping her survive. "I went into that hippy grocery store on our side of the bridge. Found some bandages. I saved them for you."

Iris's empty soup pot slid across the floor and clanged against the metal fuel can hooked to the compact camp stove.

"I'm s-sorry," Iris stuttered. A nervous smile parked itself on her face. "I pushed it too hard. I didn't mean to do that."

"'S'okay." Pip set her own soup can in the pot.

"Bandages." Whistler slurped the last of his meal, tapping the bottom of the can to get the last few beans. "What kind?"

Pip dragged her bag into the lantern's glow and dug into a side pocket where she'd stashed the paper box of bandages. The box was a little squished; she squeezed it into shape and held it up for inspection. Glittery print caught the light, throwing tiny rainbows onto the floor and Whistler's wrinkled face.

"My Little Zombie Kitten," Pip chuckled as she tossed the box.

Whistler immediately opened the box and put a bandage on. The bandage's rainbow-colored cartoon kitten, featuring sparkly gore on its legs and face, was unsettling and hilarious at the same time. Whistler used the entire box on his sore fingers and held his hands out like a lady checking her nails, admiring them.

"Thanks, Pip," Whistler said with a shy smile. He gently tapped each wrapped finger on the edge of his soup can. "You do the dishes and I'll do the portable privy." He picked up his gun and headed for the bathroom.

An awkward silence settled between Pip and Iris while Whistler rustled about with the privy's plastic bag.

"So..." Pip reached for a distraction. "How'd you get the burns on your face?"

The acrid scent of nervous sweat rolled off Iris. Pip mentally kicked herself for asking such a stupid question. She was certain Iris was going to let the question go unanswered, until Iris scooted a millimeter closer and whispered.

"Those guys with no hair."

"The Skins," Pip said.

"What?" The brown of Iris's eyes looked like a solid wall of black in the light of the lantern.

"You know, angry young guys, like skinheads—"

"'Cause of those shaved heads," Whistler interrupted. "They're like hornets, all zigzags and rage..." he trailed off.

Iris looked like she might bolt from the room. Panic contorted her face into a mask.

"Never mind," Pip said.

Iris plucked at loose threads on the violin's bow. "This needs to be rehaired. I can't play like this." She stood on jittery legs.

Pip handed her a flashlight. "Okay..."

Whistler caught Pip's eye. He didn't have to say anything. They both knew Iris had been pushed too far.

Kicking herself with regret for starting the whole uncomfortable conversation—*Why did you ask about the burns on her face, you complete idiot?*—Pip kept a tense watch over Iris as the kid scoured the back room for whatever would fix her newfound instrument. Every time Iris looked her way, Pip pretended her whole attention was on washing dishes and setting her books in order.

It took about an hour until Iris calmed and found what she needed. She sat near the lantern and took apart the violin bow. When she couldn't get something loosened, Whistler sat by her side, handing over his multi-tool. Pip sighed with relief when their heads knocked together and Iris managed a grin.

Whistler was back to winding his yarn when Iris held up the bow and broke the silence. "And that's how you rehair a violin bow."

She tucked the newly strung bow into the violin case and curled herself around the hard black sides like it was a teddy bear. She closed her eyes, and it wasn't long before she was cut down by sleep.

"Where'd you find her?" Whistler mumbled.

Pip flashed back to Iris's terrified face wrapped in dirty blankets. She cringed. "On the bridge."

"Where you killed the guy."

"Yeah."

"Hmm." Whistler rubbed at the stubble on his chin. "You said they had a moving truck?"

"And a motorcycle."

"I wonder if they're getting the gas from the air force base."

"Maybe."

"It's getting crowded out there. Too easy to get caught."

Pip thought of his missing grocery cart. They'd both been caught just trying to survive.

Whistler stretched and lay down on his sleeping bag. "If I *ever* suggest we take a day off again, end me."

CHAPTER 5

By midmorning the next day, Pip wanted to eat a handful of painkillers. Her entire right side seized with every breath. Standing in the bathroom, she unwrapped the bandage and hesitated before peeling off the tape holding the gauze pad in place. This kind of deep pain couldn't mean anything good.

The edges of the bullet graze were a vivid shade of pink. Holding the flashlight close to the wound, Pip couldn't tell if it was healing pink or better-start-praying-'cause-you're-gonna-die pink. She hissed at her bedraggled reflection and forced herself to dab on an extra-thick layer of the antibiotic cream.

Twisting painfully to apply the bandages, Pip regretted leaving Iris with Whistler instead of asking for her help to clean the wound. She half-assed wrapping the bandage over her bullet wound, struggling to secure it around her slim waist. Afterwards she leaned against the doorway of the bathroom, wiping cold sweat off her forehead.

"You okay?" Whistler asked.

"Mmm." Pip settled her shirt and gingerly lowered herself onto her sleeping bag.

She breathed painfully through pursed lips and almost choked when she noticed Kitty curled up asleep in Iris's lap. Long loops of yarn wound around Iris's hands and dangled low, brushing Kitty's ears. The little black cat didn't even flinch as Iris shifted. Pip stilled herself, waiting for the bloodbath to begin.

"Relax, Pip." Whistler threw another few wraps around the growing ball of yarn in his hands. "Kitty is the sweetest."

"Ha!"

The last loops of yarn came off Iris's hands, and Kitty's head popped up to track the end slithering across the floor. The lanky cat stretched, bumped her head affectionately against Iris's chin, and jumped off her lap. Kitty strutted away, tail waving like a banner. Pip surveyed the scene, dumbfounded. The queen bitch of all cats had gone out of her way to sit on Iris's lap. Pip blinked in disbelief. How was Iris not dead from a thousand wrathful scratches?

"Told ya," Whistler chuckled.

Kitty did a loop around the room, then jumped onto one of the barricades in the doorway.

"Where's she going?" Iris asked.

"There's big enough gaps in the metal gate for her to go outside to do her business," Whistler said.

He tossed a blue yarn ball onto the growing pile he and Iris had worked on all morning. The grin on his face didn't mask his haunted eyes. "We should stay in today."

What happened at the yarn store? Pip wondered. She'd tried to get Whistler to talk after Iris fell asleep the night before, but he'd stonewalled her. She'd killed somebody. He'd probably killed at least one person, maybe more. Staying inside was for the best.

This wasn't the first time they'd needed to hide out for a few days. They'd had confrontations before. But in the post–One Mile Cough world, the person with the worse luck usually ended up dead after a violent exchange. The consequences of killing could follow you anywhere. The music store's fortress-like quality and the quick draw of Whistler's rifle had always kept strangers at bay. But the Skins seemed more organized lately.

Should we be packing up to run? A new place farther away from the city might be for the best.

A sour note plucked on the violin pulled Pip out of her worries. "You gonna play something for us?"

Iris tapped on the string, quieting it. "No."

Pip caught a large breath of air and hissed it out her nose. Such a small defiance, and yet it landed like a punch in the guts. The half of herself that was her father's daughter wanted to lash out.

Holding her anger in check took all her strength. Better to walk away and cool off. "I need to check the street."

Making her way through the darkness of the front room, Pip stalked around piano keys and wondered if she'd done herself a favor dragging Iris off the bridge. At the time, it felt like the right thing. The *only* thing to do. She sank onto her knees and crawled to the security gate. The cool metal of Utah's dog tags bounced on her collarbone, reminding her of her promise to never leave someone behind.

Easier said than done.

Instead of waiting out the day reading one of her new books, she spent it lying on her stomach, avoiding Iris. She bided her time, counting rats and crows while listening for the sound of engines. Whistler rustled about in the music room behind her. He'd laid out maps of the city on a wide counter when they'd moved in and kept extensive notes on where they'd foraged.

Empty homes were highlighted in red. Homes full of the dead were marked with big black x's over them. The margins of the map were full of notes about where they'd run into trouble or found a doomsday prepper's cache of goods. A softly whistled tune while he worked meant he was trying to distract himself. She knew from the tone of the song that he held the purple pen. They used it to write down the locations of people they'd killed. The pen was running out of ink.

They were evolving into people who did things they never thought they'd do. Pip remembered the solid crack of the bat slamming into the man on the motorcycle. She'd almost certainly killed him. She'd done the worst and couldn't find a place inside herself that felt bad about it. That in and of itself was worrying.

The first time she'd killed to protect herself had been during her escape from Sacred Heart Hospital. Her mom had fought the delirium of One Mile Cough and begged her to leave, to save herself. On her way out, Pip caught two young soldiers locking the hospital's emergency exits. Knowing her only chance of surviving was on the outside, she fought with ferocious purpose, biting and kicking her way to the smoke-filled sunshine beyond the doors. In the confusion, she'd stolen a handgun from one of the soldiers.

She cocked, aimed, and fired the weapon just like her dad had taught her. *Bang, bang.* No more soldiers or locked doors in her way. A stampede of patients followed her out of the hospital, sick and healthy alike. There had been so many terrified people clambering over one another that she'd been knocked down and lost the gun.

She closed her eyes and leaned her face into the warm breeze running across the pavement to where she lay in the foyer. Whistler's song faded with the wind. He must have finished his tally of the dead.

A rhythmic clicking sound caught her attention. Her eyes flew open and she pressed closer to the gate, hunting for the source of the noise. She glanced up and down the street, pressing her face hard against the metal security gate until she finally spotted the source of the tapping: a herd of deer.

Mothers and spotted yearlings wandered casually down the road, pausing to nibble weeds between the cracks in the pavement. A large doe lingered near the door, her radar-dish ears swiveling. Pip chirped air through her teeth, and their heads came up. The herd regarded her for a moment, then moved on. They were unconcerned about the human lying on the ground.

Doubtless they've seen a lot of us this way.

A line of shade crossed the road as the glow of sunset lit the tops of the buildings. Pip yawned. She should go back inside. It was time to stop avoiding the kid.

Coming back into the warm glow of the lantern to hear Whistler making Iris laugh felt strange. It almost felt like home.

"What are we having?" Pip asked.

"Spaghetti, spaghetti," Iris said with a tiny grin.

"Uh…" Pip looked to Whistler. He smirked.

"It tastes so nice, you have to say it twice," Iris said.

Pip laughed. "Alright then, dish me up some."

It wasn't great. The freeze-dried noodles refused to soften. They crunched their way through dinner. Pip tossed her bowl into the dirty-dish pot. "Well, at least it was hot."

They shared a laugh, and Pip's cautious heart soared at the sound.

Whistler set his bowl next to the stove. "I'll do the privy, you do the dishes again?"

"Yeah, sure."

It was quiet after Whistler left. Pip wondered what to say to Iris. This time she would be more careful. *Should I apologize for getting angry, for hiding at the front of the music store all day?*

Iris looked up and fixed Pip with an unsettling look. "Remember when you asked me how I got the burns on my face?"

Pip cleared her throat, surprised by the vulnerable offer. "You don't have to talk about it."

"But I think I want to," Iris said.

She scooted a little closer until their knees were almost touching.

"I was in a house in that neighborhood that burned." Iris leaned a bit closer, studying Pip's face to see if she was listening.

Pip winced at the memory of yelling at Iris when she'd panicked. Now her refusal to run toward the burning houses made more sense. She'd been terrified of returning. Pip felt dumb for not making the connection sooner. "Oh."

"My parents died during the cough. It was just me in our house until the food ran out. I uh, got caught trying to steal from some teenagers, and they took me in. We were all just kids."

"In a house?"

"Yeah, one of the big ones by the sports stadium. We switched to taking turns going out for food at night because those guys—"

"The Skins?"

Iris paused so long, Pip thought she'd changed her mind about talking. Pulling in a deep breath, Iris finally continued. "The Skins started to follow us if we weren't careful. When one of our boys didn't come home a few days ago, we boarded up the windows on the lower floors and carried all our supplies upstairs to the attic. We thought the Skins might come for us."

Pip was sure she already knew the end of the story.

"A bunch of them came into the yard. The windows in the attic were small and dirty; we couldn't see anything. I volunteered to go down and look." Iris's voice went flat and distant.

"They dumped the missing boy onto the dead grass in the front yard and yelled for us to come out." Iris inhaled and tears tumbled out of her eyes. "This guy with a twisted nose, he took a gas can and poured it on the porch, told us to come out or he'd set the house on fire."

"You don't have to say any more if you don't want to."

"It caught so fast. Everyone was trapped in the attic. I could hear them screaming," Iris choked. "While I ran."

Pip longed to drag the sobbing girl into her lap. But afraid of doing the wrong thing again, she simply sat with Iris, sharing in the pain. Iris scrubbed a fist over her face, smearing tears and antibiotic ointment into her hair before lying down on her side with a sob.

"I'm so sorry," Pip said.

Iris closed her eyes. Unable to resist the feelings rising in her like a tide, Pip rested her hand on Iris's forehead. Iris flinched, then eased, relaxing under the pressure of her palm. Running a gentle hand over Iris's hair, Pip smoothed out the tangles. This sisterly feeling was a thorn in her heart. It hurt to care.

She studied the burns on Iris's face and wondered if there really was a connection between the Skins and the traders from the library. One of the traders—the younger one, Curtis—had an awfully crooked nose. Camo had yelled at Curtis; they'd argued about setting a fire. Were they the reason Iris's house had burned to the ground?

A light snore from Iris distracted Pip from troubled thoughts. She got up to wash the dinner dishes, and Kitty wove between her legs, tripping her. The black cat rubbed her head on Pip's shoe and wandered over to the ladder leading to the roof. Pip marked the cat's progress across the floor and shuddered. Kitty never touched her. And Whistler still hadn't come down from the roof. It didn't take *that* long to dump the privy bag. *Where the hell was Whistler?*

CHAPTER 6

On the off chance that Iris was awake, Pip whispered, "I'm gonna check on Whist. Stay here, 'kay?"

Pip hurried to the ladder. Kitty made a mad leap onto her shoulders, sinking her claws deep.

"Argh-oooww," Pip gasped, arching against the unexpected pain. Gritting her teeth at the agony of claws sunk into the meat of her back, Pip climbed to the roof in record time. Kitty jumped off her body the second her head cleared the opening.

Pip caught glimpses of shiny black fur weaving between the portable privy bags they'd carefully stored on the roof. It was twilight, still bright enough for someone to spot her silhouette against the darkening sky. Ducking low, she followed the cat.

They'd advanced to the middle of the roof when she noticed boots on the ground. Her breath caught, heart tripping at the sight of Whistler's feet twisted together. She rushed to his side. His legs pedaled, slow-motion swimming in the air. He was having a seizure. As if understanding, Kitty licked Whistler's twitching face.

"Some help you are." Pip rolled Whistler onto his side, propping his head on her knees to make him comfortable.

His fits could last a few seconds or several minutes. She counted the seconds until his limbs stopped seizing and his unfocused eyes rolled open.

"Northern twilight lasts forever in my heart," Whistler sang. "Her eyes like black wings on a winter's day, she was my love."

"Whist, can you hear me?" She jiggled his shoulder.

"My northern heart," he mumbled dreamily, then flinched. "Wings. So many wings. Can you see the butterflies?"

He raised an unsteady hand to stroke a flying bug, one that only existed in his head.

In the past, she would have told Whistler there was nothing there. She'd learned the hard way that denying his delusions could send him into a frustrated rage. Better to play along until he recovered his senses.

"What color are they?"

"Orange." Whistler touched Pip's cheek with one zombie-kitten finger. "Orange with black stripes and dots. They might be monarchs. Shhh. You'll scare them."

She massaged his temples while he imagined butterflies in the cooling air. Hoping Iris wasn't freaking out wondering where she'd gone, Pip let his stream-of-consciousness descriptions of fluttering butterflies paint a soothing picture against the night sky.

Soon his eyelids dropped, and he slipped into a restless sleep. Pip eased out from under him, setting his head gently on the gritty roof. Kitty came out of the growing shadows and curled up on Whistler's chest, floating on the waves of his breath.

She left the pair and climbed down the ladder. A thick snore came from the pile of Iris and blanket. Pip relaxed a bit. At least Iris wasn't worrying over why she'd been gone so long.

Grabbing Whistler's sleeping bag and a bottle of water, Pip returned to the roof. She tucked him under the down-filled bag, gingerly poking fabric around Kitty. The cat hissed, swiping at her hand when she got too close.

"Bitch."

"Don't talk to me that way," Whistler coughed.

She helped him sit. Taking huge gulps of water, he finished the bottle.

"Do you remember the song you were singing?" Pip asked.

"Hmm?"

"After the seizure you sang about"—she searched for the words—"'she was my love.'"

The water bottle fell from his limp fingers with a clatter. "You were there? In the north?"

"No. I mean, yes, I was here. You have a nice singing voice. I was wondering what the song was."

Whistler fidgeted, vigorously rubbing his hands together. "I saw a girl in blowing snow with long black hair." He struggled out of his blankets and paced to the ladder. He wobbled at the edge, then grabbed Kitty and climbed down.

"Whist, wait!"

Pip ran to the hole in the roof, sure he'd fall.

He reached the bottom and urgently gestured for her to join him.

Pip swung her feet over the lip and followed. She found him standing over Iris. A chill ran through her.

"I wasn't there to protect her in the north. She *was* alone. You had to go, to tell me if she was okay."

"Who?"

"The girl with snowflakes tangled in black hair. The girl who didn't want your protection." Whistler pointed a tremulous finger at Iris. "She's alone. You have to take her north."

He let his hand drop and started to hum the song he'd sung after his seizure. The tune was familiar. She'd listened to it while riding in the backseat of her mom's car—something on the oldies station.

Afraid he'd wake Iris and unsettled by his strange words, she pulled him to the music stands and made him climb over them. Something was happening, and Pip wanted Whistler as far away from Iris as he could get. She shoved Whistler over the top and dragged him into the front room.

"You had a seizure, Whist."

"She's alone. He'll break her if you don't…" Whistler grabbed the sides of his head like he was trying to keep it from splitting apart. "So many butterflies. YOU CAN'T LEAVE HER ALONE!"

"There wasn't a girl. There weren't any butterflies." Pip had broken their unspoken rule and contradicted Whistler's hallucinations. She felt herself getting swept up in his panic and tried to catch the edge of his coat to stop his agitated pacing. She caught his sleeve, giving it a sharp tug. "No one is alone."

"Everyone is alone!" Whistler erupted, eyes wild. Spit showered her face as he shouted.

He swung a punch at the air and fell onto the map table. Pens and maps scattered across the floor as Pip grabbed him by the shoulders, hauling him back onto his feet. They tussled against each other until Whistler lost his fight and sagged into her. She let go of him with one hand and tilted his chin so she could see his face. His gaze was unfocused, like she wasn't even there.

Then it happened. Both his pupils shrank to pinpoints before blowing wide open. Another seizure was coming. Worried he'd hurt himself in a thrashing collapse, she tackled Whistler into a hug and twisted so that when they landed she'd soften his fall. The seizure pulled him under as they hit in a clatter of piano keys. She wrapped herself around his body as he convulsed. This second fit was much more violent than the one before. She clung to Whistler until his spasms subsided, rubbing his back to let him know he wasn't alone. They had each other.

A few minutes later, Whistler mumbled, "You can let go now. I can't breathe."

Pip peeled herself away and scooted back, giving him room. Her nose wrinkled. She'd held him so tight, she reeked of him; a smell like the inside of a sweaty hat. Pip felt a nibbling of guilt for being disgusted by his smell. Whistler leaned over and vomited on the floor.

"Jesus. You okay?" She sprang to her feet, danced around the spreading puddle, and threw down sheet music to cover the sick.

"I'm sorry," Whistler said.

"That's okay, Whist. It isn't something you can control. Feeling better?"

"Sure."

They shared an ironic laugh.

She wanted to ask if Iris's presence was the reason he thought he'd seen a girl in trouble. But Iris had shoulder-length hair. It *was* black hair, he'd gotten that much right, but his visions were just that. Visions. Cooked up by a virus-addled brain. No more real than the butterflies he'd imagined on the roof.

"I need to get some sleep." Whistler reached for her to help him stand.

He almost fell off the barricade; seizures always left him

uncoordinated. Pip fetched the sleeping bag from the roof and settled Whistler next to the lantern. Only a moment lapsed before his eyes rolled shut.

"Is he alright?" Iris whispered.

Pip blew out a tired breath. "He had a seizure."

"My mom did too. Before she died."

"Life kinda sucks," Pip said, "and it isn't fair."

"Fair has nothing to do with it."

It sounded to Pip like Iris was quoting someone. She'd bet her next meal it was one of her parents.

"My dad said you are what life makes you," Iris sniffled. "Life made me Chinese but gave me a place in America. Growing up adopted made me stronger. The stupid kids in school who called me racist names, they were life making me...more."

"I can *maybe* see the first bit. But slurs turning you into a stronger person? That's just bullshit."

"Bullshit," Iris repeated firmly.

"You can say it again if you want."

Iris blushed, her cheeks flushing with blotchy pink spots. "Maybe later."

"Hey, Iris—"

"Yeah?" she yawned.

"I'd love it if you could play the violin for us tomorrow."

Iris was quiet, but the grin on her sore face spoke volumes.

Pip was awake long after Iris slipped into a sleep filled with fitful dreams. Iris's whole body shuddered, tossing with restless agitation. She moaned and thrashed in her sleeping bag until the erratic breathing of bad dreams evened out into something more peaceful.

Lying on her back next to a lantern dimmed by a red bandana, Pip glowered at shadows cast on the ceiling. Iris's words were troubling. Leaning up on an elbow, she studied the small curve of Iris's back. What kind of parent told their child they were only what life made them? Growing up at loose ends, swept from here to there, waiting for cruelty and thoughtlessness to make a person strong. It didn't make any sense. Life hadn't designed the world to make Iris suffer at the hands of hateful kids. Or One Mile Cough. Shit happened. People made choices.

Pip switched off the light. Running a hand along her side, she brushed over one small breast and the sharp hill of her pelvic bone. The first time she'd tried to look on the outside the way she felt on the inside, a circle of teens had pushed and shoved her around in the lunchroom, calling out every slur for "queer" they knew. Hate hadn't taught her anything but how to mask who she really was.

The lump of shadow that was Iris grumbled in her sleep.

On the face of it, Pip knew what Iris's father had been trying to teach her. *What doesn't kill you makes you stronger.*

But the heart was such a squishy thing. The scars of a lifetime did more damage than could be believed. Why be a tumbleweed blown about by a storm of hate if you could find your own path?

"You *aren't* what life makes you," she said to Iris's sleeping form.

She knew who she was.

No one has control over who I am but me. Pip let sleep take her.

CHAPTER 7

She was running to catch a train. The sound of the whistle whined in her ears. Her feet lagged behind, and she tripped toward the slicing disc wheel and cried out. Pip fell hard. Gravel bit into her hands. The whistle shrieked as she snapped awake.

Two high-pitched plucks and the whining notes repeated, this time blending into a faster tempo. Pip sat up, dumbstruck. Iris stood in the storeroom, fiddling with wild abandon. The hand holding the bow moved in tight arcs across the strings. The fingers on her other hand were flying.

For a second, Pip enjoyed the music. Then she remembered the store's broken glass door. The concrete walls surrounding them amplified every sound. She panicked at the thought of Iris's giddy notes making their way outside. Iris was like the Pied Piper, and anyone could follow her merry tune right to them.

"Iris!" Pip gasped and shimmied out of her sleeping bag. She clamped a hand around the neck of the violin, damping the vibration of the strings. Now it sounded like Iris was playing from the bottom of a tissue box, muffled and far away.

Iris angrily jabbed her bow at Pip. "I was playing for you! Like you asked me to!"

Whistler sat up and shook himself. "What *was* that?"

Pip held a finger to her lips and bolted for the front door. It was still dark outside, but Pip's feet knew the way by heart. She crouched at the bottom of the ramp and inched her way to lie prone at the top. The angle of the entrance made it hard to see much of anything outside, but she wasn't looking. She was listening.

A robin chirruped, announcing the morning. Other birds began to sing out, celebrating another day. Pip listened until the pounding of her nervous heart was drowned by bird song. No one was coming. They were still safe. She sagged into the floor with relief and stayed there, enjoying the fresh morning air on her face. This time they'd gotten lucky. No one had heard the bright whine of the fiddle.

Whistler elbow crawled up beside her. "I should have woken up to stop her."

Resting her head on her crossed arms, Pip yawned. Purple bags sagged under Whistler's eyes. He looked exhausted. "You had two seizures, Whist."

"Excuses get you killed."

Pip nodded.

"Hear anything?"

"Nope."

Whistler cleared his throat. "You know they know we're here, right?"

They never saw anyone watching the entrance to Myers, but Pip knew what he meant. Whistler didn't have his nickname for no reason. The gun and locks kept the strays away. At least, they had so far. Seeing the trader's yellow truck downtown had unsettled her. Things were changing. People were getting bolder.

"Fun day was a disaster," he whispered.

They shared a glance. Pip found herself discouraged by the naked fear on his face. She'd never seen him like this before. "What did you do?"

"Three."

"What does that mean?"

"The Skins surrounded me. I didn't see them until I came out of the yarn shop. They threw rocks at Kitty." Whistler held a finger to his lips.

A crow landed in the street and hopped in their direction. Pip admired the shiny black feathers ruffling in the breeze and wondered if it had fed on the carcasses of Whistler's dead men. She resolved not to ask any more questions about what had happened at the yarn shop. She didn't need to know if he'd really killed three men for taunting his cat.

"The people I saw in the library, the traders with the moving truck, they had a Skin with them."

"You think they're teaming up?"

Pip scrubbed a hand across her eyes, picking out the crusts of sleep. "Remember when we talked about moving on, finding a new place?"

Neither of them much wanted to leave the safe home they'd created in the music store. Kitty crossed the road and wove between the bars of the gate. She dropped the remains of a mouse next to Whistler. He flicked the broken body away with the barrel of his rifle.

"We have to do something," he said. "We've made too much trouble around here."

"We should've left yesterday."

"We don't know where your moving truck is. Better to give them a few days to clear out."

Pip hummed agreement. "Shall we go and yell at our little bird?"

"Go soft, Pip."

He knew her better than she knew herself. "I know, Whist."

Iris had the instrument on her lap and a worried look on her face when Pip climbed over the barricade. "I was going to surprise you."

Pip rubbed the back of her neck. "You did."

"I was too loud, wasn't I?"

"Yep." Pip flopped onto her rumpled sleeping bag. "Don't do that again."

"Once I started playing, I didn't think."

While Iris made an apologetic breakfast of blackberry cobbler, Pip took several trips to the front door to verify their home was still safe. Whistler sat by Iris in his quiet way, coaching her on the finer points of using the camp stove. They were whispering when she came back.

"Food's ready," Iris called.

"Better enjoy it—that's the last of the fuel," Whistler said.

"Smells good." She took a steaming bowl full of purple mush and dug in. Pip swallowed a mouthful. "This is so much better than dinner."

"What? You didn't like spaghetti, spaghetti?" Whistler said.

Pip snorted and opened a bottle of water. "It sucked, sucked."

Iris watched Pip drink. "I'm sorry I played the fiddle."

"Don't be sorry for playing. It was beautiful."

Iris glowed under the praise.

"Just—let's be a little quieter next time, yeah?"

Iris nodded. She looked toward the food storeroom and asked, "Where'd you get all the water from?"

Almost an entire wall of the storeroom was stacked with water bottles in every shape and size. Some were still sealed—fresh from a store shelf—but many had been refilled.

"Water heaters." Pip scooped the last of her breakfast into her mouth and checked the cooking pot for more.

"What?"

"Whistler showed me."

He paused mid scoop and grinned. His teeth were purple with blackberry seeds. Even Iris laughed.

"Every house has a water heater that's usually full of potable water. Forty to fifty gallons. There's even a drain at the bottom, makes it simple to fill the bottles."

Iris looked stunned. "All that water."

Pip refilled her bowl and poked her spoon at Iris. "'Course it won't last forever—water gets to be stale tasting. But for now, it means we can travel anywhere there's houses and be fairly sure to find water."

"We?" Iris asked in surprise.

Her stunned expression looked almost comical. Pip squinted at Whistler. He nodded.

"Well...yeah," Pip answered. Finding Iris had been unexpected, and the violin incident was dangerously stupid, but watching Iris eat her breakfast, Pip realized she actually liked the kid. It wasn't just her promise. She wanted Iris around.

"Why would you leave here? It's safe. There's food and water—"

"Things are getting thin. You saw how much food we have. Crossing-the-Bridge Day wasn't a great adventure for any of us, right?" Pip crossed her arms over her skinny chest, holding in the unease building inside. "The Skins are more organized. I don't know what that means, but it can't be good. The north side of Spokane has tons of neighborhoods to forage. Our plan is to head away from the people coming together in the city and explore whatever else is out there."

Pip heard an echo of Whistler singing his song, pleading for her to go north.

One of Iris's lower eyelids twitched, the muscle vibrating with a nervous tremor. "Wouldn't it be better to stay here?"

"That's fear talking," Pip said, picking at a blackberry seed stuck between her teeth.

Iris's bowl hit the floor with an empty metallic clunk. "I am *not* afraid," she hissed.

Pip stared at the determined set of the girl's thin shoulders and sighed. Whistler tsked and nudged her. Of course Iris was afraid. Pip was often afraid too. "I'm sorry."

Iris sniffed and covered her face, muffling the sound of crying.

The part in Iris's hair reminded Pip of combing the snarls out of her mom's curly hair while she grabbed for breath in a makeshift hospital bed. She'd called Pip by her old name. Her deadname. Of course she had. Her mom looked like she hadn't slept in years. Dark rings circled her eyes, puffed over sallow cheeks. A ropy cough brought a flush to her mom's cheeks as she reached out for Pip's hand. They didn't say much. Her mom was already dead. All she had left was the dying.

Pip told her mom about life on the streets, about scavenging for a place to sleep in the shelters during the winter. They hadn't spoken in the year since Pip had run away from home. It was her mom who brought up her dad. That's how Pip learned he was already dead. One Mile Cough took that bastard like a thief in the night. She'd never get the chance to tell him he'd been wrong about her.

Iris sniffed, wiping her nose on her sleeve. Pip knew she was hard and sometimes cruel. She'd gotten that from her parents.

"You don't have to come with us if you don't want to. We'd leave you the bike-lock keys for the front door. You could stay here and use the supplies. But I think we'd be safer together. And I'd like to hear you play that violin again. What do you say?"

"Everyone's dead," Iris cried, her mouth stretching with grief.

Her voice warbled, gaining steam and increasing in volume with every word. "Mom, Dad. Everyone I'm with dies."

Dies ricocheted off the walls, buzzing in their ears.

Iris stood with her mouth hanging loose, like the words had been knocked out of her. Eerie silence filled the music store as Pip glanced at Whistler. He placed a callused hand on his rifle, curling his fingers around the barrel. Their heads turned as one to watch the doorway. Plastic keys plinked in the front room and Kitty rushed over the music stands, her tail puffed to twice its size.

At the front of the store the metal gate rattled. Pip's blood froze.

A cheerful male voice sang out, "Hellooooo?"

CHAPTER 8

The gate rattled again, this time with more urgency. Iris's face was a pale moon, her brown eyes dilating into pools of black. Dizziness washed over Pip. She couldn't remember how to breathe.

"Whistling Man, I know you're in there," the voice crooned.

Whistler quietly racked the slide on his rifle.

Pip gestured for Iris to come to her and be oh so quiet. They walked in single file to the storeroom. Pip began stuffing bottles of water into two packs.

"What are those?" Iris breathed as Pip topped off the bags.

"Bug-out bags. Always ready to go," she whispered, holding up a pack for Whistler.

Pip threw hers on and turned off the lantern, plunging them into complete darkness.

An engine whined, turning over roughly before catching. A loud voice swore, and the report of several backfires sounded like gunshots inside the music store. Something heavy crashed into the gate with a squealing crunch. They were using a car as a battering ram. As Pip's eyes adjusted to the dim light, she seized Iris and guided her to the roof ladder. She felt Whistler take Iris's hand and heard him whispering instructions.

"Wait here," Pip hissed.

She moved silently into the room, feeling around in the dark for her bat and the violin in its hard case. Snatching at Whistler's backpack, she deftly readjusted the straps and secured the violin to the outside. She tapped Whistler on the shoulder. He began to climb.

Pip tucked her bat into a holster on her own pack as the squeal of tires ended with another horrible slam into the building. Dust rained down on their heads and Pip steadied herself on the ladder. Iris whimpered.

Pip put Iris's hands on a rung. "You need to climb."

She pushed Iris the last few feet up the ladder, thrusting the terrified girl onto the roof and out of the way. Pip pulled herself onto the roof right after, sheltering behind a reeking pile of portable privy bags.

The car backfired before charging diagonally across the street, smashing against the music store gate. The building shook and concrete dust plumed into the air. The six locks they used on the door were still holding, but Pip wasn't sure for how long. She slammed the roof hatch closed.

Whistler pointed at Iris to stay and yanked a struggling Kitty out of his jacket. He set her on the roof and gave her a rough bump on the head with his knuckles. Fresh slashes covered his neck and disappeared into his shirt. Kitty hadn't liked being shoved into his coat.

Pip piled three bags of waste on the hatch and sliced them with the sharp knife she'd left on the roof for just that purpose. Cedar shavings and sludge oozed out. The stench of an overfull porta potty on a hot day wafted over them. Iris gagged and clamped a hand over her mouth.

Rising to her knees and taking a firm grip on several poop bags with both hands, Pip tilted her head toward the rear of the building. They stayed low to avoid being seen from the street. A few feet from the edge, she set the bags down and army crawled to look down below, risking a fast peek. Two bald men stood at the corner of the building, watching the back door.

The car's engine stuttered, belts screeching from repeated crashes into the metal bars. Sand danced on the roof as the car collided again. The building shook once more. Another plume of dust. But this time, triumphant yelling carried over the engine.

She checked over the ledge. The men below punched the air in victory.

"They're in." Pip's words tasted like regret.

"This is on me," Whistler said.

Iris placed a shaky hand on her chest. "It's 'cause I played the violin."

Whistler tucked a strand of Iris's hair behind her ear. Pip couldn't believe how she calmed under his hand. "This is for the yarn store. Your loud music is a coincidence. *Not your fault.*"

Pip connected the dots from the yarn store to the roof. Three dead men had pushed the Skins to retaliate. They'd finally gotten strong enough to fight back. Whistler was right: they *were* all anger and zigzags. Whist caught her devastated expression and nodded.

"My fault," he mouthed.

The car emitted a mighty backfire, belching a cloud of black smoke.

"Crappy gas," Whistler muttered.

The roof hatch jumped and slammed down, muffling an angry scream of disgust as feces spilled into the face of the idiot who'd climbed the ladder.

A wolf's smile crossed Whistler's face. "That was a great idea, Pip."

"It won't stop them. It'll just piss them off."

He clicked off the safety on his rifle.

"What do we do?" Iris's fear breathed hot in Pip's ear.

Pip looked at Whistler. They didn't have any choice: it was time to run. He nodded, grabbed Kitty by the scruff of the neck, and tossed her off the roof.

Pip caught Iris's scream in her hand, clamping her fingers over her mouth.

"There's a shipping container about three feet from the building. It's a big jump."

Iris scrabbled under Pip's tight grip, kicking up gravel as she fought the idea of jumping off the roof.

Pip held her tight, shushing her. When she let go, Pip held up a stern finger to remind Iris to stay quiet and wriggled as near to the edge as she dared to risk another look. This close, if one of the guys on the ground was facing her way, he'd see her pack move above the roof's concrete lip. She popped her head over the little wall and huffed with relief. Both men had gone around the corner toward the front of the building.

"We're going to jump and run into the building next door. Whist made a path that takes us all the way through to the other side of the block. Just like when we ran over the bridge. Running. No stopping. Got it?"

Iris nodded woodenly. Pip tossed the toilet bags to the ground. Whistler crouched, gripping his rifle, and raised his eyebrows at Iris. He knew she'd never jump on her own. Someone needed to push her.

Pip tugged Iris up and heaved her over the ledge. She was still pinwheeling in the air when Pip and Whistler jumped after. They all crashed onto the metal shipping container at almost the same time.

Pip landed at a run, sliding off the container as if pounding her way to home plate. Iris stumbled on the container's metal ridges. Her belt caught her up before she hit the ground. Pip made quick work of cutting Iris free and pushed her toward the next building.

Snatching up toilet bags that hadn't burst from the fall, Pip was about to follow Iris when two Skins came around the corner. Their acne-covered faces and gangly limbs revealed what she hadn't noticed from up on the roof. They weren't men. They were barely teens. Neither of them was any bigger than she was.

Her grin was triumphant as she slashed a shit-filled bag with her knife.

"Hey!" one of them yelled as the bag exploded across his face. Fetid shavings splashed onto the other teen. He was still figuring out what had happened when a second bag smacked into him, knocking him off his feet with a wet squelch. The two guys collapsed under a rain of sewage.

"Whistler!" Iris screamed.

Pip whirled around. A group of Skins—four of them—stood between Iris and their escape.

Whistler grabbed Pip by the upper arm. "You need to run."

"No!" She twisted free of his grip. "No one gets left behind."

"Bullshit." Whistler racked the slide on his rifle and shot.

One of the Skins threw himself at the ground as the other three sprinted for the street. Whistler kicked the man cowering on the ground, knocking him out.

"*I'm here to protect you,*" Whistler said.

Shoving Pip out of the way, he stepped around the corner of the music store. His rifle barked: *brap-brap-brap.* A scrambling of Skins ran past the alley, sprinting for cover.

"Oh, God," Pip exhaled.

A guttural scream sent her into a flat-out run for the corner. Whistler was marching slow and steady down the street, shooting as he went. He'd pinned a few of the Skins behind the car they'd used to ram the store. Bullets punched into the side door, and the driver lay slumped over the wheel.

All the air escaped her lungs.

Each bullet landed in the car with the crunch of a crushed pop can. Echoes of the gunshots zipped between the surrounding buildings. A Skin stood up from behind the bullet-riddled car and threw a piece of concrete at Whistler. He took a careful step to the side, dodging the chunk with ease. It hit the wall not far from Pip. Flecks of concrete cut her cheek.

"Hands up!" Whistler ordered. "Right the hell up."

The concrete thrower raised his hands to the sky, and another Skin rose from his crouch by the rear bumper.

"Tell your guys to walk away." Whistler trained his rifle on the guy by the bumper.

The Skin was so young. He wasn't a bogeyman. He wasn't even older than Pip. He was scrapping for what he could find. But then again, maybe not like her. He wanted revenge. She only wanted to survive.

"You started this," Whistler shouted.

The Skin rubbed his head. The rasping sound of palm against stubble sandpapered across Pip's nerves. "You shot them over a cat!" he shouted back.

Whistler took one step closer to the bullet-pocked car and growled, "You need to leave."

Pip felt like she was having an out-of-body experience. Her fingers were numb, and adrenaline filled her mouth with the stale flavor of copper pennies. There was nothing she could do.

"Let's go!" the Skin finally shouted, voice cracking at the end.

For a moment nothing moved.

She heard the scrape of shoes over pavement as the Skins emerged from hiding. Ones and twos of scruffy guys—all with raw scalps from shaving with a dull blade—slunk past. Nine Skins made their way to the other side of the car.

Pointing his rifle's black barrel in the direction of the Monroe Street Bridge, Whistler gestured for them to leave. Shouting insults, they backed away for half a block, then turned and ran. Whistler shifted the heavy weight of his pack and peered over his shoulder, checking his surroundings before giving Pip a discreet nod.

She sagged against Myers's brick wall. *That was close.* No question—now they *had* to leave.

Grabbing the spent magazine in his gun, Whistler tugged it free and fumbled it. The metal rectangle skipped off the pavement, landing in a scattering of brass shells as he reached for a reload. He rammed it into the rifle and turned to flash Pip a triumphant smile.

She was looking into Whistler's eyes when Curtis stood up from behind the car and shot him.

CHAPTER 9

Whistler dropped where he stood.

Pip clutched the dog collar around her neck, choking herself with disbelief. Her heart screamed for blood and action. *Grab the bat, rush in, kill.* She was paralyzed. Curtis came out from behind the car. He checked his surroundings before walking to Whistler and spitting on him.

Pip touched the cool metal of her bat with one shaking finger. Iris huddled in a doorway, eyes huge, close to breaking.

"God damn you, Whist," Pip sobbed.

The sound of another shot startled her. Brick blew off the building's corner, showering her with grit. Curtis was firing at her. She launched off the wall, shoving Iris into motion. Feet pounding, they sprinted through the interlocking shops and out the other side. Seeing the street was empty, they bolted across, rabbiting into a neighborhood of abandoned homes.

They were a block from Myers Music when Pip spotted a house with a front porch that was above ground level. A white wooden lattice covered with vines obscured the supports underneath. Pip seized Iris by the arm, yanking her to a sudden stop.

"Underneath," she pointed.

Iris didn't understand.

Pip made for the yard and pulled back the lattice. "Get in."

It wasn't a request.

The air was much cooler under the porch, the dirt dry. A few straggly weeds grew in the dappled shade, but most of the space was open. Garden hoses were stacked close to the entrance. Iris collapsed on the pile with a sob.

Pip grabbed a water bottle, crawled to the front of the porch, and sat where she could observe the street. The bullet wound in her side was agony. She couldn't process what she'd seen. Whistler dropping to the pavement, blood everywhere. Dead. He had to be dead. Pip moaned and clutched her side. How could Whistler be murdered by that idiot from the library? It had to be a mistake.

"Whistler?" Iris asked.

Pip's answer was to thrust the water bottle into Iris's hands.

Iris spoke in a monotone. "He's dead."

Pip swallowed the helpless grief threatening to devour her. A half-formed grunt escaped her mouth. She mashed her fists against her eyes, holding in tears. "Just drink the water."

Iris gulped half the bottle before handing it back. Pip forced herself to drink the rest, closing her eyes as cool water splashed her overheated insides.

So many broken promises. She hadn't left him. Whistler still died alone.

"I have to go back."

"What?" Iris gasped.

"He might be wounded."

Iris's empty stare looked a lot like pity.

Pressing a hand against the ache in her side, Pip crawled to her pack and untied the bat. "I'm gonna check the music store." She shoved the lattice open and checked outside. "I'm leaving the pack. There's food."

Iris whispered, "I don't want you to go."

"I made a promise"—Pip touched the dog collar—"to never leave someone behind."

"But what about me?"

"Whistler needs me. And I will come back for you."

"But what if—"

"Enough!"

Iris cringed, knocked into submission by the force of Pip's voice.

Pip eased into the yard and pressed the lattice into place. The dog tags jingled, catching her off step, tripping on memory.

After leaving her mom in the hospital, she'd gone back to her former home and used a metal bat to bash through the sliding glass door into her parents' kitchen. They'd changed the locks after she ran away.

Gagging at the smell of her father's fly-bloated corpse rotting in the living room, she hastily backed into the yard and vomited up her breakfast on the patio. Tears spilled from her eyes. She let them fall hard and fast to the ground. Her father had never tried to understand her. Now he never would. It was a novel form of grief—raw, angry. Part of her raged at the unfairness of still loving someone she despised.

Pip spit out curses and the awful taste of death that coated her tongue. Her eyes and throat burned with regret for what she'd never have.

"Utah! C'mere, boy!"

Her scratchy voice didn't carry far. But he should've heard. She called his name again, even as hope died. Nothing moved inside the house. She sobbed and dug with a frantic hand for the VapoRub jar in her pack. Nostrils filled against the bilious smell, she picked up her bat and ran back inside the house.

She found Utah collapsed, lifeless, on a pile of newspapers. His black-and-tan fur was dull and patchy, his skin pulled tight over his bones. He was so thin. Starved. Pip covered her eyes as tears burned down her face. If she'd only come sooner.

She should have snuck him out of the yard on one of her secret visits. Taken him to live with her on the streets as a guard dog and friend. But she'd left Utah behind. She didn't have the means to take care of him. Instead she'd brought him stolen treats, slipping them through the fence when her dad let him out before bed. That warm tongue against her palm was the closest she came to a hug in all the months she'd been homeless.

Regret thrummed in her ears, muffling the clatter of the aluminum bat hitting the floor as it dropped from her hands.

"Breathe!" she'd screamed at him. Nothing flinched in the house except a part of Pip's soul.

Pip clawed her way out of the memory, shivering in the sunshine. She tore off a bit of her shirt and tied it around the dog tags, knotting the ends tight. Silencing them.

"I hear ya," she muttered.

Using parked cars as cover, she took her time carefully retracing her steps back to Whistler's body, checking her exits, always making sure there was another way out before going forward. The wind shifted, and ash fell on the street in choking drifts. She dug in her pockets for a bandana to cover her face. She tied it tight and picked up the bat. Crouching on her knees, she crawled into the alley behind the music store.

At the base of the shipping container was the violin case. Pip froze, thinking how it must have fallen off Whistler's pack when he jumped. One corner was cracked. Part of her wanted to pick it up and run back to Iris. Forget checking the street.

Taking a deep breath, she forced herself to move. She paused at the corner and pressed her hands against her thighs. Heart racing, she shook her head, wanting to deny anything she might see. *If I don't look, he'll be alive. If I walk away right now, he's fine. Looking for us*, she bargained.

A cry escaped her. She covered her mouth and looked.

Whistler was still there.

Pip pulled down the bandana and retched. His feet were bare. The bastards had taken his shoes. She spit out the yellow taste of bile and went to her friend.

He'd been rolled onto his side, the pack ripped free and emptied, pockets pulled inside out in the hunt for more ammunition. Her feet skirted the drying pool of blood outlining his body the same way her eyes skirted the gaping wound in his chest.

What if he'd been alive when she ran?

On the knife's edge of breaking, she found herself staring into his empty face. Closing his eyes, she placed a hand on his cheek and wept.

"Never again, Whist. I promise."

Barely able to breathe, Pip searched for courage and found only emptiness. She traced a line of freckles down to his neck and checked for a pulse. Nothing. Sliding a finger under the chain he always wore around his neck, Pip drew the military dog tags from under his shirt. Dried blood coated one of the tags; the other was clean.

Pip unbuckled the collar around her neck and slid Whistler's ID off its chain and onto the rusty jump ring with Utah's license. When she found the strength to put the collar back on, the weight of the tags against her chest filled her heart with failure.

Forcing herself to look at the vacant expression on Whistler's face, she cleared her throat, coughing on tears. Iris was under the porch, waiting for her to return. Pip stood up. "I won't leave her."

It was late morning by the time Pip made it back to Iris. She pried open the lattice and held out the violin case. "He's gone."

Iris crawled out and dusted herself off. She didn't say a word as she took the case and inspected the cracked corner.

"My mom hated it when I played country fiddle songs." Iris looked up. "She called it backwoods, white trash music."

"That's shitty."

Iris drummed her fingers on the case, a rapid percussion that ended with "Shave and a Haircut."

"So what do you play?"

"Fiddle music."

Pip closed her eyes. *Help me be kind to her, Whist,* she thought. "Ready for more?"

"No."

"Neither am I. Let's go."

Pip backtracked them onto a street that paralleled Monroe, hoping to keep Iris from looking back and seeing Whistler's body. After a mile of brisk walking, Pip paused for a water break. A steep cliff of basalt blocked their way. A hundred feet above, an apartment building overlooked the neighborhoods.

Pip flipped off the jagged black rock and held in a scream of frustration at their poor choices. The only other safe space she'd stocked with food was deep in the part of town that had burned. It was probably gone now. Whistler had an old hideout on the South Hill. They'd have to find a way through the Skins to get there. Dead end.

She had an idea of where they could go before it was totally dark, but that meant risking exposure on Monroe Street to work their way north. "We're gonna run for a bit."

Iris screwed the cap onto the bottle of water with a resigned nod. Picking up the pace, Pip forced herself to keep putting one tired foot in front of the other. They jogged the winding twists of Monroe Street and made quick time up the steep hill into the Garland District.

Iris waved for Pip to stop—the younger girl was a wilted flower puffing for air. Her burns were red blotches on her sweaty face as she hugged the violin case tight to her chest with both arms. Pip paused, waiting for her racing heart to calm. A persistent stitch in her side made it hard to take a deep breath. She pressed against the gunshot wound, and her palm came away wet with blood.

Wiping her bloody hand down the side of her pants, Pip took a second look at the empty breweries and antique stores butted up against houses with overgrown yards. Across the street stood the old Garland Theater. Maybe they should stop and hole up there.

A hint of movement in the alley next to the theater caught her breath. Taking a few steps closer, she saw a moving truck parked in between two buildings. A yellow one, like the one from the library. The traders were close. *What're the odds?*

"Pip?" Iris asked.

"Let's keep going."

They made it four blocks before an engine rumbled in the distance. It was behind them. Pip turned left onto a side street and jogged half a block to an alley. Holding her bat at the ready, they walked single file down the broken concrete road, passing telephone poles and the backsides of stand-alone garages.

The moving truck rumbled up Monroe—they spotted its yellow side as it passed on the main street. Pip hauled Iris behind a parked car. Dead weeds crunched under their shoes.

"Did they see us?"

"I don't think so."

"Are they following us?"

"It sure feels like it."

Pip remembered Camo saying they were looking for women and

children. Had Curtis seen them both when they'd run from the music store?

Pip took a sip of water and handed the bottle to Iris. "We're gonna stay in the alleys for a bit and walk careful."

What should have been an hour's walk turned into an hours-long trek through yards and over fences. Every time they felt safe enough to move faster, the damn yellow truck would slowly cruise past the end of an alley, and they'd have to hide to wait it out.

It was dark by the time Pip kicked in the door of a dental office that fronted Francis Avenue. They'd jogged the last half mile on Monroe, taking a straight course to race the evening and the threat of the truck to a safer location. Once inside the dental office, Pip fought exhaustion as she dumped her pack on a reclining dental chair.

Iris sprawled facedown on a chair. The violin case dangled from her hand, swinging by the handle as she lowered it the last few inches to the floor. The kid was a trooper. Not one complaint.

Pip stretched. Even with the wound burning in her side, it was easy to enjoy the peculiar lightness that always came after taking off a heavy pack. She lowered her arms. *Whistler will never take off his pack again.* She shook off the image of him sprawled in the street. Looking around the dark office, she could almost hear him telling her to check the exits.

The dental office wasn't ideal: too many windows. She turned on her heel, inspecting the exam rooms. There had to be some place, maybe an X-ray room, which would be shielded from view.

"Stay here," Pip said.

"Mmmguh," Iris mumbled into the chair.

The dental office hadn't been looted. Everything was creepily in place. Trays of tools in the prep area were organized for a day of appointments that would never come. Past a few treatment bays, Pip found the safe place she'd hoped for. A small room in the middle of the building, surrounded by thick walls with a door that locked. The X-ray technician's room.

She headed back to Iris, closing the shades of each window she passed. It was a gamble to close them; someone might notice they'd changed. Pausing with her fingers wound into the draw cord of the last blind, she shrugged, too tired to care. Nothing was certain.

In the exam room, Iris was sound asleep. A trickle of her drool dripped off the seat onto the floor.

"Ick," Pip said. She gently got Iris on her feet and nudged her toward the X-ray room. Iris lumbered down the hall, grumbling about how everything hurt. She curled up on the floor under a radiation protection blanket and was instantly snoring. Pip lay down in their new safe room, expecting sleep to dance just out of reach. It took her under hard.

The next morning when she woke, there wasn't a single part of her body that didn't complain. Even her hair hurt. She flopped onto her back, wincing at the tightness in her calves. The trip from Myers Music to the dental office couldn't have been more than four or five miles. It felt like she'd run a marathon with a knife in her side. She closed her eyes and held still, willing herself to hear a whistle somewhere in the dental office. Like Whistler had just gotten up to go exploring.

"Pip?" Iris said.

"Hmm?"

"You awake?"

"No."

Silence stretched between them. A dull ache ran from the base of Pip's throat down her wounded side, forming a pit in her stomach. She'd let Whistler down.

"Where do you think Kitty is?"

Pip ran her fingers over the old scratches on her arm. She hadn't once thought about the little black cat since she'd vanished over the edge of the roof. "Hell."

The locks on the violin case popped open. Pip rolled up on her elbow and grunted at a stabbing pain. What had been a simple wound two days before throbbed to angry life.

"You okay?" Iris was immediately at her side, worry written all over her face.

Rolling herself off the pile of blankets she'd found in the surgery room, Pip winced as she peeled up her shirt. Iris helped her unwind the long coil of bloodstained elastic bandage. The look on

Iris's face said it all. Pip needed more than a squirt of antibiotic ointment to fix things.

"You need penicillin. Or amoxicillin if you're allergic," Iris said.

"How'd you know that?"

Iris's lips tightened into a thin line. "My mom was a doctor."

"Ah." Pip eased her shirt down. "It feels like I've been bitten by a T. rex. *Chomp*."

A tiny smile winked on Iris's face for the barest second. She picked up the violin and tuned it, plucking each string with the tip of a fingernail. The sound reminded Pip of a broken wind chime. *Plink*. Pause. *Plunk*. *Twang*. Pause. Notes filled the air as Iris twisted the tuning knobs.

"So is it a violin or a fiddle?"

Iris tucked her hair behind both ears, her face serious. "Both. What you play is what you call it. Classical: violin. Hillbilly: fiddle."

"Huh."

"Kinda like me."

"What?"

"If I was in China, I'd be Xiuying. Here, I'm Iris."

"I don't understand."

"My name, the one my birth mother gave me, means 'beautiful flower.' That's why my parents named me Iris." She set down the violin with a frown. "I don't like the name Iris."

Pip nodded, understanding. "Would you prefer I call you Xiuying?"

"No!" Iris flapped her hands like frightened birds. "That isn't me either."

Pip got up from the floor and did a painful lap around the exam room. She knew the burden of not knowing who you were. Iris heaved a breath while bars of sunlight sparkled across the dust floating between them. Pip paused and traced the jail cell bars of shadow cast on the wall.

Iris wasn't the only one with two names.

CHAPTER 10

Pip tapped her front tooth in thought. "You know, you can be Iris *and* Xiuying. Or something completely different. You're the one who makes you...*you.*"

"Huh?"

Gesturing for Iris to follow, Pip pulled a food bag out of her pack. She assembled a compact one-use heating packet she'd gotten from the army-navy surplus store, splashed some water into the bag, and left it to heat. Digging in the pack for an aluminum cup, Pip poured in a measure of powder.

"Every person is like these eggs." She tipped the cup so Iris could see the sliding hill of yellowish grit. "We both know these are eggs, right? But how?"

"The powder is yellow, kinda like an egg," Iris said thoughtfully. "And you said it was an egg."

Pip hummed agreement. "Right. I've told you this is an egg, so you see an egg. You know what it will taste like—you even know what it will look like when cooked."

"So?"

Pip checked the water's temperature, then playfully flicked warm drops off her fingers at Iris. She poured water onto the powder in the cup.

Iris was confused when the scent of the dissolving powder filled the air. "Lemon?"

Swirling a spoon around in the cup, Pip scooped out a mouthful of thick custard and held it out. Iris sniffed at the steaming custard, then ate. Her face lit up with surprise. She held out her hands for the cup and spoon. She was ready for more.

Pip got another cup. "We judge a person's clothes, their build, how they stand, the sound of their voice—everything. Other people decide how we're seen and how we see ourselves."

"I get it," Iris said. "I thought I knew what the powder was because of what you said."

"Yeah. You think you're Iris because of what your parents said." Pip tilted her hand in a seesaw motion. "You think you're Xiuying because of what your birth certificate says. But what are you when you add water?"

Iris studied Pip's face thoughtfully, considering the question.

Pip poured hot water over the powder in her cup and stirred. "You take what you want and make something new. Something...you."

Iris's eyes widened as a solidness seemed to shift inside. Her shoulders relaxed, she sat taller. Her delicate cheekbones, already sharp, hollowed out her face as she smiled. There was a pride there, an understanding of self, like Pip's words had just given Iris permission to be who she wanted to be. Pip acknowledged Iris's grin with one of her own and took a chance.

"*My* birth name was Noah Philip."

Iris's mouth dropped open.

"Rocks the world a bit, doesn't it?" Pip said. "Until I was ten, I thought, I knew, I was a boy. When my period started I found out I was also a girl. Turns out, my parents knew a secret about me. Something they hadn't bothered to share, like if they kept quiet about it, I'd never figure it out. It was when they took me to a specialist—" Inhaling hard through her nostrils, Pip held the anger for a long moment.

Then she exhaled, feeling the sting of her breath against chapped lips. The question of how her parents had been persuaded not to have a surgeon rip away the female parts of her was one she'd never be able to answer. She closed her eyes for a moment and thanked whoever was responsible for that decision.

She opened her eyes and smiled reassuringly at Iris. "It was a doctor who finally explained it. I'm intersex."

"Intersex?" Confused wrinkles deeper than the Grand Canyon

crossed Iris's forehead as she spoke the unfamiliar word. "What does that mean?"

"For me, it means on a physical level, most of me is female and some of me is male."

Iris tucked her chin into the neck of her shirt and Pip hesitated, wondering if she'd made a mistake. *Tell it all. Tell her the truth: she isn't alone.* It felt like Whistler was right there, whispering in her ear, urging her to speak.

"I'm a girl, with a little extra."

"But—" Iris blurted.

"One in roughly every two thousand babies is born like me. Most don't even realize they're different. For the ones who look different on the outside, doctors and parents used to choose the baby's gender based on what their junk *most* looked like. My parents decided I was a boy. And even though I had a small vagina, the doctors told them I'd probably never get a period."

"But. How?" Iris asked. Curiosity uncurled her from the protection of the T-shirt. She raked her gaze over Pip's body, taking in all her physical details.

Pip tried not to feel like an animal being observed at a zoo while Iris adjusted her view.

See me, Pip thought with tense desperation. *See me.*

Skittery as a deer, Iris moved closer and took a deep breath, thinking.

"Does it *really* matter how?" Pip said softly. Watching the neutral expression on Iris's face, she allowed herself to hope.

"So when you were a baby you...looked more like a boy?" Iris shot a blushing glance toward Pip's lap.

"I qualified as a boy. But when the doctor told me I was intersex"—Pip smiled at the relief she carried with her every day—"I could be what I was. But in the end, my parents weren't happy with the person I became."

She got up and cracked open the blinds, letting in a little light. "By the time I was fifteen, I was more Pip than Noah Philip, more feminine than masculine."

"Pip. Short for Philip," Iris finally said.

Pip nodded.

"What did your parents do?" Iris said.

"Threw me out." She crossed her arms and considered. "Maybe I threw myself out. I hated them for not being able to see me. My father hated me for not being the son he'd always wanted. My mom—" The pain was an old wound, stretched tight, pulling at her heart. "My mom's Bible told her I was a sin. She loved me, but that wasn't enough."

"I'm sorry, Pip."

"Don't be. It isn't your fault." She ate a few spoonfuls of lemon dessert. "So, what do I call *you*?"

Iris set down her cup. "If I say Iris, will you be mad?"

Pip shook her head. "Nope."

"Even though I hate the name, I think I'm still an Iris."

Pip finished her lemon custard while Iris rummaged through the drawers in the X-ray room. A stinging pain in her side propelled Pip to her feet. Pressing a hand against the wound, she peeked through the blinds to study the grocery store catty-corner across the street. Holding the plastic slats apart with two fingers, she peered at the wreck of the parking lot and gas station. Iris hadn't been wrong. Pip needed antibiotics, and their best hope to find them was in the pharmacy in the grocery store.

Iris found a cupboard full of the molds of people's mouths and held up a model with baby teeth. The adult teeth hid just above the gums like it was a shark's mouth. It was horrifying. Iris stuck out her tongue in mock disgust. Pip's heart soared and crashed. Grief wrapped around responsibility and looped through growing affection like the tangle of yarn Whistler had carried in his pockets.

A sob escaped Pip's lips. She clamped a hand over her mouth, muscling down the emotion. "Be right back, I'm gonna check the bathroom."

She left the X-ray room and hurried down a side hall to another window, farther away from Iris. Pacing like a caged animal, Pip wrestled with her emotions. Her nose burned with unshed tears. Her throat worked against cries that fought to come out. Walking with uncertain steps, Pip grabbed her pack. She was several steps closer to the door before she'd even stopped to think. Tracing the fake woodgrain on the door with tired eyes, it was all she could do to keep from running away from her feelings. She wanted to yell. To scream loud enough to knock down the door and let herself out.

Her promise was an elephant's weight on her chest. It was hard to breathe. *How can I do this?*

The rough pack strap chafed against her hand like the collar around her neck. Whistler's dog tag was a chilling reminder that filled the hollow at the base of her throat. She'd made a promise to Utah. A promise to Whistler. A promise to Iris. She dropped the backpack on the floor. She wasn't going anywhere.

"What was that?" Iris ran out of the X-ray room and found her.

"Sorry." Pip crossed her arms, trapping indecision and covering it with a smile. "Dropped my pack."

"Okay," Iris grinned.

Dragging Iris off the bridge had been instinct. Taking her to the music store had been the right thing to do. Pip shifted the collar so the clasp pressed against the back of her neck. Making a promise was cake. Keeping a promise was the hard work that came after. Cleaning up the pots and pans and making sure the cake didn't burn in the oven. She wouldn't let Iris burn.

Heat flared on Pip's side. The intense pain had her more than a little worried. It was time they got moving.

"Time to go."

Iris retied her shoes, tucking in the laces while Pip made quick work of rolling up the sleeping bag. She pulled a change of clothes and a tent out of the pack to make room for supplies from the store.

With every movement, her shoulders screamed from the beating they'd taken the day before. Pip's body was a symphony of pain that was only getting louder. Swinging on her pack with a grunt, she poked the dental office door open with her bat and did a slow sweep of the parking lot, scanning for movement. Crossing Francis Avenue—a wide, four-lane street—during daylight wasn't ideal, but they needed sunshine to conceal the flashlight while they were inside the store. In the middle of the night, bouncing circles of light would be a beacon alerting the Skins or the traders to their location.

She watched Iris swing their military-issue flashlight a couple of times with eager confidence and suppressed an urge to ruffle her hair.

They moved in tandem, Iris mimicking Pip's every step as they wove between abandoned vehicles. Crouching by the rust-pitted bumper of a car, Pip checked all four directions, quartering the view at twelve, three, six, and nine, like on a clock. She felt the memory of Whistler standing at her shoulder. She could almost feel his callused fingers, rough through the fabric of her shirt, holding her still, telling her to watch her corners. Her throat thickened with regret as she checked their surroundings again. Just like he'd taught her.

Iris glanced at Pip, asking for confirmation that it was safe.

"Quick, like a bunny," Pip reminded her.

Iris sprinted out of cover toward the ravaged front of the grocery store. Pip let out a relieved breath when Iris reached the twisted metal of the broken automatic doors and ducked safely inside. Surveying the street behind her one last time, Pip took a chance and jogged to the entrance. A shoal of broken safety glass covered the sidewalk in front of the store. She slipped on the smooth pieces of glass as she entered the grocery store and gagged at the rotten smells oozing out of the dark.

Iris crouched next to the shopping carts and wiped VapoRub around her nose. She immediately looked relieved and handed the bottle to Pip. Once the stinging eucalyptus lotion was deep in Pip's nostrils, she ripped her bandana in half and handed one piece to Iris. They both tied the fabric over their faces as a double barrier against the nauseatingly spoiled odors wafting from the produce and meat departments.

Iris gave a thumbs-up, her brown eyes crinkling over the purple fabric tied around her face. Pip shoved her bat into her pack and clicked on the flashlight. Spilled coffee beans in front of an espresso stand crunched under their feet. Moldy bits of baked goods were on display in the counter case. Pip shoved away a wistful memory of vanilla scones and turned to check on Iris. Tears soaked Iris's bandana. Pip moved closer and tried to read Iris's mood. "You okay?"

"The VapoRub, it's making everything run." She swiped a hand over her irritated eyes.

Hairs tingled in warning at the nape of Pip's neck. The disarray of the store—the riot-tossed endcaps and rows of empty shelves—screamed danger. People had been there; perhaps they still were. She took a few steps away from the coffee kiosk and played her light over the floral department. Magazines flung from a stand fluttered in a slight breeze. Besides the dry-leaf crinkle of pages, everything was still.

"Stick close," Pip instructed.

They stepped nimbly past flipped-over carts and the remains of a small campfire. The main part of the store had been picked clean during One Mile Cough's deadly spread. Bread and water had gone first, then everything else as survivors scrounged for something to eat.

Her plan was to check the pharmacy for antibiotics before exploring the large stockroom in the back.

"Hey!" Iris shout-whispered. She held up a protein bar, the foil wrapper winking in the light. "White chocolate and macadamia nut. That's my favorite." Iris ripped open the package.

Pip moved on, amused by the mouse-nibble crunching of Iris enjoying her snack. She probably could only taste eucalyptus from the VapoRub in her nose. That didn't prevent Iris from hastily finishing the bar.

They climbed over an upturned blood pressure monitor outside the pharmacy.

"Hold up." Pip raised a hand.

Something about the hole in the security gate reminded her of the one she'd seen in the library. She looked around, shining light into corners, checking down the long hall toward the produce department. *Jumping at shadows.*

"Okay."

Iris's foot caught in the broken security gate. Vitamin bottles launched out of a display, rattling like hail in a summer storm. Iris hopped up, rubbing her shoulder.

"Sorry."

"You okay?" Pip asked.

"Tripped." Iris shrugged, embarrassed. "That was really loud."

She was starting to poke a bottle with a toe when Pip held up a hand for silence. Iris froze, one foot hanging forgotten in the air as they listened. Pip wished for the radar dish–sized ears of a deer, like the ones from the music store. She held her breath and tilted her head toward the front of the store. Was that the crinkle of pages, or furtive footsteps?

CHAPTER 11

Quiet spun out between them.

"I think we're good," Pip said. She gestured for Iris to follow.

They pushed through the jagged, chopped-off pieces of security gate. Pills of every size scattered the floor like colorful sprinkles.

Pip quietly cheered when she located a small cabinet full of penicillin while digging through the chaos. She popped the top off the closest bottle, dry swallowed two pills, and stuffed the bottle in her pocket. She dumped the rest in her pack. Even if she didn't need them all, antibiotics would make for valuable trading if they ran into other people. Pip grabbed a few inhalers and other various drugs that seemed like they might be good in an emergency.

When the empty spaces in her pack were about half full, she cinched the top. "Let's check the back."

Keeping to the rear wall of the store, they worked their way toward the oversized double doors of the stockroom. Pip checked through a wavy plastic window in the door and was pleased to see nothing but darkness. Pushing against the rubber gasket, she held the door open for Iris and silently closed it behind them.

Torn piles of plastic tangled on the floor—waves of the shiny material led toward the storage area. The warehouse had been looted, boxes ripped open, their contents spilled onto the floor. Pip shined her light along the scaffolding used to hold supplies needed to restock the store shelves.

"Jackpot!" she cheered.

None of the survivors had risked climbing for food that needed to be retrieved with a forklift. The nearest boxes were twenty feet off the ground and held bags of chips. Pip passed them by. Iris trailed behind, wistfully reading the brands.

"Pringles, Pip. And Ruffles...I'd kill for a potato chip," Iris groaned.

"Hmm. I'd kill for a cheesecake. Think they've got a box of those?"

"Ooh, gummy bears."

Pip shined her light on Iris. She'd clasped her hands together, gazing with rapture at cases of rainbow-colored candy bears. Pip soaked for a moment in Iris's innocent wonder. Flipping open her pocketknife, she jumped as high as she could and slashed at the closest box. A rainbow of gummies tumbled out of their packaging. Iris danced in the sugary rain, catching bears and stuffing them into her pockets.

Snagging a few uncut bags, Pip slipped them into her pack as a surprise for later. Iris tucked a bear under her bandana and chewed with delight.

"Alright you, enough of the junk food. Soup and powdered potatoes over this way."

She steered Iris away from the candy. Iris reached longingly toward the gummy bears like an overly dramatic B-movie heroine and grinned at her own silliness.

The soup cans were right there for the taking. Pip swallowed nervously as she gauged their height at over fifteen feet off the concrete floor. The steel scaffolding was designed for strength. She wasn't worried about it holding her weight. It was the lack of handholds that made her wary.

"I can climb it!" Iris said.

"Of course you can. But I know what kind of food we're looking for."

Pip shrugged out of her pack, made sure the knife was secure in her back pocket, and rolled over a beer keg as a boost; the metal barrel was full of liquid and sturdy enough to balance on while she figured out where to put her hands. There wasn't a clear spot on the shelf above. She shoved hard at a box and managed to move it out of the way.

Satisfied she'd made enough room to stand, Pip reached for the scaffold. The metal pipe was rough—barbed ridges of metal bit into her palms as she pulled up and hooked a leg over the bar.

She grunted with effort, and something in her bullet wound tore. It was a struggle, but she managed to get her body onto the shelf.

"Not pretty," she puffed.

"But you're up!" Iris said.

"It's embarrassing how surprised you sound."

Pip cut plastic wrappings off boxes, then tossed cans and packages to Iris. They made a game of it, with Pip faking throws and Iris pretending to fumble almost every can. After a while, Iris tugged the bandana off her sweaty face and took a deep breath.

"It doesn't smell bad in here."

Pip pulled her bandana down and enjoyed the cool air on her cheeks. "Yes, it does. You just can't smell it anymore."

"Either way, I don't care." Iris looked around.

"What is it?"

"Bathroom," Iris said.

Pip shrugged. "Pick a corner."

"Ew. There's a bathroom right back there. I saw it when we came in." Iris turned to go.

"Wait." Pip looked over the edge and knew it was too far to jump. "Wait until I get down."

Iris swept the light back to the double doors with a determined look. "I'll be right back."

"Wait!"

Iris jogged to the entrance of the storeroom and then went around a corner, unthinkingly taking the light. She left Pip up in the air in the dark.

"Shit."

Taking a firm grip on the scaffold, she eased herself down, legs dangling over the edge. She punched the nearest box in frustration. But when minutes passed, her irritation became tinged with worry. Scooting her butt closer to the edge, she looked down at the black, trying to remember exactly where the keg was.

With my luck, I'd break my leg at the same time she came back with the light.

Pip scooted forward. A muffled grunt came from the other side of the cavernous room. Goosebumps rashed her arms, leaving her cold. Boxes tumbled, and she heard quick panting and the running footfalls of multiple people.

"Iris," Pip breathed.

Someone squealed in surprise as the footfalls increased in tempo. More boxes crashed. Pip almost fell when Iris screamed.

"Pip! He—" Iris was drowned out by cheering voices and the shattering of glass.

Without thinking, Pip rolled onto her stomach and slid backward off the lip. Her sweaty palms slipped, and she barely felt the electric pain of her pinky nail peeling away as she swung down. One foot crashed into the beer keg. She got a toe on it, found her balance, and slid to the floor without making any noise.

People shouted victory in the hallway. Blue-tinged light flashed across the room. Pip winced at the sudden brightness and hustled to her backpack. Fingers shaking, she fumbled at the knot holding the bat to the pack. She yanked it loose and sprinted for the doorway. She slid behind a stack of boxes just as the intruders shoved their way into the storeroom.

"Kid isn't alone," a female voice announced.

Two silhouettes spread out, beams of light cutting across the storage area in jagged arcs as they searched. Pip lifted a box of coffee cups a few inches off the floor and moved it to block the light.

"Backpack!" a man shouted.

She risked a glimpse around the box. The man and a young woman converged on her pack. The man stepped away from the bag and shined his light on the floor.

"Looks like blood."

"Not a lot," the woman said. She paused, studying something. "Huh."

Pip looked down at her hands and finally registered the pain searing her little finger. Blood oozed sluggishly from her hand down to her elbow and splattered in small drops on the concrete. Stomach sinking, she knew they would follow her trail.

Hide or fight. She touched the dog collar around her neck. Whistler would fight. But attacking was pointless if there were too many of them. The trouble was calculating how many people were in the group. There had to be more people with Iris. At *least* four opponents. She shook her head at the odds.

Glancing around the box again, Pip realized the woman was definitely following the trail of blood. It would be a matter of seconds before she was discovered. Pip ran her hand over the floor, searching for something to throw, and landed on a bag of gummy bears. Heart pounding, she waited until the woman started to move the box.

Pip hurled the candy at the woman's face and came around the box swinging the bat. The woman collapsed when the metal cracked against her skull.

The woman's dropped flashlight bounced across the floor. As it spun away from them, crazy shadows jumped and danced in the air. Pip used the distraction to run at the remaining man, catching him in the side with the bat. Her shoulders wrenched as he clutched at the handle, fighting for control. Pip yanked hard, pulling it out of his reach. She raised the bat to hit him again.

Bright-red light flashed in her head.

Pain exploded across the base of her neck. She stumbled, crashing sideways into her pack and sliding unconscious to the floor.

CHAPTER 12

The world returned in agonizing waves. Pip shut her eyes against the torment of her brain pounding its way out of her skull. Random lightning bolts of pain zipped over her scalp, stabbing her eye with cold precision every time her body jolted.

Feels like I tried to kiss a freight train, she thought, right before something ground on the raw flesh of her pinky and sent her into the black.

The next time she rolled to the surface everything throbbed with her pulse. A blanket of pain wrapped around her head, muddling her memories, making it hard to remember anything. Pip took a deep breath—the scent of fearful, unwashed bodies assaulted her, slapping disoriented thoughts into order. She opened her eyes.

Surrounded by dirty shoes and bare feet, she was curled up on the bed of a moving truck. The toes closest to her nose had gnarled yellow nails, twisted with age. Pip rocked forward as they went over a bump, skinning her nose on a jagged nail. Gentle hands gripped her shoulders, holding her in place against the truck's jostling.

The rocking lulled her back into the blackness, even as she fought to remain awake. There was something she needed to do. Something to stay for. Someone to stay with.

"Pip." Wet-hot breath warmed her ear. Someone had called her name. "Wake up." The voice returned, this time with a pinch to her inner arm.

Pip opened her eyes to a blurry double view. Two wavering faces hung over her, mouths and eyes overlapping, twisted like a nightmare kaleidoscope. She squinted, forcing life into focus. Iris's hair formed a curtain around them that shut out the rest of the world. Her sweaty palms stuck to Pip's cheeks. Pip didn't have the energy to push them away.

"Where?" Pip croaked.

Iris hunched forward, lips touching Pip's ear. "Shhh."

The truck went over a particularly large bump and Iris lost her balance. They nearly knocked foreheads. Pip tried to push up on an elbow. Blood pounded into her temples—she quickly closed her eyes to keep them from popping out of their sockets. Strong fingers pressed hard against the sides of her head, compressing the pain.

"Ahh," she said with genuine relief. Opening her eyes to risk a look, Pip spied her savior: an elderly woman whose toothless, wrinkled face radiated troubled kindness.

"Thanks," Pip managed.

The woman tightened her grip, applying one last squeeze before letting go. This time, Pip supported her own bruised neck, wincing at random muscle cramps shooting pain down her spine. More helpful hands pressed against her back and Iris leaned into her shoulder, helping her sit up.

A blur of people huddled together, crowded onto benches in the cargo area of a moving truck. All of them had their hands resting in their laps, wrists together. Their poses reminded Pip of sitting in the back of a cop car: shoulders hunched and posture defeated. Pip blinked hard, trying to clear her vision. Stuffed under the benches were bags and backpacks. A row of milk crates lined the end of the truck bed. They were filled with books.

She swayed with the rhythm of the rocking vehicle and felt a wave of recognition.

Oh shit. This is the truck from the library. The trader's truck.

Two cool hands gripped hers. A plastic zip tie bit into the wrists of those hands, holding them together. Rusty-purple scars on brown skin traced up those arms like they'd been splashed with fire. An appraising smirk dimpled the freckled cheek of the owner of the bound hands. The young woman's perfectly shaped hair was shaved to a practical quarter inch. The delicate gold hoop curving through the septum of her nose looked like it belonged there. Pip blinked as the young woman eyed her with similar appraising scrutiny. Pip stared back, unsure if her heart was galloping from the pain of her injuries or maybe from something else entirely.

Iris roughly cleared her throat, pulling Pip's attention away from the woman. Iris had the same zip-tie handcuffs binding her hands. Everyone in the back of the truck did.

"Are you alright?"

Iris nodded. "I was worried you wouldn't wake up."

Pip rubbed the back of her neck and found a goose egg on the base of her skull.

Iris eagerly pointed to a trio of high school–aged girls bunched together in a far corner. "They're from my house, the one that burned down. The tan one with the pink pants is Jessica." Iris leaned close and whispered, "Jessica never liked me much."

Jessica held up her hands in greeting, then let them drop back into her lap. Her blond hair was tangled and streaked with soot. The skin on her face appeared loose, like she was dehydrated.

"The Skins caught them running from our house and stuck her in the moving truck. She saw you come out of the library."

"What?" *But that was days ago,* Pip thought. "You've been in here this whole time?"

Jessica gave a tired nod and closed her eyes.

The rolled-up loading door hung unevenly from the roof, leaving the cargo area open to the air. Even with the open door, the inside of the truck was a stinking pit of crushed-together humanity. The only things keeping any of them from falling out were several thick waist-high ropes crisscrossing the gap. The truck rolled along down a paved road at no more than walking speed. A motorcycle followed at a short distance behind the truck.

The engine downshifted, brakes squealing in protest, rocking everyone with a hard stop. All heads turned at the sound of muffled shouting coming from the cab. A raging argument ended with the slam of a door. Everyone in the truck tracked the crunch of boots on the road until a scowling man in a greasy camouflage jacket stepped into view. *Oh shit.* It was Camo, the trader from the library.

He bounced a knife on his palm, then shoved it into a pocket when the motorcycle rolled up and stopped. Curtis popped the kickstand and stepped off. A wave of stunned heat washed over Pip's body, filling her guts with squirming eels. Whistler's killer was only steps away. And there was nothing she could do about it.

"You four." Camo pointed at the four men in the truck and gestured for them to come to the opening.

Everyone else shuffled around like amoebas, rearranging themselves and carefully stepping around Pip so the men could get out.

Camo growled when Pip gingerly scooted on her butt to get out of the way. "Don't move."

Everyone froze.

"God damn it! I'm not talking to you morons." He jabbed his finger at Pip. "You. Come here."

She moved closer to the open door and hesitated.

"Crawl out or I'm coming in."

Pip met the intense eyes of the young woman who'd held her hand. Her eyes widened in fear at the prospect of Camo coming into the truck.

"Go," the young woman mouthed.

Pip squirmed sideways through the group and slid under the ropes. Her feet hadn't even touched the ground before Camo grabbed her hands and held them out for Curtis to zip-tie her wrists together. Her heart pounded as she waited for Curtis to realize he knew her from the music store. There wasn't a spark of recognition in his eyes. He went about his job of making her a prisoner.

"What the hell is this?" Camo yanked at the dog collar around Pip's neck. "Woof, woof," he barked. Spit flecked her face.

She clenched her fists, body tensing, crouching to fight. Camo saw her anger and sneered before slamming a fist into the gut of the man next to her. The surprised prisoner tripped backward with a whoosh of expelled air. Stunned into immobility, Pip stared at the gasping man sprawled on the pavement. A hard slap to the face almost knocked her over. Pain exploded, doubling the already crippling headache pounding at her temples.

"One of you screws with me, you all get screwed." Camo snatched at the neck of her shirt and dragged her close.

His rank breath gagged her as he unbuckled the collar around her neck and yanked it free. It hit the ground with a jingle of tags. Pip kept her eyes down, studying the weave of the collar's fabric. Just like that. Collar gone. Promise broken. She wished with all her heart for Whistler and his rifle's retribution.

Camo laughed, mistaking her rage for submission. Curtis trained a six-shooter pistol on them with a steady hand, his finger tapping lightly on the trigger guard. Pip shifted over a few inches to block the truck's opening. If the gun were to fire, a stray shot would hit her and not Iris.

"Get him up." Camo gestured for them to follow.

Pip helped the injured man Camo had gut-punched. They leaned on each other, barely managing to keep their feet.

Curtis shouted for the group to stop at the moving truck's bug-speckled front bumper. The truck was parked on a wide highway with six lanes divided by a concrete wall. Interchanges crossed over the freeway back the way they'd come. Pip knew this stretch of road: they were a thirty-minute drive north of the city. The only destinations in front of them were a couple of small towns and Canada.

Where were they going?

The passenger-side window rolled down and a sour-faced woman leaned out. It was Navvy. She pointed a dirty finger at Pip.

"What's *that bastard* doing out of the truck?"

"Didn't want him to miss out on the fun," Camo answered.

Him, Pip thought. *Things just got more dangerous.* She flashed back to her dad's rage when he realized the child he'd raised as a boy was actually a girl. Her dad started by tearing her with words. When that didn't work, he used his fists.

The muscles in Pip's back twitched, spasming at the possibility of being caught. Under Camo's watchful eyes, her shoulders hunched tight to her ears with nervous tension until she forced them down.

Do I dare go back? The thought of pretending to be something she wasn't made her mouth dry as a desert, but she picked up the shreds of who she'd been as a child and put him on. She climbed into the feeling of being Noah Philip one piece at a time, promising herself she could take him off whenever she wanted. This was only a change of who she was on the surface. She would be a chameleon, protecting herself with a shield of maleness. She'd done it before, but it fit like a badly tailored suit.

Pip changed her stance, trying to bulk up her arms and hold herself more like the teenage boy the traders thought she was. She eyed Camo. He was a big man, shaped in the same kind of mold that had made her father. Hit first and ask questions later.

Camo poked her in the shoulder, his finger digging deep into the muscle. "Navvy doesn't like you. You busted up Tami."

Imagine if Navvy knew she'd already killed someone from her crew. So many things to hide now.

Crooked teeth jutted from Navvy's lower jaw, giving her the appearance of an angry bulldog. "Move that pile of shit out of the way." She rolled up the window.

Camo jerked a thumb at the muscular black man at the front of their group. "Guess she's talkin' to you."

The prisoner was older than Pip, maybe in his late twenties. A diagonal gash cut across his pecs. Fresh blood soaked the fabric of his ripped shirt, but it wasn't slowing him down. His build reminded her of a gym instructor, one of those guys who worked out every day, so muscled they had trouble putting their arms down at their sides. She dubbed him "Muscles" and hoped she'd get to see him crush Camo like an empty can.

Camo pulled a folded map from his back pocket and consulted it. After a moment, he lounged against the truck's bumper and pointed. "New business means a new route and new pain-in-the-ass problems. *For you.*"

Not far from where they'd stopped, a collision of four vehicles blocked the road. Pip studied the remains of the accident with resignation. Sometime in the panic of trying to escape from One Mile Cough, two cars, a minivan, and a semitruck had crashed. Judging by the skeletons in and around the wreckage, the unfortunate collision had occurred quite some time ago. The northbound side of the freeway was completely blocked. Lanes going the other direction were clear, but the concrete divider made crossing over to the other side impossible.

"Why not go back and drive up the other side?" Pip asked.

Camo hocked and spit. "This is the smallest crash for miles."

Muscles cracked his knuckles. "Why are we going this way? Where are we going?"

"Shut up," Camo drawled. He nodded at Curtis, who then pointed the gun at Muscles.

The bleat of the truck's horn made Pip's heart stutter in her chest. Except for Camo, they all startled at the loud noise. Camo's giggle at their surprise was like a locked room in an insane asylum.

"Make a hole or I'll have Curtis make a hole in you."

It sounded like a phrase he'd practiced delivering in front of a mirror.

CHAPTER 13

They shuffled forward, uncertain of where to start. One of the prisoners kept favoring his right arm where a purple bruise wrapped around his elbow. Along the edge of the swollen joint, greenish yellow faded into his white skin. The arm had to be broken. Pip winced in sympathy and unbuckled her belt.

"Wait. This might help." Wrapping the middle part of the belt around his wrist, she buckled the ends over his other shoulder. He let the weight of his arm hang in the makeshift sling.

"Thanks. I'm Jack."

"Pip."

Stomach-Punched Guy raised two fingers. "I'm Ben."

The teenager opened his mouth and was interrupted by Camo's impatient drawl. "And I'm your worst nightmare. Stop pissing around."

Pip considered the danger of flipping Camo off. Instead, she gauged the space they'd need for the moving truck. If the minivan could be rolled off the embankment into the gully, maybe the truck would fit.

"Move the van." The teenager had come to the same conclusion.

Spidery cracks traced the windows, but none of them had broken. The group moved toward the minivan and tried the doors. It was locked.

Jack face-palmed. "Is this an automatic?"

"Huh?" said Muscles.

Pip had a flash of her father with his head under the hood of a car, his greasy fingers reaching for a tool. His voice nagging for her to pay attention. "If the battery is dead, can you even shift it into neutral?" Pip asked.

A rock bounced painfully off her shoulder and rattled across the hood of the minivan.

"Hurry up," Camo threatened.

Ben groaned. His face took on a decidedly greenish tone as he studied the van. He cleared his throat. "I can get it going."

Pip raised her eyebrows, and Muscles stepped closer, pulling the group into a huddle.

"How's that?" Muscles asked.

"There's a button by the shifter. You have to pry up a panel and push it. Once you depress the button you can shift into neutral. We'll get it rolling."

They examined the van. Beads of condensation covered the inside of every window, obscuring any glimpse of what waited inside. Pip counted one shadowy skull and the top of a car seat. She didn't look at the car seat for long. An entire bottle of VapoRub couldn't combat the awful stink that would billow out when the van busted open.

As the teen looked at the wide concrete shoulder on the side of the road, his voice cracked with nerves. "I think there's enough room already. Don't you guys?"

Camo pushed off the bumper and sauntered toward the teen. A mean grin spread across Camo's face as he checked the cab of the moving truck, making sure he had an audience. Quicker than a blink, he kicked Jack in the elbow of his broken arm. Jack collapsed without a sound.

"Gonna be hard to get the van moving with only four of you," Camo chuckled. He strutted back to his resting spot on the truck's bumper.

"I'm gonna kill him," Pip muttered under her breath as she bent to check on Jack.

"Not if I do it first," Muscles answered.

They moved Jack's unconscious body into the shade of the minivan.

Muscles climbed onto the hood, found his balance, and raised a broken piece of a car's bumper above his head. "This sucks," he said as he got ready to swing at the windshield. "Ready?"

Ben held a sharp piece of metal he'd scrounged from the wreckage in his bound hands. A little whimper escaped his lips as he hid his face in the crook of his arm. The teenager inhaled and clapped his hands over his nose and mouth, holding in the fresh air. Pip didn't even try to hold her breath. When the windshield finally broke, she had one goal: not to barf on her clothes or Jack. She shielded her face with an arm and waited. There was an explosive pop, followed by a sickening hiss, and they all gagged, overwhelmed by the putrid scent of the minivan. It filled her pores, soaking her with the stench of death.

Muscles kicked the fractured windshield into the minivan as Ben coughed deep, ragged coughs that turned into frantic gulping. He took Muscles's place on the hood. Tears poured from his eyes as he dove into the car.

Pip grabbed his nearest ankle, keeping him from sliding all the way into the van.

Something clunked.

"Pull me back!" Ben hollered.

They dragged him out. He landed on the pavement with a grunt. What he'd seen inside the minivan left him shuddering in the afternoon sun.

"You okay?" Pip asked.

"No. I'm not. Let's get this over with."

Muscles moved Jack out of the way, and they piled up on the rear passenger side to push. They shoved in short bursts, getting the minivan rocking on its tires. Gears squealed as the van inched forward. They yelled triumphantly when the van picked up speed and disappeared over the brink.

A horn blared, shocking them into silence.

"Let's go!" Navvy yelled.

Camo tilted his head toward the rear of the moving truck. "You heard her."

Curtis walked backward, keeping them covered with the gun. He waved the barrel, gesturing for them to hurry up.

"What about him?" Muscles pointed at Jack.

"Carry him."

Huffing an exasperated laugh, Muscles held out his bound

hands. Camo dug in his pocket for the knife, flicked out the blade, and cut the zip tie. The plastic band popped and fell on the ground. "Don't do anything stupid."

Muscles picked Jack up, tossing him over one shoulder in an efficient fireman's carry. He stared at Camo with flat eyes.

"Stop thinking, *boy*. Get him in the truck," Camo said.

Without warning, Muscles bent at the waist and hurled Jack's body at Curtis. Their limbs slammed together, sending the gun flying into the ditch. Camo took one look at Curtis trapped flat on his back under Jack and ran for the passenger door of the truck. Muscles wasted no time jumping the ditch and hauling ass up the bank.

As the big man tore up the hill, Pip realized she had a chance to grab Iris and escape. She ran around Curtis as he struggled out from under Jack. When she reached the back of the van, a gun fired and the crack of it slapped against her eardrums. Pip flinched, sliding on loose gravel. She landed hard on her side against the tailgate.

Pain burst in her wound, blinding her.

Someone grabbed her shirt and hauled her off the ground, dragging her into the truck. She barely felt hands patting her down, searching for an injury.

"Are you okay?" a voice shouted over the ringing in her ears.

Pip elbowed people out of the way to lean out of the truck. The teenager jumped off the pavement and landed hard in the ditch. He was halfway up the hill when the gun went off again. He fell on his face, sprawling in wild grass. Muscles was nowhere to be seen.

"What's happening?" Iris cried.

When the teenager didn't move again, Curtis lowered the gun. Seeing a chance to attack, Pip gathered herself.

The barrel of a rifle pressed against her left temple.

"Try it," Camo huffed.

Pip froze. Afraid to blink. Iris crouched right beside her, panting in fear.

"You don't want to do this," the young woman with the scarred hands said to Camo. She knelt by Pip's other side and gently pulled her away from the rifle.

Camo's laugh was the squeal of a fork grinding against a plate.

"You." He pointed at Ben crouched on the pavement next to the rear of the van. "Pick him up."

Ben wobbled to his feet. He gathered Jack's limp body like a sack of potatoes and tried to shove him onto the truck. Pip and the scarred girl hauled with all their might. It took all three of them to get Jack back on board.

Camo banged on the side of the truck and the engine shuddered to life, exhaust backfiring with a cloud of black smoke. Curtis waited until the truck started to roll before holstering his gun and starting his motorcycle.

Pip made herself study the teenager's body while they bumped over the rocky shoulder and pulled away. She hadn't even known his name. She reached for Utah's collar and closed her fist around empty air. Pip bowed her head. She'd left her promise to Whistler and Utah on the side of the road. She'd left the collar behind.

The prisoners rocked, their bodies knocking together as the van weaved haphazardly between abandoned cars. It wasn't long before they bumped over railroad tracks, passed a school, and were suddenly surrounded by farms. The road wound into gently rolling hills. None of the fields were cultivated, and weeds grew in last year's furrows.

Iris pointed. Some of the houses had smoke trailing from their chimneys.

"People are living here," Ben said. He sounded as surprised as Pip felt. Unlike in the city—where everyone hid from each other, protecting their own space with tooth and nail—the homes they passed seemed normal. Like before One Mile Cough. It felt unreal.

One house even had laundry hanging on a line, blowing in the warm breeze.

"Where are we?" Jessica asked.

"Green Bluff," said the young woman with the gold nose ring and scarred hands. "It's mostly family farms. We used to come up here to pick strawberries and pumpkins when I was a kid."

"Me too," Pip said with regret.

Iris beckoned for Pip to come closer.

"Her name is Fly," she whispered.

"Fly?"

Fly scowled at them, all spiky and don't-ask-about-my-name. "I'm Pip." *God*, Pip thought, *she's stunning.*

The truck turned, lurching off pavement onto a gravel road. Green fields of young wheat rolled into the distance on both sides of the truck. Most of the region around Spokane was rural: farmland for wheat, corn, and lentils. There was plenty of food to be had if you knew how to grow it.

Curtis rolled closer to the truck and pulled past, roaring up the gravel road with careless speed. Not long after, the truck lurched to a stop and they heard Camo talking. The engine started with a belch of smoke and they rolled through a gate protected by an armed guard, who closed it after they passed. Curtis stayed behind to talk with the guard.

Someday you'll pay for what you did to Whistler. Pip held onto the anger, planting it deep.

They passed ramshackle outbuildings, warped and leaning like fun-house mirror reflections. Plowed fields with hundreds of parallel lines ran unbroken to a tall chain-link fence in the distance. On the other side of the truck, children herded goats through an orchard of blooming trees.

Pip inhaled, relishing the clean scent of fresh-turned earth as the truck stopped next to a red-washed barn. Chickens chuckled in the long grass growing near its base; she watched them scratch at the dirt and envied their empty-headed, busy work of living.

Curtis rolled up to the barn on his motorcycle, scattering the chickens as doors on both sides of the truck slammed. Camo and Navvy untied the ropes across the opening, roughly coiling them and tossing the sections into the truck.

"Whatcha got?" A fit, thirty-something white man walked up to Camo and shook his hand. He sported a bucking-bronco belt buckle and an easy grin, both intended to charm but neither quite hitting their mark. At least not for Pip.

"Just like you ordered—a few men and a couple of kids and women," Camo said.

A person beyond their view cleared their throat. "Get them out of that truck."

"You heard the lady," Camo said. "Ride's over."

CHAPTER 14

A pair of women stepped into Pip's view. The older one was gray like a wood fence with years of weathering. The younger woman was bright and cheerful. *Like a sunflower,* Pip thought. The sunny woman took one look into the back of the truck and withered. The look of shock on her face was an easy read. What she saw wasn't what she'd been expecting.

A look of compressed rage crossed the face of the older woman. "*Why* are their hands bound?"

Belt Buckle stepped into the uncomfortable silence. "What the hell, man?"

"The children have their hands bound together." The woman was incandescent with fury. "Get them out of the truck now!"

"We haven't discussed my fee," Camo announced.

"Fee?" the prim older woman asked, swelling with righteous indignation. "I will never pay *anything* for people."

"Hold up! This is a misunderstanding." Belt Buckle snapped his fingers.

Three men carried baskets of fresh vegetables out of the barn. They set them down and went back inside, returning with what looked like a case of ammunition. All three men carried rifles— the kind that made Whistler's look like a party favor.

"Come on. I think we both know this could have gone better, right?" Belt Buckle said to Camo.

Camo sniffed and made a show of digging in his pockets. "I need some men. Let me keep a few of them."

"We need men too," the older woman said. "You can't have them."

Ignoring the negotiations, the sunny woman approached the truck and moved Navvy aside with a glare.

"I'm Heather," she said as she reached for a child, plucking him up.

Grubby hands wrapped around her arm in an instant. Pip suspected it would take an act of God to get the kid to let go.

Heather reached with her free hand to help Iris out of the truck and waved for the rest to follow. Iris jumped down in a puff of dust. Fly followed, casting a wary glance at the standoff between Camo and the older woman.

"I'm Veronica," the older woman said. "You are welcome here."

A stampede of eager prisoners overwhelmed Navvy. Pip sat on the lip of the truck and eased herself out, hissing over the pain lancing her gunshot wound.

"Not you." Navvy took the gun from Curtis's holster and pointed it at Pip's face. "You stay."

"What's this?" Veronica worked her way down the line of prisoners, using a small knife to set them free. The twists of plastic zip ties made a haphazard pattern in the compact dirt of the courtyard. Pip watched Navvy with a nervous eye.

"He injured one of my people. I'm keeping him."

Veronica crossed her arms. "To what end?"

"None of your business."

"The way I see it, you have a revolver with six shots, and I have three men with at least ninety bullets between them."

Navvy paled as she considered the threat of overwhelming force.

"Did he hurt someone while you were 'asking' him to ride in the truck?" Veronica pointed at Jack's unconcious body. "Did *he* get knocked out at the same time?"

"This is—"

Veronica clasped her hands together, smacking the palms with a clap so loud that people flinched. "I told Granville we needed help running the farm. That we needed women *and* a few more men to balance the population. Any children who wanted a home would be welcome."

Pip felt the weight of Veronica's gaze. The woman was intense— she crackled like a storm. Veronica drew her knife from a sheath at her waist and held it out as if to cut Pip free.

"He looks sick, but sturdy. I need him more than you do."

"No," Navvy growled.

Heather gathered the children together and hurried them into the barn. Iris struggled against the flow of the group, trying to stay nearby. Fly took Iris by the hand and made her go.

"I think we need to calm down," Belt Buckle said.

"Granville," Veronica said his name like a curse. "This isn't what we agreed to."

He took a step back. "How 'bout we ask if anybody would be interested in leaving with the truck?"

Who in their right mind would leave with these three? Pip thought.

Veronica opened her mouth to argue. Navvy cocked the gun.

Camo quickly stepped to Navvy's side and slapped his hand into the gap between the hammer and the firing pin. He howled as it made a meaty click against the webbing of his thumb. Tugging back his hand, he ripped the gun out of Navvy's grip and gave her a hard shove, sending her sprawling. He pulled the webbing between his thumb and pointer finger out of the pinch of the gun's hammer and gave it back to Curtis. "You owe me one, Granville."

Veronica sawed through the zip tie around Pip's numb wrists. When the plastic landed at Camo's feet, Pip remembered Utah's collar lying on the side of the road and resisted the urge to spit in his face.

"I'll arrange the supplies if you want to take him inside," Granville said with a nod in Pip's direction.

Veronica gestured for Pip to follow. Pausing at the wide barn door, she turned. "Unpack the supplies and leave. Make no mistake, Granville—they are *never* welcome here again."

Granville's nod was noncommittal, his expression distant. Something about him was off. Pip knew the intricate dance of hiding things. The belt-buckled man reminded her of a fox sidling up to a henhouse.

Pip gathered her unsettled feelings and followed Veronica into the barn. Squinting in the dim light, she waited for her eyes to adjust and wished for the solid feel of Whistler at her back, holding her up, checking the exits. She'd have to do that for herself now.

She stepped into a tight semicircle of people. Her fellow truck-mates were gathered together just inside the barn, waiting for instructions. Iris crashed into her, wrapping her arms around her waist. Agony from Pip's swollen wound made her want to howl, but she didn't try to push Iris away.

Even with the doors closed, the large, open space wasn't gloomy. Light shone from windows in the rafters, illuminating specks of dust that floated around groups of people sitting at pine tables. Pip was surprised at how many of them were young children. One towheaded girl's encouraging smile was mostly gaps. The faces seated at the tables were overwhelmingly friendly. Their kind welcome was unmistakable.

The scent of fresh sawdust mingled with the irresistible smell of food. Each table was covered with it. Saliva squirted into Pip's mouth with a strange, dry squeak, loud enough to be heard.

Veronica stopped next to Heather: sunshine and storm, they seemed an unlikely pairing. Veronica cleared her throat.

"When I asked for more help on the farm, I thought we would have volunteers. I wanted them to bring children who were lost and needed a home." She touched a little boy's hair, brushing it into place. "I thought the traders who brought you here would explain how Thistle Hill is a place of safety, growing and blooming in accord with nature. We need men and women like you to preserve this balance. Believe me when I say that everyone will have a place and a role. One Mile Cough might have tried to wipe us off this planet, but we will build again. As the Lord said, one man is united to one woman in matrimony, and the two form a family. Someday, perhaps, you will find that person here and make a commitment to rebuild what we have lost."

Despair settled for a passing moment across Veronica's face, like clouds over the sun. Heather took the older woman by the elbow, bolstering her up against some inner pain.

"I am *so sorry* for how you have come to be here. All I can offer you by way of apology is to welcome everyone to Thistle Hill Orchard and reassure you that you will never be treated like that again. This is my farm. And if you choose, your new home."

"If we choose?"

Heads turned. A toddler cried out in the sudden quiet. All attention was directed at Fly as she spoke. Her voice carried in the tense stillness.

"I was fine where I was before they picked me up. Then they stuffed me into that stinking truck and brought us here. Some of us were prisoners for more than a week. The people who work for *you* snatched us out of our lives and you talk about choice? Who the *hell* are you, anyway?"

"I'm Veronica Robinson and this is Heather Anderson. Thistle Hill is my family farm. And I thought we could help people who needed help. I didn't know." She frowned at Granville as he entered the barn. "I didn't think you would come here this way. Again, I'm sorry. But I am glad you're here."

A look of inspiration crossed Veronica's face. "'Thus said the Lord of Hosts unto all that are carried away as captives, whom I have caused to be carried away, build ye houses and dwell in them; and plant gardens and eat the fruit of them.' Jeremiah 29—"

"What are you talking about?" Fly said.

"I'm sorry for the trials you have suffered. But take heart," Veronica said, taking the time to look at each of the newcomers one by one. "You have not come here by choice, but there is still a plan. Just as we need a perfect ratio of bucks to does to ensure the healthy vigor of a herd of goats, so we reach out into the world with the hope of keeping that kind of balance among ourselves. Our work is more than just survival."

A look of pain crossed Heather's face. Discomfort at Veronica's words appeared to put her on the defensive. She didn't interrupt, but she did hold the boy in her arms a little closer.

Veronica surveyed the group of prisoners with a careful eye, then turned her attention to Iris. "What's your name?"

Iris looked to Pip for direction, her brow furrowed in confusion. Pip shook her head; she didn't understand what was happening either. Iris gulped and took a step forward. "I'm Iris."

Veronica bent at the waist and spoke directly to her. "Will you promise to work your hardest so we can thrive?"

"I—" Iris paused. Longing drew her eyes toward the savory steam rising from the nearest table.

Pip stepped to the front. "What happens if she says no?"

"She won't say no."

But what if she does?

Pip felt a keen sense of obligation to Veronica. After all, she'd saved her from Navvy's wrath at her own personal peril. But the repopulate-the-world craziness Veronica spouted set Pip's teeth on edge. Did Veronica seriously think she'd picked up a truckload of people who couldn't wait to pair up and make more kids? The religious quoting didn't sit any better with her. Pip's fingers itched to grab Iris and run for the door, but Navvy might be out there, waiting for her chance at revenge. Outwardly, Pip kept her emotions on a tight leash. She owed Veronica the chance to speak. "Why not let us leave?"

Veronica looked confused. "Thistle Hill is safe. We have food and medicine. We are a family. We can offer you a real life here. Why would you *want* to go?"

Where have we landed? The farm seemed safe in the same way petting a strange dog was safe. Everything would be fine until it wasn't. It was like being at home with her parents again, waiting for their religion and misunderstanding to lash her with hate. There was no way she could ever openly be herself at Thistle Hill. Pip's stomach boiled with a stew of anxiety.

Veronica knelt in the dirt before Iris like a supplicant. "Will you stay?"

Pip shuddered, constrained by a decision she couldn't make. Yes or no, Pip felt bound to Iris by more than just her promise to never leave someone behind.

Iris shuddered, face pale and drawn. "Yes."

Veronica clapped with joy; the sound rang out sharply. "Join the other children at the table, Iris."

Pip's heart tumbled to her toes as Iris walked stiffly to a table and sat. A boy who looked barely older than four handed her a biscuit. Iris accepted the food with eager hands and settled herself deeper into the group. In that moment, Pip's chest tightened as she took an involuntary step forward. Her heart wanted to stay even if it put her in danger. Veronica noticed the motion and fixed her with an appraising stare.

Sunlight sparkled in Iris's hair, picking out shiny blue highlights. Something about the single-minded way Iris tore into the food, crumbs tumbling down the front of her shirt, broke Pip. *She doesn't need me.* Disconcerted, she touched the empty spot at her throat where she'd gotten used to the rough scratch of Utah's collar. Loss settled into the empty place.

One by one, the next four teenage girls in their group introduced themselves to Veronica and chose to join the farm community. When Veronica came to Fly, the mood in the barn turned from cautious optimism to the crackling suspense of a grenade without its pin. Oblivious to the change, Veronica offered Fly her hand.

"I don't trust you," Fly said, refusing the handshake.

Incomprehension furrowed Veronica's brow.

"There's been a misunderstanding." Heather moved the sleepy boy she held to her other hip. "I'm sorry for how you were treated in the truck. We aren't like that—"

Veronica held up a hand to silence her. She and Fly faced off, snake versus mongoose. Veronica was the first to look away.

"I'll stay," Fly said. "For now."

Veronica moved to the next person in line, pretending the confrontation hadn't happened. She quickly worked her way through the remaining ex-prisoners and sent them to sit at the table. The hurried munching of people eating turned Pip's hunger into a hollow gnawing in her belly.

She looked down the line of prisoners who remained and realized Veronica had left the men for last. Pip did a quick headcount of the people in the barn. Like Veronica had said, there was a disturbingly even distribution of men and women when it came to the adults. Caught out and feeling exposed, she wanted to hide. Indecision was making her sick.

"If you men decide to stay, there will be forty-three of us at Thistle Hill. Forty-three souls who need protection and guidance. Healthy men such as yourselves are an asset."

Veronica looked directly at Pip. "And it's the main reason you are here. You are the foundation we will use to rebuild."

A trickle of nervous sweat eased its way down Pip's spine as she crossed her arms over her breasts. The leader of Thistle Hill

Orchard thought she was a boy. A boy expected to grow into a man and father. Pip contemplated pointing out the misunderstanding, explaining away any awkwardness by acknowledging how easy it was to mistake the sex of a tomboy. But her supposed maleness was clearly what had caught Veronica's attention. It had saved her from Navvy's revenge.

Given the nature of Veronica's beliefs and plans for the farm, coming out to her would be a spectacularly bad idea. A profound sadness sidled up to Pip, filling her with a sense of loss. Thistle Hill seemed like it could be a real home for her and Iris. But only if she found a way to continue passing as a boy.

It was a hard pill to swallow.

The Bible-quoting introduction to the farm plucked at the edges of Pip's thoughts. It wasn't the religion in particular that troubled her. She had fond memories of Deacon Stephen, the man with a ready laugh who'd run the Catholic midnight outreach in downtown Spokane. He'd been quick with a blanket and a joke, handing out peanut butter sandwiches to anyone who needed a meal. She wasn't blind to the good that Christians could do.

What she couldn't forgive was the way her mother's church had treated her like a blight. A weed to be pruned. The support the church had given her mom for turning Pip out of the house still stung, even now, after they were all dead and gone.

What if Veronica also found out she was bisexual? Fly stood off to the side, observing their interaction. Pip was drawn to her in ways that made her uncomfortably warm. Two girls pairing off wouldn't fit in with Veronica's world-repopulation plan. Not at all. She couldn't risk Veronica discovering she'd chosen a queer girl instead of a young man, at least not until she had a better lay of the land.

Let Veronica believe whatever she wanted. It would be safer to keep her mouth shut.

"I must have your word that you'll be peaceful," Veronica said. "No funny business. No pairing off without my permission. Until you've proven yourselves, you will be under constant supervision. The safety and harmony of this farm isn't something I will compromise. I want to trust you. Will you trust me?" She rested her hands on her hips and waited.

The words were harsh, and there was no doubt: Veronica was uncompromising. Pip considered the leader of Thistle Hill. She was fiercely protective of the kids. That was to be admired. Even so, something about Veronica was like tinfoil in the mouth. Bitter and unexpected. Pip didn't trust her any more than Fly did. Veronica felt too much like her parents: religious and inflexible in a way that made her uneasy.

"I'm in," Ben said. Veronica waved him over to the tables.

"And you?" Veronica asked Pip.

Pip searched the barn tables for her main reason to stay at Thistle Hill. For a moment, she couldn't find Iris. A pressure like all the air being sucked out of her lungs left Pip breathless. Panic bloomed with the frantic beat of her heart.

A small hand snatched at her wrist, fingers clutching so hard that two heartbeats pounded in the pressure. As Pip looked into Iris's pleading eyes, relief surged through her. She gave Iris's hand a reassuring squeeze and nodded. Pip's heart was with Iris, so she would stay on the farm.

The shreds of Pip's dead life as a boy chafed hard against her skin, taunting her. Pip grabbed tight to who she knew she was and held her deep inside. She was strong enough to do what she must. For now.

"I'll stay," Pip said in the deepest version of her voice.

CHAPTER 15

Iris gave Pip's sleeve an eager tug, dragging her toward the nearest table. A few steps from the seated children, Pip pulled Iris to a stop. "They think I'm a boy. Make sure you call me 'he.'"

"But…"

Not knowing if they could be overheard left her too unsteady to be polite.

"Just do it," Pip insisted. "It's safer this way."

Iris swallowed her objections and followed Pip's wishes when introducing her to the group of children sitting at the table. They made room for one more while Iris loaded a plate with a hearty bean casserole and fresh greens. She set it on the table in front of Pip like a gift.

Her first bite was crunchy. Concern over their uncertain position at Thistle Hill stepped aside as she moaned with delight over the crisp snap of salad between her teeth. Even without ranch dressing, every mouthful was perfect. Within minutes, she devoured her first helping. Not even close to full, she breathlessly reloaded her plate, taking two biscuits slathered with butter and honey. As her teeth sank into their creamy sweetness, she wondered if the meal was an exception in honor of the new arrivals.

"Do you always eat like this?" she asked a young girl across the table.

"We have one big meal every day. Usually at night," the girl answered. "Do you like the honey? My job is bees."

"Cool!" Iris said.

"Does everyone have a job?" Pip asked.

"Except the littlest kids. Heather watches them and the twins help her." The girl pointed at two lanky black girls with braids. Matching orange and yellow beads on the ends of each braid clacked when they moved. The girls were perfectly identical— two cheery-faced kids in clean clothes who, like all the children, seemed relaxed and unafraid.

As the meal wound down, some of the adults started clearing the tables. Others gathered the older children in ones and twos, ushering them out of the barn, smiling indulgently at their half-hearted complaints about evening chores.

As the residents of Thistle Hill filed out, Pip stayed in her seat. Excitement drained out of Iris. Without the comforting buffer of other children, she deflated. Pip gave her wrist a reassuring squeeze. Iris scooted closer, her elbow scoring a direct hit into Pip's bullet wound.

Gasping for air, Pip sagged in her seat, letting her head rest on the table.

Heather was at her side in an instant. "Is that blood on your shirt? Let's take a look at that."

Pip opened her mouth to argue but relented at Heather's stern finger shake. Pip let Heather pull her to her feet. Her side throbbed from hip to shoulder.

Veronica closed the barn door and clapped twice for attention. "Women and children will go with Heather to the main house."

"I'm taking..." Heather shook her head. "I didn't get your name."

"Pip."

"I'm taking Pip with me to the house, he's wounded."

"Send him to the sleeping barn when you're done. Ben and Jack will be coming with me. Your building is almost full, so you might have to bunk in the old horse barn," Veronica said.

"Excuse me?" Ben pushed back from the table and stood. He placed a proprietary hand on the shoulder of a raggedly dressed young woman. "My girlfriend and I want to stay together."

Creases traversed Veronica's forehead as her eyebrows raised for miles. A deep flush bloomed on her cheeks.

"Your...girlfriend?"

Defiance exaggerated the thrust of the young man's jaw. He stepped around the table. "Nothing—*nothing*—is going to keep us apart."

"That's not how things work on my farm." Veronica's voice gained strength as she continued. "Hebrews 13:4: 'Marriage is honorable in all, and the bed undefiled: but whoremongers and adulterers God will judge.'"

"What's a whoremonger?" Iris muttered to Pip.

"Uh…someone who kisses someone when they aren't married," she fumbled.

"Ew."

"What the hell?" Ben clenched his fists. "Alison is not going to the 'girl's house.'"

"Are you married?" Veronica asked.

"No."

"With a commitment, of course my answer would be different. But as you two are not married—"

"What does that have to do with anything?" Ben interrupted.

The strength that had carried him headfirst into the rotting minivan propelled him forward. He vibrated with fear-tinged rage. The fight blew out of him when his girlfriend spoke.

"Ben," she said his name in the timidest voice Pip had ever heard. All breathy and light, like a subtle perfume. She wrapped her arms around his shoulders. "I'll go with Heather. It'll be fine."

"But—"

"I'll be safe. Don't worry," Alison consoled him. "They fed us such a nice meal and the children seem happy. I think it's okay." She gave him a lingering hug.

"Thank you for understanding. I just want everyone to be safe." Veronica cleared her throat and gestured for Ben to follow. "The men's house is this way."

Outside, slanting afternoon light cut around the buildings. Pip shaded her eyes and let herself be swept along with a chattering group of kids to the side door of a sprawling clapboard farmhouse. Multiple rooflines and strangely placed windows gave the white house a haphazard quality. Generations of families must have added rooms to the main structure as needed.

The house was filled with the scent of cooking, savory and rich like biscuits browned in the oven. Heather led them through a giant kitchen with two wood-burning stoves and paused in the foyer. The main part of the house was shaped like a square with four big rooms, one in each corner, split by a stairway to the second floor. Two young women set down their mending and joined them.

"Everybody needs a place to sleep," Heather said.

Dimples poked deep into Heather's cheeks when she smiled. She handed off a drowsy toddler to one of the women and nodded for everyone to follow them upstairs. Iris hung back, staying at Pip's side.

"I think it's okay," Pip said.

Iris thrummed with nervous energy and shook her head.

"No worries, you can help me fix him up," Heather said.

She led them to the rear of the house, through a large room full of books. Several children were already deep in study, working on what looked like geography while their teacher shelved books from Camo's left-behind milk crates. Iris paused by a globe on a metal stand and gave it a spin.

The teacher—the oldest person Pip had seen for a long while—pushed up his glasses and held out a piece of paper to Iris. "Would you like to take the test? Eighty percent or better gets a ride on the llama."

Eyes wide, Iris snatched the paper out of his hand. She didn't even look up as Pip left the room. She was deep into winning that llama ride.

They took three stairs down and then one step up into an addition off the back of the house: the infirmary. Neat shelves full of medical supplies and bottles of pills paired strangely with herbs hanging in bundles from the ceiling. Heather pointed to a hospital bed complete with stirrups folded down at the sides.

"Have a seat."

"It's like an apothecary in here," Pip mused.

Brushing past a low-hanging bunch of dried white flowers with bright-yellow centers, Heather laughed. "Old-school medicine. Our doctor is a midwife. Marty came to Thistle Hill the same time I did. She's out with a birth on another farm."

"Did you come in on a truck?"

Heather stiffened. "Absolutely not!"

She set down a metal tray with a bang. Rubbing alcohol splashed, and bandages hopped onto the floor. Tying up her long red hair, she tucked loose ends behind her ears, settling herself before shutting the door of the infirmary and cleaning up her mess.

"One Mile Cough hit Green Bluff all at once. We'd tried to quarantine, but someone got sick. When it was done, we couldn't run our farms alone. Veronica's farm was the largest, so we came together to survive."

"But...why bring us here?"

Heather gestured for Pip to lift her shirt. A rash of goosebumps prickled up Pip's arms. Afraid of being discovered, she carefully kept her chest covered, rolling the fabric out of the way before crossing an arm over her breasts.

"Hold still." Picking at the blood-crusted metal clips holding the bandage in place, Heather worked the gauze free. "Winter was hard. We were hit with a flu. A lot of people died."

Pain flared as the last of the gauze peeled out of her wound. Pip gasped.

"Sorry."

"'S'okay."

"Anyway," Heather continued, dabbing rubbing alcohol in the wound, lighting up Pip's side with liquid fire, "Veronica's daughter, Elizabeth, died in December. When she went, Veronica stopped talking for almost a month. We had to force-feed her to keep her alive. Hold this." Heather pressed a square of gauze over the bullet wound.

Pip thought she might vomit. Her body shook with the sting of Heather's practical cleaning. She had the kind but no-time-for-pity bedside manner of a nurse. While Pip gingerly pressed the gauze into her side, she took a shuddering breath through her nose.

Heather snapped a sprig of rosemary off a hanging bundle and held it out. "Deep breaths."

The resinous scent of the herb helped. She still felt like dying, but at least it smelled like pizza. She missed pizza. It had been a long time since she'd eaten pizza.

"When Veronica started speaking again, all she'd talk about was saving children. Bringing them home to the farm and building new families. It seemed like a good idea."

Heather washed her hands with a rough bar of brown soap. Pip lay back on the bed and stared at the ceiling. Shock made it feel like she was floating. A bell-shaped lamp hung over the bed. She squinted at the bright light bulb.

"You have power?"

Heather wheezed a laugh at the astonishment in Pip's words. "Solar panels. We only have enough to run the pump for the well and a few lights. But it's nice, isn't it?" She sobered. "It's one of the few *good* things he's brought to Thistle Hill."

"Him." Pip sat up. "Granville."

The door was shut, but Heather still checked over her shoulder. "He showed up during a blizzard in January. Veronica was lost in her Bible, grasping at straws for comfort. We didn't know what to do. By March she couldn't make much of a decision without him. That's when he brought men with guns and built the gate. It wasn't always like this here."

The door cracked open and Iris peeked in. The smile that split her face told Pip everything she needed to know.

"Looks like someone is going on a llama ride."

Iris did a little dance with her test. "Can I go?"

Pip rolled down her shirt. "Sure. I've got to figure out where I'm sleeping tonight. You ride the llama, and I'll see you later."

A girl bumped into Iris, dragging her away from the door. Pip's heart soared to hear their easy laughter.

"She's sweet, your Iris," Heather said. "Is she your sister?"

Pip was caught off guard. She'd been so busy protecting herself, she hadn't planned an answer to that sort of question. "Kind of. I mean...I found her, and she needed help. She's *like* a little sister." Pip winced; she was babbling.

"Well, she clearly thinks of you as kin. She's got a real spark about her." Heather leaned on a table, fixing Pip with a critical eye as she eased herself off the bed. "It's too bad we don't have antibiotics. That's what you really need."

The bottle of penicillin she'd stuffed in her pocket after raiding the pharmacy was long gone. "I had a whole pharmacy's worth of drugs in my pack when Navvy and her crew grabbed us. Did they leave my stuff?"

Heather opened the door. "I don't know, but I *will* find out."

They ran into Veronica on their way out of the white house.

"The packs Granville unloaded weren't things they'd found," Heather said. "Those traders stole their belongings."

A light breeze tugged a few loose hairs out of Veronica's tight bun, and they waved around her face, softening her edges. She looked into the sky, then fixed Pip with her light-gray eyes. "I'll make sure you get what's yours."

"I had medicines. The farm could use them."

"Thank you."

Veronica was formal and polite to an uncomfortable degree. Pip tried to imagine the leader of Thistle Hill relaxing by a fire with a smile, a child on her knee. She couldn't do it.

"When I find the meds, I'll get you some pills," Heather said, leaving on a mission. Pip pitied anyone who got in her way. Heather looked ready to wrestle a bear.

"Let me take you to the men's barn."

Pip followed Veronica into the tilting second barn. Faded wood planks of many shades patched the old building. Despite the structure's drunken lean, the roof looked sound. Pip thumped the doorframe as she walked inside, a little surprised when the barn didn't collapse.

"It's an old dairy barn we've been trying to keep up," Veronica explained. She paused next to an empty cot.

The dirt floor had three drains evenly spaced down the length of the building. Each of the old stalls held a makeshift bedroom with one cot and cobbled-together furniture. The room stank of straw and the spicy sweat of men. The stall closest to Pip was open to the rest of the room, the dividers barely chest high. Hiding her secret in the close quarters of the barn would be nearly impossible. She gulped, anxiety cranking to eleven before busting off the knob. She fervently hoped she wouldn't be stuck with a bed in the communal space.

"I have ten beds in here, but they're already taken. I've put Jack in the last one." Veronica pointed to where Jack sat in bed. His broken arm was bandaged, and he looked much improved. Ben sat on a chair pulled up by his side. He waved.

"There's an outhouse halfway between this barn and the white house, and the water pump is on the other side of the farmyard. Please don't try to run the pump until someone shows you how. We'll go over that tomorrow." Veronica gestured for Ben to get up. "You two, come with me."

They recrossed the farm, passing the red barn and heading to one of the fun-house shacks Pip noticed during the ride in on the truck. They ducked inside a low doorway, and she breathed a sigh of relief. A dividing wall went all the way to the roof, creating two crude rooms that shared a pitted dirt floor. Ancient spiderwebs trembled in the rafters, and both bays had a deep drift of freshly chopped straw piled in a corner.

"I'll have someone bring you a few wool blankets," Veronica said.

"Thanks," Pip said.

"Of course." Veronica turned to go.

"Wait," Ben said. "Can we talk outside?"

Veronica agreed and followed him out.

Pip sank into the straw, tucked an arm behind her head to keep the tickly ends off her neck, and tried to eavesdrop on their conversation. They must have walked quite a distance from the shack, because she couldn't decipher their indistinct mumbling.

CHAPTER 16

Pip woke in the deep darkness of night covered with a heavy blanket and serenaded by the frantic, high-pitched cheeps of frogs in search of a mate. Straw pricked her skin. She rolled onto her side in a fruitless attempt to get comfortable. Frustrated, she got up and flicked the blanket onto the straw, hoping it would serve as a protective barrier. The blanket thumped onto the pile and bits of straw blew past her feet. She felt around the space as she arranged the blanket, her fingers recoiling each time she brushed rotten wood. The cracks in the walls were probably crawling with bugs, or worse, spiders.

She hissed in surprise when her guts twisted. The unusually rich food was fouling up her digestion. Nature was calling. She turned on the spot and headed in what she thought was the direction of the door. Hopefully the stars would provide enough light to help her find the outhouse.

A warm glow came from behind the red barn, emitted by a lit bulb dangling from the roof of the outhouse. Moths fluttered around the fixture, smashing themselves with wild abandon against the only light for miles. Slapping fluttery bugs aside, she opened the door of the two-seater privy. Someone inside screamed.

Pip knocked her head against the light, and the door slammed shut against her shins. Shadows jumped crazily around the inside of the outhouse. In the strobe flash of light, Pip saw Iris perched on the seat farthest from the door.

"Iris!" Pip clutched at her chest. "Are you trying to kill me?"

Iris barked out an embarrassed laugh and snatched the door shut.

After Iris was done, Pip used the facilities, then walked to the washing station next to the outhouse. She scrubbed in the bucket labeled "wash," then held out her hands for Iris to pour a cup of clean water from the "rinse" bucket.

"How's the house?" Pip asked, shaking excess water off her hands.

"I'm sharing a room with five kids. Except for Jessica and her two friends, I'm the oldest. It's kinda nice."

Pip wanted to ask how Jessica managed to survive their house in Spokane catching fire, but she didn't want to upset Iris. "How's she doing?"

"Okay, I guess. She's one of those girls who always gushes about boys. We don't talk much."

"Ah."

A moth bumped into Iris's forehead, tangling in her hair. Pip trapped the moth with her fingers and unwove it from the thick strands. Two feather-shaped antennas sprouted from the top of the moth's fuzzy head. They tickled her palm as the insect struggled inside her fist. As the moth's rusty wings flapped against her fingers, a chill ran through Pip. This fuzzy night-flyer didn't look a thing like the orange butterflies Whistler had described, but still. It felt like he was right beside her, telling her something she couldn't quite understand.

"Careful!" Iris admonished. "Don't touch the wings."

"I got this," Pip said. She pulled the last of Iris's hair out of the moth's tenacious grip. "See, it's fine."

Wings flapped frantically within the cage of Pip's fingers until the moth settled upside down, clinging to her thumb.

"He's beautiful," Iris said.

She was so close that her breath blew gently on the moth. His wings fluttered in the gentle breeze, and he took off. As his shadow faded into the stars, Iris leaned against Pip; her affection warmed the chill of the night better than any wool blanket ever could. Pip tried to wrap an arm around her, but Iris pulled away and dug deep into a front pocket. There was a subtle jingling. Pip inhaled with shock at the sight of Utah's collar stretched across Iris's palms. Pip opened her mouth to speak, but nothing came out.

"It was in the dirt by the side of the road, and we were all alone so I got out of the truck," Iris blurted out in a breathless rush. "They tried to pull me back. Fly made them let me go."

Pip could almost hear Fly ordering the prisoners to shut up. She would have been gentle with Iris though, watching her back as she got the collar.

"You could've been caught."

Iris placed Utah's collar in Pip's hand. "I had to."

"What are you talking about?"

"It's important to you. *I had to.*"

"A dog collar means nothing compared to your safety."

Pain bloomed in Iris's eyes, and Pip mentally punched herself. The act of recklessness was already behind them. Lecturing was pointless now. Iris had known the collar was important, and she had risked getting caught by Camo or Curtis to retrieve it. She deserved better than a reprimand.

"Thank you, Iris."

"Uh." Iris scuffed a toe in the dirt. "Is Utah your dog?"

"Yes. He *was.*"

Pip turned the collar over. Whistler's tag had a slight bend in it—a curve that fit the palm of her hand. Shuffling the pain of his death aside, she touched the other tags on the collar. The once-shiny metal was now edged with a rough tinge of rust. She didn't need a light to read the largest tag: *Retired Military War Dog: Utah T593.* She brought the collar to her nose and sniffed the memory of its stale taco-chip dog scent.

"We adopted Utah when he was decommissioned. He was my best friend—" Pip choked on the words but forced herself to explain. "I'm the reason he died."

"You killed him?" Iris stuttered.

"As good as." Pip's voice broke.

"What do you mean?"

"When my mom was in the hospital, Utah was trapped in the house with my dad. After she died, I went back to the house and found them." Pip closed her eyes against the memory of Utah's ragged fur under her hand. "He starved to death waiting for me."

"But...why did you take his collar?"

Pip settled it around her neck—the cool band of woven cloth felt comfortable where it rested on her chest. The latch closed with a satisfying click, and she tucked the tags into her shirt. The collar's familiar weight marked her mistakes. She wore it as a reminder. She thought of her mom withering away in the hospital and the nameless teenager shot on the side of the road. So many dead. She clenched her fist around the dog tags, relishing the sting of the metal edges against her palm. First Utah, then Whistler. The pain of their loss hurt more than the stiffening wound in her side.

"It's my promise."

"To never leave someone behind." Iris took a few wobbly steps out of their circle of light before sitting down.

She curled forward, holding her stomach like she was about to be sick. Pip rushed to her side. Iris gulped huge, chuffing breaths like hiccups.

"What is it?"

A storm of emotions poured out of Iris in a mess of snot and tears, but she didn't make a sound as it passed. Not knowing what to do, Pip began to murmur calming nonsense, discussing the color of the stars and whether the red-tinged one close to the horizon was a planet, maybe Jupiter.

"Mars," Iris sniffed.

"You sure?"

"Mars looks like a red twinkle light."

Pip squinted at the sky. She was right, it *did* look like a red Christmas light up there. Iris sniffled and lay down in the grass. Pip shifted so she could see her face.

"Are you alright?"

Silence floated around Iris like a bubble.

"Iris?"

"Did you mean me?" Hope hung on Iris's words, with the promise of more tears.

"That I would *never* leave you?" A sad half smile played over Pip's face as she discovered the truth. "Yes, I did."

Iris deflated with relief, sagging into the ground. Pip awkwardly patted her on the hip.

"Where I go, you go. Okay?"

"Okay."

When Iris calmed, they walked together back to the main house. Pip waited on the porch until the door locked. Not long after, a curtain twitched in a window on the top floor, and Iris waved. Taking her time returning to her bedroom shack and pile-of-straw bed, Pip felt too exhilarated to go back to sleep.

Rescuing Iris from the bridge was probably the best thing she'd ever done.

CHAPTER 17

Pip spent the rest of the night seesawing between remembering the rough caress of Fly's hand against her own and wondering what the future would hold. It was a restless wait for dawn. The tantalizing scent of frying bacon finally lured her away from the dent she'd made in her pile of straw.

Roosters were crowing up the sun as she took her place at a table. Farther down the long bench, the three girls from Iris's burned-down house huddled together like thieves picking through a stolen purse.

"Excuse me, you're Jessica, right?" Pip asked.

The group tightened ranks as the blonde girl looked her way.

"Yes. Why?"

Pip slid closer. "Iris said you were in her house. I'm glad you made it. She thought she was the only one."

"I don't want to talk about it," Jessica said.

"That's okay, I just wanted to—"

One of the other girls poked Jessica in the side. All three looked toward the barn's open double doors. Granville walked in, and Jessica beamed in response. She was delighted to see the cowboy. He caught their admiration and tipped his hat before turning to talk to a man at another table. The girls cooed. Pip sucked her teeth and slid back to her spot farther down the table. *What are they playing at? Granville is a grown-ass man.*

Iris ran to the table. "Pip, I've got a job!"

"A job, huh? What is it?"

"Chickens and ducks."

"How...fowl."

Iris groaned as Veronica and a few other women came into the barn. The leader of Thistle Hill carried a jug of water. Condensation ran down the sides and dripped splashes of water onto the dusty floor. She set it on Pip's table and bowed her head.

Faces in the barn dipped in answer, except for those of the people who'd arrived on the moving truck the day before. The newcomers gradually understood their role and joined in. Pip refused to pray or bow her head. Granville noticed. He rolled his eyes at Veronica while taking off his stained baseball cap and holding it to his chest with feigned piousness. Pip chuffed a laugh.

Two tables over, Fly picked up a slice of bacon and slowly ate it. Pip watched her defiant chewing. Eating had never looked so sexy.

Living near Fly might just kill me.

When the barn was still, Veronica began to pray. "For food in a world where many walk in hunger, for faith in a world where many walk in fear, for friends in a world where many walk alone, we give you thanks, O Lord. Amen."

"Amen," the group echoed.

"You may eat," Veronica intoned. "Welcome again to all who joined us yesterday."

She spoke over the eager sounds of people gathering food onto their plates. "For you newcomers, Granville will be coming 'round the tables while we eat. Please tell him of any skills you have. We need to find everyone a place."

Granville moseyed over to the two prettiest young women from the moving truck and laid on the charm. One of them simpered as the rugged cowboy leaned in.

"Eggs?" Iris interrupted Pip's troubled thoughts.

"Mmm, yes. They look great." Pip accepted the platter and scooped a few dollops of buttery scrambled eggs onto her plate.

She held herself to one solid helping of food instead of the waistband-busting amount she'd consumed the night before. Iris poured honey into her bowl of nutty oatmeal and shoveled it down quickly. She vibrated with excitement while keeping an eager gaze on another table where a slightly older boy was chewing at a more leisurely pace.

"Who's that?" Pip nodded toward the boy.

"That's Dusty. He's in charge of the chickens. I'm working with him today."

"Do you need to go over there?"

Iris was alight with anticipation. Pip knew she desperately wanted to join the older boy and pick his brain about her new job.

"Go ahead, I have to talk to Granville." Pip didn't like the taste of his name in her mouth.

Iris sprang out of her seat, flashed Pip a thrilled smile, and speed walked to the boy. Pip shook her head at Iris's impatient excitement, then stacked Iris's empty bowl on top of her plate. She poured water from the cool pitcher into her glass and took a sip, savoring the clean, almost-nothing flavor.

Granville paused near Jessica on his way down the table and flashed her a thousand-watt smile. He was an obvious flirt, but this was the second time he seemed to be turning on the charm for a teenager. It made Pip uneasy. He moved through the barn, chatting up the newcomers until he rambled up to her end of the table.

"What's your name?" He asked.

"I'm Pip."

"Pip?"

"Granville?"

He pushed the brim of his hat with one finger and laughed. "No need to bust my balls, little man. What can you do? Farming, taking care of animals—how about hunting?"

"My dad and I hunted. I've never done much with gardening or raising animals, but I can find my way out of the woods. I was a Boy Scout."

"So, you sold a lot of popcorn," he sneered.

She ignored the bait. She had a black belt in putting up with assholes.

His tongue fiddled with a lump of chew while he thought. "We need supplies to repair solar panels on the lower well. I'm headed out this morning; you can tag along. If you suck at scrounging, I'll bring you back to shovel shit in the pigsty."

"Sounds fair."

Veronica placed her hands on the table between them. "Everything alright?"

Granville stood. "Yes, ma'am."

"Yep." Pip took note of how polite he was around Veronica.

Granville was malleable like clay, shaping to match people's expectations. His personality felt fluid. It made her wonder what he was like when he thought no one was watching.

"Meet me at the pickup parked out front in five," Granville said. He tipped his hat to Veronica and left the barn.

"Be careful out there," Veronica said.

Pip gathered her dishes. "Always am."

Heather trotted across the barn with a rattling prescription bottle. "They gave us the drugs, but I couldn't find your backpack." She popped off the lid to show Pip the pills. "Penicillin. The midwife said you're to take one twice a day."

Battling disappointment over the loss of her stuff, Pip dry swallowed a pill. "Thanks."

"Sure."

She pocketed the pill bottle and went to wait by Granville's dusty black pickup, lightly punching the truck when she remembered Iris's missing violin. Another mark against Camo. *That bastard.*

Dwelling on what had been taken was a hopeless exercise. Pip leaned on the sun-warmed metal of the truck and hoped for an opportunity to collect supplies while away from the farm. Top on the list was a double-wide bandage to bind her breasts. She'd tightened the thin straps of her sports bra as far as they'd go and reused the wrap from her gunshot wound. Binding with a bandage wasn't great. It could cause damage if she bound too tightly, but she figured her odds of finding an honest-to-God binder during their scavenging were slim to none.

A bandage should be enough; she was practically flat in the boob department. She was fortunate in that sense. Being small-busted made her breasts easier to hide. At least the shirt she had on was loose. Pip tugged down the hem of her shirt and stepped up on the rear tire to climb into the truck bed.

"Hi."

is Clack. Dumber than a bag of hammers, the both of them, but they sure can pull a load." Clare jabbed a callused thumb at the bed of her truck.

Several sheep and goat carcasses were piled by the tailgate. Jagged gashes full of congealed blood disfigured their flanks and faces.

"Something raided one of my pens last night. Killed this lot and only took one. I'm hitting the farms on the bluff to see if anyone wants any."

"What was it?" Granville leaned out his window for a closer look. "Coyote?"

Clare blew a scornful breath. "Only if coyotes are black-and-orange striped."

Black and orange, like Whistler's rambling description of black-and-orange butterflies after his seizure.

Granville snorted. "Who're you kidding? A tiger?"

"What I saw slipping into the woods had stripes." Clare shrugged at Granville's mocking smile. "Whatever it was, the past few nights something's been roaring and screaming out my way. I'll be locking up my animals. Tell Veronica she should do the same."

"Mmm." Granville nodded. "Could be one of the cats from Cat Tails. Think they got out?"

Pip had only been to Cat Tails once on a field trip in third grade. The place styled itself as a retirement home meets game preserve for ex–circus cats and other predators stupidly kept as pets. There were lions, tigers, and bears...*oh my*. She sincerely hoped no one had been rash enough to let out the inmates of the wildlife refuge.

"Could be," Clare said with resignation. "Anyway, want the meat?"

"I'll take the sheep," Granville said. He waved for Pip and Marcus to load the sheep into the truck.

Pip stood behind Clare's wagon and surveyed the pile of dead animals, walling off the part of her mind shrieking in response. It didn't matter that she'd hunted with her father, killing deer with ease. The pile of sheep was too much like dead people piled in the streets after the outbreak. The scent of blood was strong in her nose. Marcus raised an eyebrow. Pip nodded. The farm needed food; getting squeamish wouldn't help anybody.

A magpie flicked its black-and-white wings, cackling on a useless power line above them while Pip helped carry the heavy carcass. The sheep's legs were hard, like stiff clay wrapped in flannel. She deliberately watched new wheat bending in the wind, trying to ignore the rhythmic slap of the head knocking against her thigh as she walked.

They tossed the body onto the bed of Granville's truck and went back for the rest. Clare had gutted the animals. Blood dripped sluggishly from gaping holes in their abdomens. A gruesome trail of crimson between the two vehicles grew thicker with each trip. By the time they'd retrieved the last sheep, Pip's hands were tacky with drying blood, and the incessant buzz of flies made her want to vomit. She squatted by the side of the road, waiting for the nausea to pass, rubbing her hands in dirt until the grit left them dusty but clean.

"I'll swing by the farm later today to settle up," Clare said, shaking the reins. The mules danced sideways, then leaned their powerful shoulders into the weight of her wagon truck, getting it moving. Hooves clopped loudly on the pavement as they made their way along.

Granville raised a hand in goodbye, then slapped the door.

"Hop in the back," he said to Pip.

"You've got to be kidding."

Granville's reflection in the side mirror smiled at her.

She hoisted herself up on the rear tire; the bloody snowbank of sheep waited for her against the tailgate. Granville gunned the truck's engine just as she swung her leg to climb in. Pip lost her balance as the vehicle jerked. She landed on her knees, nearly tumbling into the sheep. Granville bellowed a hearty laugh when she flipped him off. Working with Granville was going to be a different kind of nightmare.

They only made two stops to scrounge in homes closer to Thistle Hill before the day warmed and the sheep began to stink. Gore dripped from the tailgate onto the gravel driveway as they pulled up next to Clare's wagon behind the big red barn.

"I'm not cleaning that up," Granville said, tossing the keys to Marcus.

Pip couldn't scramble out of the truck bed fast enough. Her skin crawled with the sensation of flies. She'd managed to dodge most of the muck leaking out of the sheep, but her shoes were a bloody ruin.

Heather and Jessica came out of the barn with a group of the farm's youngest children. Heather's nose wrinkled at the smell, but she looked pleased. "I'll gather some people to help unload."

"Perfect." Granville dusted off his hands. "I could use some lunch."

Heather opened her mouth to object, but Granville interrupted her reproach by sweeping his arm through Jessica's. "You look hungry."

Jessica giggled, simpering under his attention.

Warning bells rang loud in Pip's head as she watched Veronica's second-in-command escort the teenager into the red barn.

"What was that?" Pip asked.

Heather turned to watch them go and frowned. "I don't know."

CHAPTER 18

Granville's alarming flirtation with Jessica hounded Pip's thoughts as she scrubbed gritty soap against her blood-caked fingernails. Nudging the pump handle with an elbow, she was rinsing her hands when Iris shouted her name from over by the livestock barns. Down a long slope from the main house, the farm's goats, cows, and horses were kept in three large sheds.

Holding her hands under the cold splash of water from the pump, Pip rubbed off the last of the soap and shook her hands dry. "What?"

"Clare needs you." Iris waved for Pip to hurry up.

She jogged downhill through a field to the sheds. Iris's face was flushed from more than the heat of the afternoon. "Are you okay?"

"One of the goats is kidding."

Pip had a flash of a goat standing on a stage telling jokes and laughed.

Iris had no time for nonsense. "Come on!"

The inside of the shed was surprisingly dim after the bright early-summer sun. Woodchips and straw covered the floor, spilling out of four goat pens. A squeaky grunt came from the farthest pen. Something flopped hard against a wooden partition, tossing bits of straw into the air. Another grunt, deep and guttural, was followed by a bleat that was answered by a small herd of goats fenced outside.

"*Kidding* like having a *kid*?" Pip asked.

"Duh. There are two kids tangled together inside, and we need someone to hold the goat's head. I wasn't strong enough."

Clare and Fly knelt in the straw next to a pregnant goat. The poor animal had swelled nearly to bursting with kids. Her sides heaved and her back legs stuck straight out as she pushed. Her head twisted back over her white body at a weird angle as she grunted again.

"Fly's going to help her stand. I need you to hold her collar." Clare opened the gate. "Every time I stick my fingers in there to sort things out, she tries to buck."

Pip sank into the straw and grabbed the goat's collar, hauling her head around to the front. "Like this?"

Clare barely noticed. Her whole attention was on the other end of the goat. *The business end*, Pip's dad would have said with a rude grin. Fly wrapped her arms partway around the goat's middle, pressing her cheek against the white hair. She winked at Pip, then shifted to watch Clare work.

Clare handed Iris a clean towel from a stack piled next to her. "Okay, I'm going to push one of the kids back when she has her next contraction, so they don't get stuck trying to come out at the same time."

The goat strained, bleating a long, grassy breath into Pip's face while Clare's hand slid inside the goat up to the wrist. There was a wet splash. Pip closed her eyes and tried not to think about being trapped in a truck full of dead sheep. In a matter of moments, Iris was cooing over a newborn goat.

The smell of birth was raw and bloody. *Nope. Never having kids. Never ever.* Pip risked a peek as the goat gave a mighty heave. She took one look at the fluid-filled sack peeking out of the goat's backside and slammed her eyes closed. *Gross.*

"You're missing it, Pip!" Iris said.

"Scoot over," Clare ordered.

Pip opened her eyes as Clare set a damp kid in the straw. The new mother chuckled deep in her throat and licked the little one.

"That was cool!" Iris cheered as she handed Clare another towel to scrub the second kid.

"You can let her go."

Fly helped the goat lie down without squishing her two new children and slid down the wall next to Pip. She gave the pleased mama a scratch between her long, floppy ears and smiled. Pip couldn't help but grin back.

"You closed your eyes."

"It was disgusting."

"It was cool."

"I've had enough of seeing the insides of animals on the outside today, thank you very much."

Fly had a gap between her two front teeth; Pip couldn't stop enjoying how cute it was when Fly smiled.

Clare folded a towel and held it out to Fly. "Could you give the smaller one another rubdown? He's coughing more than I'd like."

"Sure." Fly bent to give the little brown-and-white-speckled kid a brisk rubbing.

Iris scooted closer and rested her head on Pip's shoulder. "You shouldn't've shut your eyes."

"I'm good."

"Some idiot left the females boxed up with the males in the middle of winter—no doubt you'll have another chance to see a kid being born." Clare dusted bits of straw off her pants and palpated the mom goat's side. "I can't tell if that's it."

"There's more?" Iris jumped to her feet, eager to midwife the goat.

"We'll give her a bit to think about it. She needs some molasses water. Iris, run up to the house and see if Heather has any to spare."

"Aww." Pip knew Iris wanted to get her hands on the newest members of the farm.

"She needs the iron and sugar. Hurry up. And if there's a third, I'll let you help with the birth."

Iris left the shed so fast her feet barely touched the ground.

"Smooth," Pip said.

Fly reached over to pluck a piece of straw out of Pip's hair. Her fingers brushed against Pip's forehead, leaving a trail of unexpected warmth. A goofy grin planted itself on Pip's face.

"You two need to watch yourselves," Clare said, startling them both.

Fly's hand dropped like a stone. Anger burned on her face for a fraction of a second before she buried her feelings. "Mind your own business."

"This isn't Spokane anymore. This is Thistle Hill Orchard. Everyone minds everyone else's business," Clare said. "Veronica's had a rough go of things—her patience and understanding aren't what they used to be. I'm not so sure you want to be doing what you're doing."

"What are we doing?" Fly asked. Her words were defensive, but her tone said she knew exactly what Clare was saying.

Right here and still out of reach. Pip ached for Fly and wanted to hit something at the same time. It wasn't fair. She stomped out of the shed to cool off. Iris was moving with slow deliberation down the hill with a bucket full of brown water. Her tongue stuck out as she tried to hold it steady and not spill a drop.

The joy on Iris's face quenched Pip's anger. Iris loved being at Thistle Hill. She'd changed so much since they'd escaped the yellow moving van. A splash of brown molasses water sloshed onto Iris's boot, and she paused to blow an irritated breath. Pip cheered her on and slid her hands into her pockets. *What Iris needs might be more important than my feelings.*

"You okay?" Fly came up from behind and brushed her fingers across the back of Pip's arm.

Everything inside Pip jumped. The tingly sensation of Fly's touch buzzed like bees in a lavender field on a hot summer day.

"I made a mistake."

"No, you didn't." Fly waved at Iris, then stepped in front of Pip, blocking her view. "We might have bad timing, but you *did not* make a mistake."

A yellow butterfly swooped between them, dipping its wings in the air, fluttering like a broken toy. It circled and landed on Fly's shirt, right over her heart. A peculiar sadness crossed Fly's face.

"It's a swallowtail," she said.

The wings' delicate edges were laced with black and little spots of iridescent blue. When it took off, they felt the wind of its flight. It spiraled into the air, following a current. Pip heard a faded lyric, sung by Whistler on the roof of the music store: *wings on a winter's day, she was my love.*

She hadn't let herself think about Whistler much, because every time she did, she saw Curtis standing up from behind the car to shoot. Closing her eyes, she imagined Whistler's monarchs surrounding her and Fly in a field, erasing the anger, giving her the courage to say what she felt even if it seemed impossible.

When she opened her eyes, Fly was still, watching the swallowtail fluttering away.

"You don't understand—"

"Neither do you." Fly picked up a bag of grain and carried it into the field for the rest of the goats.

Iris sloshed up beside Pip, splashing more molasses water onto her shoes.

"Is she mad?" Iris asked.

She's pissed. Pip exhaled a long breath. "Nah."

An urgent grunt came from the goat pen, and Clare shouted for Iris to hurry the hell up. Pip took Iris's heavy bucket. "Guess there were three kids after all."

CHAPTER 19

"Mutton yesterday, mutton today, and it looks like mutton again tomorrow," Ben said with a meaty burp.

It had been funny the first time he'd said it days ago. Pip pushed around her breakfast of sheep cheeks and eggs, hoping to catch a glimpse of Fly. Pip was surprised by how much she missed her.

She pushed away from the table and waved to Iris as she hurried past. Sunburn mixed with tiny freckles on Iris's cheeks. The frightened bags under her eyes had faded. Every evening they met at dinner, and Iris gushed about her day. Words poured in a torrent, filled with wonder and excitement for a life that, for the most part, Pip wasn't a part of.

Hiding in plain sight was wearing on her soul. She couldn't be who she was. Couldn't love who she wanted to. Thistle Hill was turning into one giant compromise where she couldn't win.

Every morning she wrapped bandages around her chest, clamping the material down tight on her breasts, tamping down her ambivalent feelings about her new home. She knew her deception wasn't sustainable but couldn't figure out what to do about it. What if she told Veronica the truth? What if Veronica found out about her yearning for Fly? Would it be another showdown like the one she'd had with her parents?

"Let's go, loser," Granville said on his way out of the barn. "Get Marcus, he's in the crapper."

"Charming."

Pip realized pretty quickly that Marcus wasn't Granville's right-hand man just because they were brothers. It went deeper than that. Marcus was always where he was needed. Ready with a tool or a helping hand. He also turned a blind eye to the overly affectionate attentions Granville paid to all the teen girls on the farm.

What had taken her longer to understand was why Marcus wouldn't talk to her. On that first day of scrounging, each time she'd asked Marcus for help, he acted like he hadn't heard. It took Granville snorting with glee while signing directions to Marcus for her to figure out the puzzle.

Marcus was Deaf.

Pip spent the rest of that day feeling like a fool. While unloading the sheep from the truck to the barn kitchen, Marcus had explained—with toddler-speed signs for her benefit—that Granville loved watching people make idiots of themselves trying to communicate with him.

She found Marcus washing up by the outhouse and poured rinse water over his chapped hands. He signed his thanks while he mouthed, "Thank you." He was teaching Pip ASL.

"You're welcome," she signed. "Time to go."

Marcus nodded and waved his hands rapidly in the air with an ironic smile on his face. Pip laughed; he'd explained the hand-waving sign the day before. He was clapping. But with the smirk on his face, she knew he was being sarcastic. They were going to spend the day hooking up a pair of solar panels to a well pump on the far side of the orchard. It promised to be a tedious day of Granville telling them he didn't need any help and swearing at them when they didn't help.

Marcus signed that Granville had already taken the truck and equipment down to the well. Walking the rutted road through blooming trees, Pip caught a glimpse of a yellow swallowtail and tried not to think about Fly. She failed miserably. She was almost always thinking about Fly.

The orchard ended where the woods began. Taking a side road that cut into the woods, Pip and Marcus stepped into a clearing and found Jessica pressed between Granville and his truck.

Disgust wrenched Pip's guts. "What's going on?"

Jessica flinched and slid out from under Granville's arm. "I brought him a lunch for later."

Granville bent and picked up a small woven basket, holding it up.

"God damn," Pip said. She marched on wooden legs into the clearing and shouted to Jessica. "You need to go back to the barn." Blushing furiously, Jessica looked to Granville for direction. "Go on." He patted her on the butt, and she took off, sprinting around Pip and Marcus.

Pip slapped her hand on the truck's hood. Granville was impassive, his expression neutral, like a snake before it struck.

"Did you know?" she signed to Marcus.

He made a few half signs, words she couldn't make out. He dropped his hands into his pockets and looked to Granville for instruction before turning away.

Granville moved toward her with the ease of a predator. Limbs swinging loose with anger, he walked like a fighter. Pip took an uneasy step back.

"You need to watch yourself," he said coolly.

"How many little girls are you grooming on the farm, you disgusting piece of crap? I'd bet Veronica doesn't know about you making the moves on fifteen-year-olds. Does she?" Pip pushed.

Granville crossed the space between them and spun her around. She slammed against the truck. Tobacco chew peppered her face. Pip tried to jerk free and hit her head on the door with a dull *clonk*.

His weight pushed hard against her chest. Granville leaned in close. "Does Veronica know about those?" he asked, gesturing at Pip's bound breasts. Pip's blood ran cold.

"Didn't think so, *little man.*"

Their eyes met. Pip read the pent-up violence there and knew her only chance was to punch first.

She snapped her head forward, mashing her skull against his nose. The top of her head went instantly numb. Granville grunted with pained surprise as blood spurted from his nose. He shoved her away and pinched his nostrils flat, stopping the crimson flow.

"Bitch!"

They panted in the harsh sunshine, facing off like gunfighters waiting for high noon. Sweat prickled Pip's hair and soaked into the binding wrapped around her chest while she waited for

Granville's next move. He held his nose pinched shut and paced in front of the truck, spitting blood and throwing menacing looks her way. Marcus kept his eyes averted.

Granville pulled his hand away from his nose with a snap, sending an arc of blood into the dust. He sniffed wetly, cleared his throat, and hocked up a bloody clot. He spit again and pulled off his shirt, tossing it on the hood. Flash tattoos covered his chest—poorly inked renditions of naked women, knives, and skulls. Pip focused on the mustache of blood drying on his upper lip and tried to calm her frantic heart.

Granville gingerly pinched the bridge of his nose. "You didn't break it."

She pursed her lips against any pity she might have felt for the pain she'd caused. Granville retrieved his shirt and mopped at the blood on his face.

He looked toward the road Jessica had taken to the farmhouse. "I need another shirt."

Pip moved to stop him from following Jessica. Granville pointed a bloody finger at her.

"You won't hit me again."

They were at an impasse until Marcus opened the passenger-side door of the truck and tossed over a greasy T-shirt as a replacement. Granville caught it out of the air with a growl and pulled it on.

Pip spit blood on the ground. She'd bitten her tongue hitting him in the nose. Landing that bull's-eye had been no more than luck. He hadn't expected her to fight back. She could scrap with the best of them, but Granville was much bigger than she was. And people had accidents every day.

Veronica probably wouldn't worry overlong if a newly pledged member of her farm was killed in a work-related accident. Marcus wouldn't help her; he'd deliberately looked away from their confrontation. As the younger brother of a charismatic bully, he wouldn't lift a finger for her sake.

Her thoughts flew to Iris. What would happen to her if Pip never returned? Given what she'd just seen with Jessica, Iris wasn't safe around Granville. None of the young girls on the farm were. Suddenly her course was crystal clear. Everything depended on convincing Granville she'd keep her mouth shut.

"I didn't see anything..." Pip ventured after a wary pause.

Hands on hips, Granville considered. His gaze tracked up her body until he met her eyes.

"I've seen you making eyes at that girl. That Fly. Remember that too, *little man*. I can *destroy* you." Granville walked into Marcus's field of vision and signed for him to grab their tools.

They rewired the solar panel to the well's pump motor in a silence pregnant with anger and unspoken accusations. Whenever Pip caught Marcus alone, she tried to get him to explain why he hadn't tried to stop Granville. Marcus's signing was sharp, angry. Rapid swoops of his hands shaped words she couldn't follow. She asked him to slow down, but he'd shake his head no, his face resigned. Every time she signed Jessica's name, Marcus refused to acknowledge anything had happened.

By the middle of the afternoon, Granville's expression was a landslide right before the dirt gave way. Full of energy and right on the edge. Pip sat in the back of the truck holding onto the sharp lip of an extra solar panel that filled almost the entire bed. Every hard and fast turn made on the way up the rutted road through the orchard sent the rough metal edges jabbing into her side. The old bullet wound wept from the abuse. Her shoulders ached. And, so help her God, if Granville slammed on the brakes one more time, she was going to snap that cocky bastard's neck.

The road to the barn was blocked by a herd of goats. Granville honked the horn and swore before making a tight U-turn under the trees. They circled around the orchard and wound up all the way back at the farm's gated entrance. One of the guardsmen waved for them to stop. He had colorful flowers tucked into the band of his dusty cowboy hat.

Granville poked a finger at the guard. "What's with the plants on your head?"

Embarrassed by Granville's ribbing, the guard brushed his fingers over the red petals of a miniature rose. "The girls did it. There's gonna be a wedding tonight. Wait 'til you see the barn. Oh! Almost forgot. Park in the back or Veronica'll kill you. Clare tried to unload some meat in front of the barn. I could hear the argument from here."

"Good to know. Thanks, princess."

Clenching her teeth, Pip chewed on anger. Every time that belt-buckled Neanderthal opened his mouth, more hate fell out of it. She'd promised to keep her mouth shut about Jessica in order to save herself and ensure Iris's safety. But the more she stewed in her decision, the more bitter it tasted. Every fresh jab of the solar panel tilted the balance a little more in favor of spilling everything she knew to Veronica—damn the consequences.

CHAPTER 20

Thistle Hill Orchard bubbled with bubbled with a party atmosphere. Near the big barn, people stacked hay bales out of the way while children tumbled about in the loose straw, enjoying freedom from the adults who were too busy to give them anything to do. Granville slowed the truck to a crawl, and Pip spotted Iris carrying a bucket of tools. She was following a woman weighed down by an enormous armful of purple lilacs.

"Iris!" Pip waved.

Iris's serious, I've-got-a-job-to-do face split wide with a joyful grin when she saw Pip. "I'm helping make the centerpieces! You should come see."

"You got it," Pip tried to say. Most of her words came out as a wheeze as Granville stomped hard on the brake before he turned off the engine and hopped out.

"Hey, pretty lady!" Granville hid the scowl he'd worn most of the day and turned up the charm as he approached the woman weighed down by flowers. He scooped blooms out of her hands and kissed her on the cheek. The startled woman took back her flowers and pushed him away. Thrilled to see someone fighting back, Pip shoved the solar panel off her lap and jumped out of the truck. Pressing a hand against the bruised pain in her side, she went to give Iris a quick hug. Granville got there first.

"I should have said...pretty *ladies*." He nudged Iris with a hip.

She blushed bright red. Granville noticed the glow and nudged her again, playfully pushing her off balance. Tripping over her own feet from the force of his attention, Iris tried to skip out of his grasp. Thinking of Jessica pressed between Granville's body and his truck, Pip wrapped a protective arm around Iris's shoulders. Granville shrugged off her interference and went inside the barn. *If they only knew. He's a monster in a man-shaped sack of skin.*

Inside the barn, tables were haphazardly shoved against the walls, leaving a long rectangle of space in the middle. Bouquets of flowers in mason jars covered every flat surface, and a lectern stood at the far end. Heather was arranging a pile of lilacs into a large vase on one side of the lectern; she gestured for them to bring their flowers.

"Almost all the decorations are done. The men need to finish repairs to the second shed before tonight or the happy couple won't have anywhere to sleep. Granville, could you get the slackers moving?" Heather asked.

"Sure." He tipped his hat. "No problem."

I'll find a way to end you, Pip thought with a sneer. Granville noted her expression. Pausing next to Iris, he plucked a white peony from a mason jar and tucked it behind her ear. Catching Pip's eye, he smoothed Iris's hair, then tilted his head so Pip would be the only one to see his deliberate wink.

"You should go too, Pip," Heather said. "Unfortunately, you'll have to move. Ben and Alison get the shed. Veronica wants your things in the men's barn. We'll make you a bed there."

Pip's stomach sank to her feet. She tried to keep dismay off her face while nodding agreement at Heather. "I'll get my stuff."

Granville hooked a thumb toward a side door and grinned. "Let's go...*man.*"

Pip swallowed the words she wanted to slice him with and went to collect her stuff.

The scent of newly cut wood and sawdust filled the ramshackle horse shed. It smelled like honest work and reminded Pip of when she'd been her dad's helpful shadow. Soda pop and gasoline fumes—the taste of them on her tongue was the sweetest memory she had from childhood. After a hard day of outside chores, she and her dad always hid in the garage to sneak the fruity sodas forbidden by her mother.

She'd lived and breathed for her dad, loving every second they spent together. Even an afternoon spent waiting for him to ask her to pass him a tool while he worked under the car was fun. The day Pip got her first period, her dad's attitude began to change, and a gradual, slow-growing tumor of hate took root in his heart. Chores they used to do together became filled with excuses. He'd pull on work gloves and wave Pip off when she approached, saying the work was too hard or too dirty. She'd tried to explain she was still the same person, but all he could see was that this girl—Pip—had taken away Noah, his son. If she wasn't Noah Philip, she wasn't anything he wanted.

Pip paused in the run-down shed's doorway. She was surrounded by men. As she pushed past two guys hauling a bed frame inside, she admired their easy, joking manner. Sometimes she had to admit that she'd missed the easy camaraderie that came with being a guy.

Pip retrieved her things from where they'd been carelessly kicked into a corner and shoved them into a bag, thankful no one had noticed the small container of pads and tampons she'd scrounged for her next period. She cinched the bag with trepidation. Moving into the men's barn was a spectacularly bad idea. But unless she was willing to risk telling Veronica at least part of the truth, there wasn't any way around it.

Granville was waiting for her just outside the men's barn. Stripped down to a surprisingly white undershirt, he stood in the hot sun with hands on hips. A deep-purple bruise was blooming across the bridge of his nose. She studied his muscular physique with apprehension. His tattooed body hid a rotten core.

She squeezed past him into the men's barn, wincing at the thrust of his hips against hers. Granville threatened with masculinity in a way that made her physically ill. Pip checked out his nose while sliding by; she should have done more than bash it with her forehead. She should have fought until one of them couldn't stand.

Steeling herself against the feeling of being exposed, Pip shoved her hands deep into her pockets to keep them from trembling. The men's barn was littered with dirty socks and the lingering smell of farts. She paused, looking for her empty cot, hoping against hope that it would be in the deepest, darkest, most out-of-the-way corner of the barn. Granville walked the row of stalls ahead of her and wolf whistled when he discovered where her new bunk was.

"Imagine that. Right. Next. To. Mine," he drawled.

Slapping a thigh with raunchy enthusiasm, Granville nodded his head. He untied his overshirt from around his waist and shook out the wrinkles before shrugging it on. He sauntered toward Pip while doing up the buttons.

"From now on, I will do as I please, and you'll keep your mouth shut. Understood?"

Fuck you, Pip seethed. She swallowed her hate, and it settled in her core like molten steel.

"That's what I thought."

Without a backward glance, he stepped out the barn's doorway with a self-satisfied chuckle.

Pip stomped on wooden legs to her bunk and sat gingerly, as if the cot was made of glass. Making a deal with that devil wasn't sitting well at all. Pip could see the decision to keep her mouth shut branching out before her. There would be consequences no matter which path she chose. If Iris was safe, the rest of the girls at Thistle Hill wouldn't be.

What am I willing to live with?

A pebble rolled along the floor and bumped against Pip's boot.

Pip picked up the pebble and tossed it back. "Sneak."

"Nice house, Pip," Iris mocked while she walked down the aisle. "*Way* better than your falling-down shack."

Mustering up a smile, Pip set her bag on the bed and hugged Iris.

"It smells kinda like the outhouse in here," Iris whispered in her ear.

Pip laughed. "You're right. Let's go."

She followed Iris into the grassy courtyard between the men's barn and the big white house. Puffy clouds did a slow cruise across the blue sky. Pip shaded her eyes and looked up, marveling at the lack of contrails. She hadn't seen an airplane in so long.

"Pip!" Iris tugged her along. "I need you to help hang the laundry."

"Oh, I see how it is. You only like me for my muscles." Pip flexed her skinny arms.

A freckled girl of about five ran up to them. Clothespins bounced out of the cloth bag she held in one fist. The little clothespin litterbug had a smile full of gaps.

"Is this your brother?" she asked Iris.

Pip caught her breath. *Brother?* The word stung and staggered in equal measure. She was no boy, not inside. She looked at Iris's sheepish smile and attempted to feel the love behind the word. After all, she'd been the one to tell Iris to call her 'he.'

"Stella, this is Pip." Iris held out her hands like she was showing off all of Pip's better features.

Stella clapped her approval, dropping more clothespins in the process. Pip suspected they spent more of their time picking up after Stella than they did hanging laundry, but with Iris snapping the wrinkles out of shirts and Stella selecting the best pins to use, they somehow made a dent in the job. They were on their last shirt when Heather stepped onto the white house's porch.

"I gave you a stepladder for a reason, Iris." She laughed at the chagrin on both girls' faces. They'd been caught.

Stella giggled. Everyone knew that no one was in trouble.

"But we love Pip," Iris said.

"Yeah." Stella wrapped her arms around Pip's thighs. "We looove Pip."

Heather tsked. "Time to get ready for the wedding, you two. If you move fast, you'll get hot water to wash up in."

"Race ya!" Iris shouted, flashing a bright grin at Pip before sprinting to the door.

"No fair!" Stella yelled. She let go of Pip's legs and took off after Iris.

Right before they got to the door, Iris slowed to let Stella catch up. Heather waved them inside with a shake of her head.

"Would you mind helping out with chopping wood? We're planning a bonfire for later tonight."

"Sure." Pip said.

"Thanks. They're behind the big barn." Heather looked thoughtful. "You've got a great way with kids."

Pip soaked up the compliment like a dried-out sponge. It felt good to be seen. "Thanks."

As twilight climbed into the sky with a chill, Pip dumped an armload of chopped wood into a rusty wheelbarrow next to the fire and rubbed muscles sore from the unfamiliar job of swinging an ax. The preparations for the wedding were done. Outside the red barn, a bonfire flickered its welcome. The toothsome smell of roasting meat and fresh-baked bread filled the air with the scent of people managing to do more than just survive until the next day.

Inside the barn, hands clapped in unison, keeping up with the bright chirping of a fiddle running through a fast-paced reel. Dusting woodchips from her clothes along to the beat, Pip stepped into the warmth of the barn and laughed with joy at the sight of Iris fiddling with happy abandon. She was surrounded by people dancing in the glow of candles and firelight. One song ended and Iris smoothly moved into another, picking up the pace with a wide smile.

Iris leaned into the music, and Pip smiled with more than a little pride, wondering where she'd found the fiddle. That kid was a magnet for stringed instruments. A hand waved at her from the other side of the room. Pip's heart did a nervous flip when she saw Fly trying to get her attention. Fly gestured around her head and pointed at Iris.

Iris's hair was braided in an elaborate crown, and her skin glowed in the firelight as she played. Fly made the gesture again. Pip had no idea what she was saying.

Moving through the crowd, Fly ambled over to stand beside Pip. They stared at each other for a long moment.

"I'm sorry for what I said at the goat barn," Pip murmured. *And what I didn't say.*

"You were afraid."

Fly wasn't wrong about that. Her words stung anyway.

Iris finished a song and Fly clapped. "I braided her hair."

An unexpected burst of jealousy warmed Pip's cheeks, and she hated herself for it. Was this how her mom had felt every time *she* had been excluded on those boys-only afternoons? Tucking away the bitterness, Pip smiled at Fly. "It's beautiful."

"She wanted to surprise you."

Veronica stepped to the lectern and clapped her hands,

gradually getting everyone's attention. Dancers broke apart and settled around tables, shushing younger children.

Wearing a modest blue dress with long sleeves, she opened a leather-bound Bible. "Bring those who would place themselves in the hand of God."

Ben was shoved out of a crowd of men. Ribald snickers followed him until Veronica fixed the revelers with a motherly stare. Someone had given Ben a haircut and found him new clothes. He looked miles better than when he'd tumbled out of the truck with zip ties around his wrists.

Iris performed a happy trill on the violin, then began a stately waltz. Keeping her steps in time with the music, Alison walked into the barn carrying a single early rose. Her hair was sectioned into neat twists layered around her face like a lion's mane. Barefoot and wearing what looked like a high school girl's prom dress, she managed to look regal and radiant in a barn full of picnic tables.

She took Ben's hand and they stood together. Pip's chest tightened. She did not allow herself to so much as glance at Fly as Veronica shepherded the couple through vows and blessed their marriage. When Alison turned to Ben with a thousand-watt smile, Pip wanted to cry.

Two feet away and miles apart. Pip desperately wanted Fly to know she wanted her to be more than a friend. The want burned deep. The pressure of Granville's secret, the bandage around her chest, the feelings she had for Fly—it was too much. *Not here, not ever.* She clenched her jaw as tears threatened. Gulping loneliness through a throat filled with unshed tears, she stepped away from Fly and moved through the crowd, searching for Iris. The kid's devotion had to be enough. It was the only thing she'd ever have at Thistle Hill.

A cheer from the crowd startled her. Pip flinched as a group of whooping children pushed past. Another yell from the group startled pigeons in the rafters when Veronica pronounced the young couple man and wife.

"Handsome couple, aren't they?" Clare gestured toward the newly married pair. "Of course, everyone looks radiant when they get married, at least for a little while."

Pip watched Ben kiss his bride on the cheek. "They do look good."

"Maybe that'll be you and Fly one day, huh?" Clare stepped into Pip's bubble with a gentle smile. Pip tried to step back, but Clare caught her arm. "Relax, kid, your secret's safe with me."

Pip's lungs collapsed like windless sails.

"What secret?"

"As I see it, you've been a girl a little too long to be passing as a boy, that's all. And either way, you're sweet on Fly and that's a whole other mess of trouble barreling down the pipe at you."

Pip choked. Words caught in her throat.

"We should talk. But first, I'm gonna stir up the hornet's nest," Clare offered her a wink and turned her attention to the crowded barn. "There's nothing more entertaining than an elderly woman clutching at her pearls."

Pip tried to laugh. Hard to do when her insides were a deflated balloon.

Clare chirped air between her teeth and tapped her glass with a spoon. "Time for a toast."

A chorus of rapped cups and vases answered Clare's, then tapered off as the older woman stepped into the aisle. Pip sagged into a chair, relieved by the loss of Clare's laser-focused attention. People parted before Clare—the sheer weight of her personality forced people out of the way.

Clare's rough voice carried over the burbling crowd as she raised her glass in honor of the newlyweds. "There was once a philosopher called Plato. Way back in ancient Greece, he said that in the beginning of creation, each person was one creature with two sexes together."

Pip's heart lurched. She was back in her bedroom listening to "The Origin of Love." Clare was speaking right to her heart. She felt exposed, like a cockroach when a late-night snacker flicked on the kitchen light—trapped on the counter, wondering which way to run. Veronica looked poleaxed.

Strolling up to the happy couple, Clare continued her speech. "The gods thought humans were too powerful. They ripped us asunder, tearing male from female, male from male, and female from female."

Veronica's lips parted, gasping shocked air.

Clare was undaunted. "Each pair was broken and lost without their better half. The gods hoped that in being separate, people would become weak. Separated from our other halves, we are alone and lost, eternally searching for the person who can make us whole. Today, Ben and Alison re-embrace their other, better halves. I hope they will forever be stronger for it. Congratulations!"

Cheers filled the rafters as Alison enthusiastically kissed her new husband.

Disoriented by Clare's perceptive words, Pip wove through the merriment to refill her glass and wound up at the refreshment table with Heather. Pouring juice with an unsteady hand, she offered Heather the jug. The fiddle started up again with a swaggering tune that begged for dancing. This time an older gentleman with a turkey feather in his hat took a turn with the bow.

Accustomed to hiding her true feelings, Pip stuffed them down for later reflection and put on the camouflage of a smile. She clinked glasses with Heather.

"Where'd you get the fiddle?" she shouted in Heather's ear to be heard.

"It came with you."

A man cut in, taking Heather's glass and handing it to Pip. He took both of Heather's hands and spun her onto the dance floor. Pip resisted the urge to throw the extra glass to the floor as Granville waltzed by with Jessica on his arm. He lifted his chin toward Iris, letting Pip know he was keeping his eye on her. The threat was clear. Pip slammed the two glasses onto a table, sloshing the contents over her hands.

She stepped out of the barn, standing near the bonfire to escape from Granville. Ears filled with the snap-crackle of burning wood, she stroked the reassuring weight of the dog tags around her neck. Even with Granville fucking everything up, it had been good to see Iris playing the fiddle again.

Heat baked through her clothes, making her skin sting and prickle. She turned her back to the flames and sparks flew overhead, winking out over the orchard.

Whistler would've loved this.

Laughter tumbled out of the barn and she gazed inside. Iris twirled in the middle of a group of dancing children, spinning in a circle to the rapid beat of the fiddle. Even without alcohol, the mood was festive and a little wild; couples paired off in the shadows, taking advantage of the tumultuous atmosphere to sneak a kiss without Veronica catching on. An older couple kissed over the head of a sleeping toddler—a wilted bunch of lilacs hung from the child's limp fist. Loneliness caressed Pip's heart as she wondered where Fly had gone.

Clare's speech had sent her adrift, spinning like a leaf trapped in the rapids of a frigid river. Did never being divided from her male or female half mean she was already complete? She didn't want to be an island of one. She wanted a person—someone who would love all of her.

Torn between staying outside and diving back into the party, Pip noticed a girl whose dress barely contained her developing curves bouncing on Granville's knee. His hands wrapped possessively around her waist. The teen threw back her head and laughed at something he whispered in her ear. Sickened by the view, Pip resisted the urge to make a scene and pull them apart. The wolf in sheep's clothing wasn't even bothering to hide his desire to take advantage of the girls on the farm.

She didn't know if she'd found a family in Thistle Hill, but watching Iris's joyously innocent face cleared her path forward. She knew what to do now. Veronica had to be told. Adjusting the rolled edge of the bandage that held her breasts flat against her chest, Pip scratched at a rash spreading under the confining wrap. In order to expose Granville, she'd have to at least tell part of the truth about herself—that she really was a girl.

The way forward was treacherous, the path uncertain. Trusting people didn't come easy; her parents had made sure of that. Whatever Veronica's reaction, sticking Granville with punishment for his sick abuse would be worth the consequences.

Pip tapped her front teeth in thought as Iris tumbled to the ground with another girl, dizzy from spinning. Without warning, the full-throated scream of a woman in pain burst from the dark woods. The music faltered. Pip looked over her shoulder at the forest. Rough tips of silent treetops broke the indigo skyline like torn edges on a piece of paper. Holding up her hand to block the glare, she stepped away from the bonfire, ears straining.

"What was that?" Jessica cried.

People poured out of the barn. Someone shushed the children while everyone waited for the terrifying noise to repeat.

"Sounded like a woman, didn't it?" Ben murmured.

Guttural screams to their left fractured the night, and every head turned. Another raw voice called, a horror-movie yowl that trailed off into a low growl.

"It's the tiger from Cat Tails!" One boy grabbed another, making him shriek.

"It's gonna eat us!"

Heather separated them, gripping each boy by the shoulder. "That isn't a tiger."

"Mountain lions," Clare said with calm authority. "Looking for mates."

The screams gradually drifted nearer to the perimeter fence. The farm was large; the cats were acres away, and yet the hair on Pip's neck stood straight up at the primal sound. Even at a distance they were too close.

"If they're this near, I'm worried about the livestock," Veronica said. "Granville?"

Pursing his lips in thought, he adjusted his hat and nodded. "Get your guns and meet back here."

Most of the men ran to retrieve weapons from their bunks. It wasn't long before they returned, armed to the teeth and ready for battle. Pitchforks and slop shovels were handed to any of the men who didn't own guns. Standing with her hands on her hips, Pip was lost between the two groups. On one side, women herded the children back to the main house, keeping them safe in a protective circle of lantern light. On the other was a boiling sea of testosterone, locked and loaded, intent on protecting the farm.

Iris came out of the barn and ran toward Pip. "What is that?"

"Cougars."

"Let's go," Fly said to Iris. She'd gathered together a group of older teens. Jessica stood in the middle of the group, glaring murder at Fly.

"I don't want to go to the house," Jessica's voice was petulant.

"I didn't ask what you wanted." Fly's don't-piss-me-off expression couldn't be denied. Properly cowed, the whole group made for the house.

"But—" Iris protested.

A cougar scream, deep and full of longing, came from the fields closest to the fence. Iris shut her mouth and nodded at Fly before running to catch up with the teens.

"Thank you," Pip said.

"I'll keep her safe."

"Take this." Clare thrust a pitchfork with wickedly sharp tines into Pip's hands. The older woman unbuttoned her flannel shirt. She wore a T-shirt and a shoulder holster with a concealed handgun underneath. Pip admired Clare's ready-for-anything attitude.

"With all the noise these morons are making, they'll scare off the mountain lions before we even see them. But just to be safe, you two watch the kids." Clare tilted her chin toward the white house lit by a single bulb on the porch.

"Okay," Pip agreed. Hefting the garden tool's reassuring weight, she and Fly trailed the teens to the house. They were almost to the front porch when Fly spotted Jessica sneaking into the shadows.

"God damn that girl." She set off at a trot to intercept her. Fly wrestled Jessica to the front door and thrust her inside. Not envying the tongue-lashing Jessica was going to get from Fly, Pip stood guard against the soul-cringing screams of big cats in heat.

Just as Clare predicted, it wasn't long before their haunting calls fell silent. But just because they weren't screaming for each other didn't mean the cougars had left the area. Pip shuddered. Moving the bloodied corpses of sheep from Clare's truck had given her a more than healthy respect for sharp-clawed predators.

A series of rapid finger taps on a nearby window was followed by a crescendo of giggles. Three faces smeared across the glass, squishing back and forth, stretching noses into pig snouts and transforming smiles into ghoulish grins. Brandishing the pitchfork and jabbing it toward the window, Pip was rewarded with hysterical screams as Iris and the two other kids tumbled out of view. Iris popped up again not a second later, hair mussed and cheeks flushed. She blew a sloppy-looking kiss. Pip slapped it onto her cheek with a flourish.

"Go to bed!" Pip said, shaking her finger in playful anger when the whole trio stuck out their tongues.

The curtain drew back and Heather loomed into view. Her reprimand must have been of sterner stuff, because the hooligans were soon off to bed.

Soft steps through the grass sent Pip's nerves into high alert. She whipped around, tines at the ready.

"Watch it!" Clare knocked the pitchfork to the ground so hard that Pip's hands stung with the impact.

"Jesus! I'm so sorry! Are you okay?"

Bending with a grunt, Clare picked up the tool. She made a show of dusting off the handle and handed it over with a laugh. "You guys, always poking with the sharp end before you stop to think."

Pip jabbed the fork into the ground.

"Or maybe I should say...that's what *men* do?"

Pip searched Clare's face for her intentions. This was the second time she'd gone out of her way to question Pip's identity.

"That bandage you've wrapped around your chest looks pretty tight."

Pip's stomach tumbled into free fall.

"I saw the outline through your shirt when you were holding the goat."

"I was shot."

Clare pursed her lips. "Whatever you've got under there is gonna bruise if you don't loosen it."

Pip checked the window, making sure no one was listening before attempting to speak. "What are you saying?"

"I'm saying, if Veronica knew about the binder and that crush you've got on Fly, you wouldn't be welcome here anymore. And with Granville all but running the show...he isn't one to be crossed." Clare thoughtfully licked her upper lip. "And I think you know that."

Pip shuffled her feet. Clare's comments threw her completely off balance.

"Let's get right to the point. People used to come to the farm of their free will. Things changed when Veronica's daughter died. Granville's making Thistle Hill into something dark, and Veronica is too broken to do anything about it." Clare flicked her gun's safety and holstered it. "So why are you passing?"

"I beat a woman pretty bad when the traders captured us. They weren't going to let me off the truck. Veronica thought I was a guy. With her whole 'girl, guy, farm balance' thing, it's part of why she made them let me stay."

"So you were stuck."

"I made a promise to Iris that we'd stay together. I couldn't be sure everything would be fine if I told the truth. And then it was too late."

Clare's expression turned grim. Frowning in anger, she squatted, gesturing for Pip to join. Smoothing out the dirt between them, she drew a rough sketch of the farm and the surrounding area. With a steady hand, Clare traced out roads, many of which Pip recognized from the scavenging expeditions for Thistle Hill.

"I'm well over twenty miles from here." Clare tapped the dirt barn at the center of the farm. "You go north. Always north." Tracing a path with her finger, she recited more directions. "Dunn. Right on Dusty Gulch. Left on Day. Right on Cedar. Left on Bickett. About two miles along Bickett is a tangle of brush I've built to obscure the old road we sometimes used to bring in supplies. Go around the woodpile and follow the rough track through the woods to my house."

Pip studied the crude map and parroted back the words, memorizing the twists and turns. She hadn't been on Cedar or Bickett but thought she'd be able to follow Clare's directions.

"Why are you telling me this?"

Clare stood and scuffed out the map with a heavy sigh. "My husband had a thing for strays. He was always bringing home bedraggled critters in need of a few square meals and a bath. Human and animal alike. It didn't make any difference to his heart. Before the Cough took him, I promised to see things his way."

"He sounds like a good person," Pip said.

"Better than me, that's for sure."

Deep voices rumbled in the distance. The men were returning from their hunt. Straggling along in twos and threes, their shadowy forms went to the barn. Granville and Ben came from the other side of the house. The rifle hanging over Granville's shoulder made Pip more than a little nervous.

"Lost the cats in the woods," Ben explained.

"Too bad. Would have made a nice wedding-night gift," Granville joked.

Pip's chuckle was all politeness. Clare's blank expression didn't change.

"Tough crowd," Granville shrugged. "See ya in the bunk, *roomie*."

Pip's heart sank deep, dragging her down.

Ben reached to shake Pip's hand. "I haven't thanked you for giving up your spot in the little shack. It happened so fast after we went to Veronica and told her we wanted to get married. When she agreed, we had no idea it would happen the *same day*."

This time her smile was genuine. "Of course. Congratulations."

"You should get your bride. She's in the house," Clare suggested.

Ben beamed and eagerly knocked on the front door. Alone for the moment, Clare turned serious. The grin she'd put on for Ben melted away.

"If a time comes when you can't stay here, remember the map, get your little Iris, and come my way."

"Clare—"

"I mean it. The location of my house is a secret—you'd be safe. As a boy or a girl. I couldn't care less."

Rocked by Clare's honesty and kindness, Pip could only think of the many times she'd been shamed for being herself. Not long after she turned twelve, her father came home early one day. He caught her wrapped in a ruffled duvet, wearing carefully applied lipstick. The slap he'd delivered to her tender cheek left a mark darker than the drop-dead-red color on her lips.

"You're a boy!" he'd shouted. Her ears buzzed with the memory.

No one in the family had cared about Noah Philip needing to be called "she." They had wanted their boy to stay a boy. They ignored the developing parts of her body. Every day was a fight against doubt, wearing at her heart like the ocean turning stone to sand.

A doctor saved her. He told the angry middle schooler with too much black eyeliner ringing her eyes that she wasn't a freak. He'd looked at Pip like she was a person, not the self-destructive circus sideshow she'd feared she'd become.

Clare looked at her now the same way the doctor had then.

"Thank you," Pip said. It wasn't enough, but there wasn't anything else to say.

Yanking the pitchfork out of the ground, Clare nodded at Pip's gratitude. "I'll take this back to the barn. I'm heading home tonight."

"Tonight? Aren't you worried about the mountain lions?"

"With two mules who'd stomp a cat into the dirt?" Clare's chuckle was dangerous. "I'd like to see them try."

CHAPTER 21

The front door opened, and the newlyweds emerged. Ben and Alison waved goodnight as they walked with eager steps toward their new home.

"Sorry to bother you." Heather leaned over the porch rail. "Iris rushed to the outhouse without waiting for someone to go with. I don't think she's feeling good. Pip, could you check?"

"Tummy ache?"

Heather shrugged. "She was fine a minute ago, and then she wilted. Her forehead wasn't hot, so it isn't a fever…"

"I'll check and bring her back." Pip turned to Clare. "Sorry—"

"No problem." Clare patted her on the shoulder and muttered, "Remember the map."

A chill breeze tugged at Pip's clothes, whistling around the well's pump equipment, pushing her toward the outhouse. Picking up the pace, she tucked clinking dog tags into her shirt, grimacing at the sting of cold metal stealing heat from her skin.

The outhouse door was locked. "Iris, you in there?"

A chesty cough came from inside. Pip tried the knob the same instant the door opened. Surprised by the lack of resistance, she stumbled backward. A deep bark of mocking laughter rang out.

"We've gotta stop meeting like this." Granville stepped out of the outhouse and took his time running the leather strap of his belt through the ornate buckle.

"Where's Iris?"

"The china doll? No idea."

Heart pounding, Pip scanned the small confines of the out-house. "Big help. Thanks."

Granville's lips pulled away from his teeth in an expression that was all bite and no smile. "Anytime." Shouldering into Pip, he knocked her aside, bruising her upper arm with casual ease.

"Bastard," she snarled.

Taking a second look inside, she took a step onto the wood decking of the outhouse floor and heard a muffled cry through the wall. Jogging around the ripe outhouse, she found Iris crumpled on a bench.

"Are you hurt?" Pip tried to gather Iris to her chest and got shoved away.

"No. I've got blood on my pants."

"From what?"

Iris gave her a long-suffering look. "I got my period."

Relief bubbled up from deep inside that it wasn't something more serious. She hugged Iris tight, then let go.

"Everyone will see."

Pip took off her overshirt and held it out. "Not if you tie this around your waist. Just wash your pants with cold water and the stain'll come right out. I'd get you some of my pads, but if the guys saw me...you'll have to ask Heather."

"Ew. No way."

"Every person in that house over the age of fifteen has been right where you are."

Iris snagged the proffered shirt from Pip and tied it around her waist. "Fine."

On the short walk back to the white house, Pip was struck with a dawning fear. Iris wasn't a little kid anymore. What would happen when Granville figured that out?

Heather answered the door before Pip had the chance to knock. The caretaker of the children was clearly worried. Whatever Pip thought about Veronica's blindness over Granville grooming the young girls, she had to admire the concern and care Heather had for her charges.

Iris went inside with a resigned "goodnight."

"Goodnight." Pip remembered the first time she found blood in her own underwear. Her mom had looked ashamed. As if Pip's biology was a disgrace. Her mom had explained periods, but they'd told her it would never happen—that Pip's vagina was superfluous, that she could have it "fixed" when she got older.

Her period caught her completely by surprise. Messy, inconvenient, and world changing. It took a few months for Pip to decipher her feelings. Her mom had said that Pip was a boy who had periods. Her mom was wrong.

"Is she alright?" Heather asked.

"She got her first period."

"Oh. But why—"

"It got on her pants."

"The shirt around her waist. Good thinking." Heather smiled. "I told you that you're good with kids, right?"

The compliment was like hot chocolate on a freezing day. "You did."

Heather smiled again and closed the door.

Stepping off the front porch, Pip looked up at Iris's window. Moths batted against the screen, attracted to the flickering light of a candle. The sound of their wings rustled like rain on leaves. Even though her chest was tight with the ache of missing Whistler, Pip refused to let herself cry. She was afraid she'd never stop. He'd been her family. They'd held together through the collapse of everything they'd ever known.

Pip waited to see if Iris would come to the window, then reluctantly turned toward her new sleeping arrangements.

Most of the men had already called it a day, exhausted from the evening's tramp through the woods. Dimmed lanterns cast spider-webbed shadows across their sleeping faces. Pip sat on her bunk as if it were a land mine, unable to relax. She fiddled with the binding around her chest. Sleeping bound was not a good idea. Just a few hours with the fabric compressing her breasts was uncomfortable. Trying to sleep would be torture. She wanted to loosen the bandage but knew it wasn't safe. She was considering spending some time in the outhouse with the bandage off when Granville popped up from behind the wall between them.

"Find the china doll?"

"That's racist, you prick."

Granville hocked a glob of phlegm onto the dirt next to Pip's shoes. "Blood on the toilet seat. Our little gal all grown up now?"

"Stay away from her." Pip's voice deepened into a feral growl.

Granville laughed as heads appeared over partitions all around the room. "Don't worry buddy, she's a *little* too young for me. For now."

Anger boiled in Pip's veins as the muscles in her arms twitched, urging her to action. Granville recognized her rage and snickered nastily. "Lights out people, we've got work to do tomorrow."

He stared at her while darkness filled the bunkhouse. The last thing she glimpsed before blackness engulfed them was the bright shine of his eyes.

CHAPTER 22

Pip spent the night clutching an unsheathed knife between her bound breasts. She flinched at the warbling cry of the first rooster crow of the morning and sat up. Tossing the blanket aside, she sheathed the knife, tucked it into the back of her pants, and snuck past the limp feet of snoring men. Pushing open the barn door just enough to slip through, she stepped outside with an exhausted sigh.

Instead of sleeping, she'd counted Granville's breaths in the dark, finding consolation in the even rhythm. If he was asleep, he wasn't dangerous...but he would always be a threat. He was grooming girls at Thistle Hill right under Veronica's nose.

That's probably why he wants to run the farm, so he can turn it into his disgusting harem. The thought of Granville touching Iris churned Pip's stomach. Even if she wasn't worried for Iris's safety, doing nothing to protect the girls of Thistle Hill wasn't right.

Pip's hiking boots left footprints in the dewy grass. She stopped, turning back to study her shining trail leading away from the men's barn. Granville knew her growing love for Iris was a weakness. If she kept quiet, he would escalate his attacks to stay in control.

"I won't let *anyone* be a victim," Pip muttered. It was time to talk to Veronica.

The head woman was elbow deep in bread dough when Pip found her in the large barn's communal kitchen. Two woodstoves ticked as the metal warmed, creating a wall of dry air and welcome heat. Her sleeves were rolled up over surprisingly muscular forearms. Veronica kneaded the dough with a practiced hand. She tore a loaf-sized chunk from the mass in the bowl and transferred it to a board layered with flour. When she noticed Pip, her mouth thinned to a fine line. She brushed her hands clean.

"Pip."

Her name sounded like a swear word. There weren't enough woodstoves in the world to ward off the prim woman's chill. Experience taught Pip to hold her tongue in situations like these.

"You lied to me."

Pip cringed. During the mountain lion confusion, Granville must have outed her to the head woman. "What are you talking about?"

"You let me believe you were male." Veronica punched down the dough.

"Ah." Pip stalled for time while she considered. "Granville talked to you."

"He did."

Pip steadied herself on a table.

Twisting the dough into an elaborate knot, Veronica placed the braided loaf onto a baking sheet. The head woman's cheek muscles worked furiously, chewing on words. She returned to the large bowl of dough and ripped off another chunk.

"Right now, our most pressing concern is your safety."

"My...what?"

"As you are a young woman, I can't in good conscience allow you to live in the men's barn. I *should* have moved you last night. If I'm entirely honest, when I learned of your lie, I left you in the men's barn last night to punish you." Veronica ripped off more dough, smearing flour onto her dress. "That was wrong, and I *am* sorry. We can't lie to each other. If the community of Thistle Hill can't trust you—"

"Can't trust me?!"

The dough fell out of Veronica's hands and plopped on the floor.

"Did Granville tell you we fought over him making moves on a fifteen-year-old?" Pip hissed.

"I will not discuss Granville with you. Not now, not ever." Veronica clasped shaking hands. "Don't push me. I'm trying to do what's best, but my tolerance only goes so far."

Pip set her jaw. Another kitchen, another ultimatum.

Nearly two years before, she'd come home from school looking forward to a shower. Instead of an empty kitchen, she'd found her parents and the family pastor waiting.

Pip's first impulse was to bypass the three worried adults. Avoid her mother's tear-filled eyes and stay in the bathroom until Pastor Mike gave up and left. She'd even gone so far as to walk out of the kitchen. Confronted by the shadowy pictures of Noah Philip in the loving embrace of his family on the living room mantle, she changed her mind.

Thumbing a headphone into her ear, she cranked the volume. Metal throbbed with righteous anger. Emboldened by the defiant anthem playing in her head, Pip took a seat at the table.

"Noah, it's important for you to listen while your parents and I explain," Pastor Mike said with a pointed stare at the headphone cord dangling from her ear. He pulled a linty tissue out of his sleeve and gently handed it to Pip's mother. She dabbed at the tears streaking her makeup. Already crying, already giving in. Pip looked away and reached out a hand to Utah, sinking her fingers deep into his fur, grabbing for strength.

"This has to stop," Pip's dad said with barely concealed disgust. "I want my son back."

"Silas," Pastor Mike cautioned. "We talked about this. Anger gets us nowhere."

Her dad slouched like a circus bear forced to ride a unicycle—he performed as told and waited for the instant when the whip-wielding trainer might look away. His frustration and scorn slashed at Pip with burly claws.

"Noah, we love you." Pip's mom looked to Pastor Mike for direction and was encouraged by his nod. "We want to help."

"That's right," the pastor interrupted. "Laura, Silas, and I want to guide you from the self-destructive wilderness you're lost in, Noah."

Pip's spine popped when she sat straight in her chair. "My *name* is Pip."

Silas huffed and glared with contempt at the tabletop.

Pastor Mike tried again. "You feel that—"

"You have *no idea* what I feel." Pip stared him down. When the pastor looked away, she faced the only person in the room she cared about. "Mom. You know I'm right."

Out of nowhere, a slap knocked Pip out of her chair. Utah danced out of the way, barking at her dad as Pip crashed to the tile. Pastor Mike was out of his chair, grabbing her dad by the arms. He was a smaller man, so he struggled to pull Silas out of the room.

Pip stared at them with blurred eyes and welcomed the clarifying pain. It wasn't the first time her dad had struck her in anger. But it would be the last. Utah nudged her, and his wet nose left a trail of cold spots down her arm. She wrapped herself around his neck, hugging tight until he whined. He slipped out of her grasp and went to the back door, kicking it with his front foot like he always did when he wanted to go out. Pip got the message loud and clear. It was time to leave. Pressing a cooling hand over her stinging cheek, she stood.

"Mom."

"Don't talk to her. Don't you dare," Silas wheezed.

An agony of minutes ticked by on the family clock while Pip waited for something to happen. Her mother twisted her tissue into a tight ball. The pastor held her father in check. It was a standoff Pip knew she wouldn't win. As they squared off, her father's face turned a blotchy shade of purple. Veins throbbed at his temples.

Pip's view of the kitchen flattened, like she was watching from a distance. Her heart finally admitted what her mind already knew. Her father would never accept that his son was a girl. And her mom was too afraid to.

"Noah Philip is dead." Pip's voice sliced through them all.

That moment had been months in the making. It was only a matter of days after the kitchen confrontation before she dropped out of school and ran away. No one would ever tell her who she was again. She'd rather live on the street than pretend to be something she wasn't.

Pip watched Veronica coiling the last loaf of dough into a braid and refused to get twisted into her demands. Not talking about Granville wasn't an option.

"He's one step away from raping a child."

Veronica wouldn't meet her eyes.

"He's changed things. This isn't how you wanted the farm. Heather said—"

"Heather said what? That my daughter died, and I went crazy?" Veronica's face was a picture of agony. "Gossip is a sin."

Talking to her was like trying to pick up a greased quarter, all round and slippery, turning in her hands.

"Rape"—Pip jabbed her finger into a braided loaf, ruining the pattern—"is a sin."

Veronica pulled at the torn pieces of bread, trying to fix the damage Pip had done. But it was too late.

"Throw him out."

Turning the loaf over in its mold, Veronica patted the smooth new top. She looked at Pip with tearful eyes. "I don't know how."

Pip suddenly understood. Veronica wasn't so different from her mother. She was a cowardly woman trapped by bad choices. Granville had infiltrated Thistle Hill after the death of her daughter, using grief to weasel his way in. She might rule the day-to-day operations of the farm, but Veronica was no longer the queen of Thistle Hill. Granville held the power with his men and their guns.

There had to be a way to stop him without being tripped up by Veronica's skirts and her fear. If Veronica couldn't make Granville leave, Pip would take Iris and leave instead.

Reaching under her shirt, Pip awkwardly unhooked the binding holding her breasts against her chest. As the bandage spiraled onto the floor, she exhaled the deep breath she'd been holding since she'd escaped her bunk. She gathered the sweaty bandage in a bundle and shoved it into the trash. Forcing the mass of fabric into the overfull can felt like a boot on her heart. From here, there was no predicting what could happen. Everything could burn up in a giant fireball of disaster.

Veronica held perfectly still. "What are you going to do?"

"I'm done pretending."

CHAPTER 23

A group of chattering young women pushed past Pip as she left the barn. Two of the younger ones flirted with her and smirked when Pip rolled her eyes. Allowing herself an instant of self-pity, she watched their loose hair swishing back and forth and wished they could see her for who she was. If only everything could be that simple. Flirt, fall in love, and find a way for everyone to get along.

A man leading a harnessed horse to the pastures smiled at her as he passed. Dust flew up from the horse's hooves, scattering a flock of chickens.

The surface of Thistle Hill was peaceful. Perfect. A happy ruckus of children boiled out of the big house, swirling like a flock of birds while playing a crazy game of tag. Iris was in the middle of the group, shouting directions like a mini-dictator. An ache filled the hollow inside Pip's chest. How could she rip Iris away from her new home? Taking a deep breath that tasted of freshly turned earth, she lost herself in worry.

"You alright?" Preoccupation had masked the sound of Heather's approach.

Pip smiled, her cheeks heavy. "Just thinking."

"Want to talk about it?" Heather asked. She shook her head, reading Pip's expression. "My daughter gave me that look all the time; the thousand-yard stare at adults who just don't understand."

"It's not that—"

Heather patted Pip's arm. "I'm giving you a hard time. Breakfast won't be for an hour. If you change your mind, my ears are open."

Wistful sadness made Pip's eyes sting with unshed tears. For the most part, Veronica had managed to collect a decent group of people at Thistle Hill Orchard. Having to leave wasn't fair. Leaving them with a monster in their midst wasn't fair either. She'd put up a good front with Veronica, but she didn't *really* know what to do. Walk up to the front gate and ask to leave? *No way would Granville let that happen. There'd be too many questions.* She turned away to hide her desperation from Heather.

"Thanks," was all she could manage.

She wandered aimlessly from Heather's unexpected sympathy toward the farm's flowering orchards. Aisles of closely cropped grass grew between the blooming trees—a sublime invitation to stroll beneath intertwined branches. The droning hum of bees gathering nectar from delicate flowers surrounded her in a comforting wall of white noise. Leaves rustled in an intermittent breeze—one pink petal floated free and stuck to her shirt.

Pip flicked off the petal. It fell in a lopsided spiral to the dirt. Her fingers tingled with tension as she thumbed the snap on her knife's sheath. As she drew the blade, sunlight winked on the silver metal, refracting triangles onto the trees. Using the surface as a mirror, Pip studied her tired eyes, then tipped the blade to examine her hair in its reflection.

A shaggy mess tangled across the top of her head. Long strands hung over her ears and covered her piercings. She didn't look like herself. She tilted the knife, studied her profile, and finally recognized the face staring back at her. She looked like her mom.

I won't be weak or helpless.

Impulsively grabbing a fistful of bangs, she sliced at the hank with angry vigor. Ragged bits of hair tumbled to the grass. Clenching the cut strands in her fist, Pip checked her reflection again. She'd trimmed the hair to an uneven inch. She dry-heaved and dropped the cut pieces of her hair, leaving the frightened parts of herself littering the ground.

Chopping with a vigor that threatened her scalp, she cut away more hair. Mangled ends stuck in the tears running down her cheeks, but she refused to wipe away their irritating itch. Tossing aside the knife, Pip lay down and rolled onto her back. She stared at the fluttering undersides of tiny flowers until her vision blurred and the entire world narrowed to a soft pink.

Breathy, inquisitive quacks woke her from a troubled doze in the orchard. The slap of webbed feet surprised her into sitting up. Startled quack-squeaks and the percussive flap of panicked wings shattered what little calm she'd found in the refuge of sleep. One duck careened off a tree, nearly knocking Iris over.

Iris neatly caught the duck by its feet. Strong wings beat against her thighs as she calmed the terrified bird. Iris tucked the duck's head beneath a wing and held the now quiet bundle of feathers under one arm like a football. Her proud smile faded the instant she noticed Pip's raggedy hair.

Taking in the distant knife and the shoal of hair surrounding her friend, Iris's brow furrowed. "What did you do?"

Words failed her. Pip studied Iris's face; an entire field of freckles covered her cheeks and the bridge of her nose. "Veronica knows I'm a girl."

Iris carefully set down the duck and its silky neck remained tucked under the wing. Nudged by Iris's boot, the duck raised its head and wandered back to the flock, grumbling with clucky dissatisfaction. Drawing her knees to her chest, Pip rested her forehead in the crook of an elbow, searching for the trick of the duck's underwing trance.

A warm hand rested on her bare neck and brushed away the itchy pieces of hair that stubbornly clung there. "You made a mess," Iris said as she finger-combed the stubble on Pip's head.

"It's not important."

"You look like a plucked chicken," Iris said.

"Iris…"

Iris retrieved the knife and studied Pip's hair with a critical eye. "Hold still." Tilting her head like a quizzical bird searching for a worm, she carefully trimmed hair until Pip waved her off.

"Enough. We have bigger problems than how I look."

Iris twiddled the blade, running her finger along the hair-dulled edge. "I know."

Taking the knife, Pip wiped it clean on her shirt and put it away.

Clouds slipped to the west, leaving the orchard in bright sunlight. The shadow of flowers covered them like a blight.

"We have to leave—"

"No! I have friends here."

"Iris plea—"

"No!" Iris cut her off with the sweep of a hand. "Why are you doing this? It's not like back in Spokane. It's safe here."

Pip didn't know what to say. She felt like she was drowning.

Iris stomped off toward her wandering flock of ducks. Pip dropped her hands, letting them slap against her thighs. She only wanted what was best for both of them. Pip noticed how Iris's shoulder blades rolled under the thin fabric of her shirt as she walked. She was small and vulnerable but growing in confidence with every passing day.

"Iris, wait. Let me explain."

Flicking her long black hair over one shoulder, Iris reluctantly turned around. The breeze returned, blowing ebony strands across her face. A storm of loose petals showered over her in a swirling mass of white. Surprised by the change in color, Pip marveled at her friend. The trees around Iris were covered in white flowers. Petals twirled around her like tentative flakes of snow.

"I want to stay here," Iris pleaded.

"Granville isn't what he seems. Veronica can't do anything to stop him."

Iris picked up a duck and smoothed the white feathers. "Please, Pip. Let's stay."

They were divided from each other by rows of tree trunks, imprisoned by their own needs.

Pip growled with frustration. "Why can't you just trust me?"

Iris shuffled her feet. "I'm taking the ducks back."

Pip knew the sound of resignation—she'd felt it enough in her own life. "Okay. Maybe we can talk later?"

"Whatever."

Iris's sarcastic, disappointed tone filled Pip with the urge to strike out. To knock some understanding into her thick little skull. Making an effort to relax her fists, Pip mastered herself and walked away from the confrontation. Stalking through the orchard kicking at trunks wasn't a real solution. It felt good to vent her frustration until she kicked too hard and stubbed her big toe.

"Damn."

She flopped to the ground with a sigh. Iris was in the distance herding her ducks out of the orchard. Scooping a handful of bruised white petals out of the dirt, Pip let them trickle between her fingers. White roses had been her mom's favorite flower. Stroking a silky-smooth petal, Pip remembered the crepey skin on her mom's hands at the hospital. Every blue vein and tendon had pushed prominently against the backs of her hands, cracking the surface like a brittle leaf.

Her mom hadn't protected Pip from her dad's petulant rages. Yet somehow, Pip managed to keep loving her. Sitting at her bedside that day, serenaded by the off-kilter beeps of vital signs on machines, Pip felt the shadow of looming death giving her mother the first real strength she'd probably ever had.

"You need to leave before you get sick...Pip." Her voice was raspy from intubation.

Their eyes met, and Pip embraced the recognition she saw there. Her mom saw *her* instead of Noah Philip. It was the first time she'd used Pip's name.

Phlegmy coughs shook her mother's frail body until the oxygen -level alarm sounded. Helping her mom sit up, Pip willed help to rush into the room and rescue them. Nobody came. Besides the intermittent alarm, the only other noises she heard were coughs.

Managing a tiny, blue-lipped smile, her mom tugged her hand out of Pip's grasp. "I love you, Pip." She inhaled a shallow breath, marshalling what little strength she had left. "Now run."

Scooping another handful of petals, Pip tossed them into the wind.

"I loved you too, Mom."

CHAPTER 24

Pip rubbed at a spot of dirt on her palm. Her thoughts ran through twisting corridors and blind alleys in search of alternatives. She was trapped in the middle of a maze, and all the paths to safety led away from Thistle Hill Orchard. Each time she decided the best way out was to kick down a wall and leave, she remembered Iris's accusing brown eyes framed with blowing white petals.

How would she ever persuade her?

A tractor rumbled by the orchard, filling the air with the scent of combustion. The driver caught her eye and blew on his hands like it was a chilly day. Pip shook her head, confused. The temperature was somewhere in the mid-sixties, squarely nestled in short-sleeve weather. She walked the row of trees to the road and peered back at the orchard. A warning chill tingled down her spine.

So many flowers had fallen that her footsteps made a trail through what looked like fresh snow. A whistled tune lilted, itching at the back of her mind. The remembered notes pitched in time with the drifting of white petals. Leaves rattled in a sudden gust, mixing pink and white into a blushing cloud. Pip gasped when the memory fully emerged. Whistler on the roof singing a song. His distress over the fate of a girl with snow in her hair had triggered a second—more violent—seizure.

Pip stumbled under the canopy of fruit trees. Using a trunk for balance, she leaned her head against a flowery branch filled with the monotonous humming of bees. Thick and ebony, Iris's hair now touched her shoulders. Her hair had tossed in the breeze, blowing across her face while she sneered with fearful contempt at the thought of leaving. Even as Iris walked away, errant white petals clung to the thick strands of her hair like snow.

"Iris? He saw Iris?" Pip turned on the spot, staring at nothing. "Is that even possible?"

Her fingers dove into her newly shorn hair. It had to be a coincidence. He'd imagined a girl lost in snow and claimed she needed Pip. What had he said? *A girl who needed help but wouldn't take it.* Surrounded by visions of orange-winged butterflies, Whistler had pleaded for Pip to understand. She felt her forehead, checking for the clammy sweat of a fever. Her fingers came away cool and dry.

A bee with jodhpurs of orange pollen landed on her open palm. Tiny feet tickled as the bee waddled in a lazy circle, following her curving lifeline. Standing delicately on the webbing between Pip's pointer finger and thumb, the bee fanned her wings before taking off with a rumbling hum.

She marveled at the minuscule fortune-teller and exhaled. Had Whistler been a crackpot of coincidence or a truth-telling oracle? In the end, his vision was nothing more than another sign. Thistle Hill wasn't the haven she'd hoped for. All that mattered now was convincing Iris that leaving was the right thing to do.

"I hear you, Whist," Pip muttered. "I hear you."

Thistle Hill Orchard was immense; there were miles of places to hide while she planned their next step. With the barn and main house in the center of the farm, she could take Iris through the orchard and into the woods. They could hide until dark and escape into the hills around Green Bluff.

But what about Fly? Pip's heart whispered. *Is there time to find her? To ask her—beg her—to come with us? Is that crazy?*

The lunch bell ringing goosed her into action. Whatever happened, she'd need supplies. With everyone in the big barn eating the midday meal, she'd be free to pack her things and find a place to stash her bag. After that, if she had to carry Iris out over her shoulder, then so be it. She wasn't getting left behind.

Pip waited at the threshold of the orchard until most of the people on the farm trickled into the barn. Fairly certain the coast was as clear as it was going to get, she walked with feigned casual confidence, holding her breath as she skirted the main buildings.

She rounded the corner of the men's dorm and bumped right into Granville and Marcus.

A feral expression crossed Granville's face. He shot her with finger guns and spit a thick glob of brown saliva at her feet while walking by. Marcus stopped in his tracks and eyed Pip with caution. He clawed two fingers on his right hand like bent bunny ears, knocked them against his cheek and then the side of his chin.

Pip didn't recognize the sign. "What?"

Since the showdown over Jessica, she hadn't seen much of Marcus. She'd managed to corner him in the barn last night in an attempt to get him to explain why he tolerated Granville's monstrosity. He'd pulled a small notebook out of his pocket and flipped to a page half-filled with writing. Folding over the page so she couldn't read what was already there, he'd used the nib of a pencil to write.

Safety. Food. Home.

What about the girls? she had written back.

Marcus's eyes were hollow. *What do want from me?*

It isn't safe for them.

He searched for another blank page and wrote: *He's my brother. It's safe for me.*

She'd slapped the notebook to the ground.

This time Marcus's hands jabbed in murderous arcs before Pip even got the chance to speak. Words flew too fast to translate. Judging by his facial expressions, she knew he was shouting. Again, he made the clawed finger sign.

Pip was flummoxed. She mimicked his finger-bunny sign and shrugged.

Rolling his eyes, Marcus chopped his hand to and away from his chin, an aggressive gesture that made her take a step back.

Making the chopping-hand sign again, he spoke. "Bitch."

One word. And it stung.

She shoved him. He fell hard against the barn and refused to meet her angry gaze.

She spoke through gritted teeth. "I saw your face yesterday. You knew about Jessica. You did nothing. You're mad at me for lying about being a girl? Are you kidding?" She yelled the last word so loudly that Marcus felt the vibration. Even if he couldn't hear her, he could feel her anger. He pushed out of her grip, flipped her off, and hurried after Granville.

"Damn it!" she swore and kicked the door to the men's barn. Stomping up the dirt corridor, her blood sang for the distraction of a fight. Rage curdled into nausea when she reached her bunk.

What few things she had were tossed around her bed like trash. Her clothes were ground into the dirt floor. Granville had stuck all her scrounged period supplies to the top sheet of her bed. Each pad was pulled open, and they were arranged to make a large circle. Tampons formed the eyes and grinning mouth of a hateful smiley face.

On the pillow, a frilly black bra bulged around the binding she'd trashed in the big barn. Folds of fabric were wadded into the rounded cups, filling out the lace undergarment. Pip moved without thought, swatting the stuffed bra into the air with an openhanded slap. It came away from the pile of bandages and sailed onto another man's bunk. The binding landed in a tangle over a partition like spilled intestines.

Pip flipped her bunk upside down. It crashed against the divider with its legs pointed at the ceiling like a dead beetle. Even if she couldn't see it, the pad smiley face was still there. Granville was trying to ruin her, to rip her world apart with insults and threats.

She remembered her father striking out with his fists, trying to knock the girl right out of her. It hadn't worked then, and Granville wouldn't stop her now.

Flipping the bunk back onto its feet, she salvaged as many pads as she could. They'd be useless for medical emergencies, but—even slightly dirty—they'd still be fine to use during her period. She shook the dirt out of her clothes and stuffed them into a backpack. Her cheekbones hurt from the pressure of withheld tears, but she refused to cry.

Snatching a water bottle off the floor next to someone's empty bed, she made a hasty circuit around the men's barn, hunting for supplies. Luck smiled on her when she found a seven-inch hunting knife under someone's pillow. She pulled it out of the sheath and grinned fiercely. The blade was wickedly sharp. Trading it for her haircut-dulled knife, she buckled the new weapon onto her belt, snapping the guard over the pearl handle.

Four half-full canteens were piled by the door, so she shoved them into her pack. It would only be a matter of moments before the lunch crowd went back to farm business as usual. If Granville had poisoned Marcus against her, there was no telling if anyone was safe to talk to. What if they *all* hated her for disguising who she was? She took one last look around the barn and snuck out the back door just as a chatting pair of men entered the front.

She snuck out the barn's rickety back door and set off at a brisk trot for the well. She could go without food. Not having water was a compromise she couldn't make. Stomach grumbling over the savory smell of food in the big barn, she forced herself to keep moving. No one stopped her; everyone who crossed her path only waved and nodded pleasantly. When she reached the well's creaky hand pump, Pip found herself searching the buildings for signs of Fly. Of *course* she wasn't anywhere to be seen. Neither was Iris for that matter.

Setting down her pilfered water bottles with a sigh, Pip unhooked the lock on the well. Green paint flaked off the pump handle—the latest layer of color added from years of use and repair. After a few squeaky cranks to prime the pump, cool water flowed over her fingers and into the waiting bottle. Soon all the containers were full to the brim. She was screwing on the last lid when a rustling of feathers followed an inquisitive quack. A line of ducks eagerly approached the standing water around the well. Their webbed feet squelched into puddles and quickly turned the area into a mess of mud.

Surrounded by the deep chuckles of pleased ducks, Pip felt her stomach dip when she saw who trailed the flock. Iris noticed Pip and dropped her half-eaten biscuit. A stampede of hungry fowl crowded around her feet. Gently nudging her way through the bread-gobbling throng, Iris registered the line of full bottles by Pip's pack and immediately understood.

Her voice was toneless. "You're leaving."

The air was redolent of fresh duck poop—everything smelled as crappy as Pip felt. "I can't explain right now, but *we* have to leave."

"Why?"

"Because—"

"You don't start a sentence with 'because,'" Iris interrupted.

Oh my God, Pip thought. Was this what love felt like? Wanting to throttle someone and hug them at the same time?

"I've learned disgusting things about Granville. He knows that I know. It all got complicated really fast, and Veronica is *not* on our side. We can't stay. And you won't be safe from Granville if I leave."

Iris pursed her lips in thought.

It took every ounce of control to not toss Iris over her shoulder and make for the fence. "I *wish* I could give you more time. Granville took all the time away."

Iris shook her head and turned to leave. Pip grabbed her wrist. Yanking like an animal with its foot caught in a trap, Iris slipped in the mud and almost fell. Still holding on, Pip grabbed her by the back of her shirt, dragging her away from the well and out of sight behind a building.

"Let go," Iris hissed.

"I can't."

It would only be a matter of moments before they attracted the wrong kind of attention.

Pip laid everything on the table. "Listen to me: I gave up trying to be Noah Philip between my freshman and sophomore years of high school. That summer, I called myself Pip and told everyone to call me *she* instead of *he*. I grew out my hair and wore a bra with a bow between the cups instead of binding like my parents wanted. I even experimented with mascara and lipstick."

Iris stopped struggling. Pip was getting through to her.

"The first day of school, I argued with every teacher over my change of name. I got beat up in the hallway behind the cafeteria before lunch. A football player split my lip so deep, it left this scar."

Iris looked at Pip's mouth, eyes bouncing across one of the few pieces of damage Pip carried on the outside.

"Everywhere was hate. My parents made me meet with their church pastor. The school guidance counselor told me to stop acting out. I fought them all. I was miserable and angry, and I made confrontation my bitch. Every. Single. Day."

"But…" Iris huffed and pointed to where her shirt bunched between her shoulder blades. "Let go already."

Pip relaxed her grip and Iris waved for her to continue her story. She'd given up trying to escape.

"It wasn't long before a bunch of jackasses figured out that I was using a private bathroom near the teacher's lounge. A girls' bathroom."

"Oh no."

Pip rubbed the scar on her lower lip, deciding how much might be too much. "Before they knocked me out, I fought back. One of them lost part of his ear, and another almost lost an eye. I woke up strapped to a gurney in an ambulance covered in a blanket and blood. All four of us were suspended from school for fighting. When we came back, the other kids celebrated those three jocks as heroes. It was a nightmare."

"I'm so sorry, Pip."

Pip acknowledged the apology with a nod. "Before the attack, I reported graffiti scrawled on the doors of every girls' bathroom, faced down every bully, and argued the patience out of every authority figure in the entire school district. But when they turned on the ambulance's sirens to take me to the hospital and I realized I was naked, I crumbled. The medic said I'd been found without clothes."

Iris gasped. "They took your clothes?"

"Took my clothes. Stole my dignity. Obliterated my fight."

"They should've gone to jail."

Pip threw her hands up in frustration. "That's what I'm trying to tell you. In the end, nothing happened. There was no justice. The abuse only got sneakier. Instead of harassing me in a group, they attacked me one-on-one. *The bullies went after my friends.* And it wasn't long until all the friends I'd had were gone."

Pip could still feel the crisp white stretcher sheet covering her skin. "Granville is exactly like one of those jocks from my high school."

"What do you mean?"

"Leaving someone bloody and broken and avoiding the consequences is what he does."

"I'd protect you." Iris curled her petite hands into fists, settling them on her delicate hips.

Pip exhaled. "He wouldn't have to touch me to ruin me, Iris. Granville would find a way to turn *you* inside out and make me watch."

"I don't understand."

"I know." Pip suddenly understood how her mother had felt trying to explain to her son why he'd gotten a period. She remembered burning with hate when she understood the lies her parents had told. Her mother broke everything that day. A few words changed Noah Philip's simple world into something different and unexpected.

Pip's stomach cramped. She didn't want the power to destroy part of Iris's childhood. She only wanted to save her from assholes like Granville.

"Remember how I said Granville wouldn't need to touch me to hurt me?"

"Yes."

"He likes young girls."

"What do you mean?"

"He's been making moves on teens not much older than you. Jessica is one of his favorites. I caught them together yesterday. He's threatened me into silence by flirting with you ever since."

Disgust flashed in Iris's eyes. "We can tell—"

"When I told Veronica the truth about Granville, she did nothing. She's just as trapped as the girls on the farm. She's scared of him. Which means we aren't safe here. Not anymore."

Iris looked into the middle distance as she considered Pip's revelations. Pip waited in suspense, wondering how much she'd broken and if she'd ever be able to fix it.

"He's like a rotten apple," Iris finally muttered.

Pip tipped her head in question.

"Shiny and red on the outside, but after you swallow that first bite, you find half a worm 'cause you've eaten the rest."

"Gross."

Iris walked to the pump and touched the handle, picking off a flake of green paint. "Okay."

"What?"

Iris sighed. "I'll come with you."

Pip looked at her friend with a mix of relief and regret.

"But...I have to take the ducks back first."

"Iris," Pip warned.

"If you want to sneak out of here, I have to herd the ducks into their pen first. Animals are checked by an adult right before dinner. No kid eats until missing animals are found. Two days ago, one of the boys forgot to put away his goats—he got double duty mucking out the stalls." Iris held up a hand to forestall any argument. "Please, Pip."

"It's hours until dinner. We should go."

"I'm wearing flip-flops." She pointed at the anvil-shaped clouds rising high and dark off to the west. "What if we get caught out in that? I need better shoes. I'll get my boots, put away the ducks, and grab some food. Be back before you know it. Promise."

Pip studied Iris's plastic flip-flops and reluctantly agreed. "Fine. But don't stop to talk with anyone. Unless you see Fly. She needs...I want her to know...she should..."

A fragile smile flashed across Iris's face. "I want her to come too."

The dog tags shifted out of Pip's shirt. On impulse, Pip unlatched the collar and yanked until its diameter was smaller. Holding it out like a fine necklace, she gestured for Iris to turn around. She swung it over her head and pushed the latch home. Iris stroked the tags, then tucked them inside her shirt.

"Stay away from Granville and Veronica. Don't even let them see you. Understand? I'll wait for you in the woods at the end of the orchard. We've hooked up solar panels out there to run another well. There's a path to the fence. Get your stuff and come back to me," Pip urged.

A hug caught her completely by surprise. Iris wrapped her arms tight around Pip's middle, squeezing and lifting at the same time. Her boots left the ground for a moment, unbalanced by love. The hug was over too soon.

"I'll find you," Iris said.

She touched the collar and turned to herd the ducks back to their enclosure.

CHAPTER 25

Pip shoved the water bottles inside her pack and checked to see if anyone was looking. Her first instinct was to find Fly and warn her. But Granville. What would happen if she ran into him again? She couldn't risk Iris's safety.

Swallowing her frustration, Pip set off at a brisk walk. It took her almost twenty minutes to reach the clearing where they'd wired the solar panels. She stepped out of the trees, then paused like an animal caught in the blaze of headlights. Granville's truck was parked by the panels. He wasn't anywhere to be seen, but Jessica was.

"You again?" Jessica wore a cute dress and her hair was done up in a fancy bun. A picnic basket waited at her feet.

Pip took a cautious step closer. "He isn't what you think."

"Shut up."

The sound of snapping twigs and the dull thuds of feet on soft dirt interrupted anything else Jessica might have said. Iris ran full tilt through the orchard into the middle of their argument. Fly was tight on her heels, and both of them were flecked with flower petals.

Iris slid to a stop. "I brought Fly." She smiled with pride, then frowned as she noticed Jessica. "What's she doing here?"

"None of your business," Jessica said.

"She's waiting for Granville." Fly checked inside the truck. "Or is he already here?"

Just like that, Fly was on their side. No questions asked, no explanations needed.

"What the actual fuck is this?" Granville sauntered up the trail from the fence while buckling his belt. "I leave to take a whiz and now it's a party?"

"Go back to the farm, Jessica," Pip said.

"Excuse me?" Granville ran his tongue across the inside of his lower lip. "I told you before, *little man*, you don't tell anyone what to do."

He growled low in his throat and lunged. Pip shrugged off her pack and threw herself at him. They collided, and her half-healed gunshot wound exploded with pain. Catching an elbow in the ribs, Pip howled incoherent words while struggling to move out of the range of his fists. They scrabbled in the dust, coughing on the dried leaves they kicked into the air.

Fly grabbed a metal thermos out of Jessica's picnic basket and swung it at Granville, knocking off his hat. When he stumbled, Pip went on the offensive and dove at his knees. The two of them landed in a heap next to his truck. Pip snatched the thermos off the ground and smashed it against Granville's temple—once, twice. His head snapped back, his Adam's apple pushed tight against the stretched-out skin of his throat.

Jessica screamed. The high-pitched note buzzed in Pip's ears as she tried to shield herself from the searing pain of Jessica's fingernails tearing at her back and shoulders.

"Enough!" Fly shoved Jessica, knocking her into the side of Granville's truck.

"You bitch! You killed him."

"He's still breathing," Iris announced. "He's just unconscious."

Jessica grabbed Granville by the shoulders and shook him. "Wake up!" Her voice was frantic.

"He's *at least* thirty-five. He does *not* love you," Fly growled at Jessica. "He's a predator."

"You don't know him like I do." Jessica dashed angry tears off her face, smudging her cheeks with dirt and blood from Pip's back. She pushed on Granville's chest, trying to wake him. Blood from her hands stained his shirt, painting him with scarlet handprints. Jessica stared with disbelief at the marks she'd made and shot off the ground, launching onto her feet like she'd been electrocuted.

She tucked her hands into her armpits, hiding them. She glanced at Pip, her mouth sagging open with a gut-wrenching sob.

Pip slumped against the front wheel of the truck with her legs sticking out. Her back stung where Jessica's nails had flayed skin. The slow movement of Granville's chest as he breathed made her think of Whistler up on the roof singing his sad song.

There aren't butterflies here, Whist. Only blood and pain.

A farm dog barked in the distance. Pip's heart skipped at the sound. Surely people at Thistle Hill had heard Jessica yelling. It was only a matter of time until someone investigated.

Fly gestured at the thermos and pointed at Jessica, miming knocking her out with the container. Pip pushed off the side of the truck, using it as a crutch to get up. Her whole body ached, but she made herself walk to the thermos and kick it under the truck. They weren't going to hurt a victim.

Jessica took a shuddering breath and held out her shaking hands before setting them on her thighs. "I won't tell them where you've gone."

A dog barked in the orchard. It was far too close. They'd run out of time.

"Let's go!" Pip urged.

Fly, Pip, and Iris raced for the fence. Iris hit it first and clambered up the six-foot-tall chain link. She leaned her belly over the jagged triangles of metal at the top and dropped with a surprised squeal to the ground on the other side. As she helplessly grabbed the fence, Pip's stomach clenched when Iris hit the dirt in a sprawl. Pip was at her side almost at once—she had no memory of climbing the fence. She ran her hands over Iris's arms and legs, dusting her off and hoisting her up while Fly scaled the fence with ease.

Holding a picture of Clare's roughly drawn map in her head, Pip recited the directions to herself. "Dunn. Right on Dusty Gulch. Left on Day. Right on Cedar. Left on Bickett."

Dunn dead ended at Thistle Hill Orchard, which made it too dangerous to use. Tracing a different route, Pip was too keyed up to hold the map in her head. She oriented herself in the direction she thought they should go and guessed they could cut cross-country to a road that joined Dusty Gulch many miles from Thistle Hill.

"Hurry, Pip," Fly urged.

"This way." Pip took off at a trot through the woods.

As they pushed their way deeper into the forest, Cicadas whined—their droning made everything feel hotter. The air was muggy and heavy like before a storm. A rumbling in the distance made them all pause. Fly mopped sweat off her forehead with the hem of her shirt and held up a hand for them to listen.

"Was that a car?"

Another rumble rolled across the sky.

"No. That's thunder," Pip said.

Wind thrashed through the forest, bending the tops of trees by the time they made it to a road. Gloomy clouds hung low over open fields. A startling whip flash of lightning lanced through the sky with a report that shook their bones. Nature was laughing at them.

"Of *course* it's gonna rain," Fly muttered.

Lightning flashed again, splitting the sky with a crazy web of white. Thunder crashed hard and fast on its heels. They had to get out of the oncoming storm. Less than a quarter mile to the north stood a one-story ranch house in the middle of fallow wheat fields. Not much wider than two trailers stuck together, it was the only cover for miles. Pip took the lead and they all sprinted toward it.

Thunder pounded their ears as rain swept toward them. Raindrops hit the ground so hard that they bounced. Blinded by water that stung where it hit exposed flesh, they stumbled along the gravel road as the ground beneath them turned into boot-sucking mud. Propelled by the worsening storm, Pip dragged Iris off the road into a muddy field. There wasn't time to search for a driveway.

They crossed the field under a hail of dime-sized ice pellets. Shielding her face from the worst of the weather, Pip hissed in pain as welts blended across her shoulders into one huge bruise. All three were battered by the time they reached the safety of the home's porch. Unable to hear anything over the hail crashing like bullets onto the metal roof, Pip nudged Iris aside and tried the doorknob. The door was locked.

Her mind numbed from the icy pounding, Pip couldn't decide what to do next. Fly grabbed a rock out of a flower bed and used it to break the pane of glass closest to the doorknob. She dropped the rock, reached her hand through the jagged hole, and flicked the deadbolt. Pip held up a hand to stop Fly from going straight in.

"Wait!" she yelled over the din of hail ringing on the metal roof. Pip prodded the door with her foot and took a hesitant sniff. The house smelled stale, like her grandparents' musty root cellar. Not a trace of decay lingered in the air. Pip hoped there wouldn't be any unpleasant surprises waiting for them inside.

Iris dumped her pack on the porch and handed over a flashlight. The bright beam shone on a tidy entryway with rubber boots lined up from small to large. Pip forced herself to not think about the smallest boots. Odds were, the child who'd once worn them didn't need them anymore.

Past the entry, an entire wall in the living room was piled to the ceiling with cords of firewood. A monstrous woodstove sat in the place most families would have hung a television.

They stayed in a tight group, exploring every room. The home was compact with no basement; the search didn't take long. When they'd verified the house was empty and corpse-free, Pip sagged against a wall in the hallway. They were safe, but something important was missing. The confident squeak of Whistler's shoes as he searched.

"Clear," Pip said.

"What?" Fly asked. She looked too tired to do anything more than breathe.

Iris solemnly reached for the flashlight and tiptoed into a small office. Opening a closet they'd skipped, she shined the light inside, checking every corner. Light reflected off shiny boxes and a collection of DVDs. She closed the door with a nod and handed back the light.

Her voice was quiet when she replied, "Clear."

"You two are nuts," Fly said. "I'm getting the woodstove lit."

Alone in the hallway with Iris, Pip remembered how she'd humored Whistler every time he'd gone into a building first, risking his life to protect her. "I used to think saying 'clear' was dumb."

"He was telling you he cared."

Pip's eyes burned with unshed tears.

"Some help would be nice," Fly grumbled from the living room. "You should warm up," Pip told Iris. "I'll look for matches."

Iris squished onto the nearest couch and wrapped herself in an afghan with a relieved groan.

Water pattered onto the floor from Pip's clothes, dribbling a trail behind her. Noticing a large buffet in the dining room, she forced her exhausted body to shove it down the hallway to barricade the broken front door.

Concerned over the chill burrowing into her bones, Pip found the bathroom and snatched at a stack of fluffy towels. She shucked her wet clothes and briskly rubbed the goosebumps and welts covering her arms and legs. It was painful but restorative. Wrapping a beach towel around herself, Pip brought some extra towels into the living room.

"Where are the fucking matches?" Fly was deep into the spiderwebby crevices around the woodstove, hunting for the matches by feel. "Ha! Found 'em."

Pip tossed a few towels on top of Iris. "You should get out of those wet clothes."

"Is one of those for me?" Fly asked.

Pip was suddenly aware she had nothing under her towel except a sports bra and her underwear. Heat bloomed across her face and chest, banishing the chill.

"Are you blushing?" Fly lit a match and set fire to a wad of paper she'd wedged into the stack of firewood. A curl of smoke wound out of the woodstove. The fire sputtered and died.

Pip knelt next to Fly and stuffed a crumpled piece of newspaper under the ashy wood. She struck a match on the brick and touched it to the paper. Then she closed the stove doors to only a crack, and air whistled through the gap as the flames leapt high. Soon there was a cheerful blaze crackling in the stove's belly. Pip opened the doors wide and leaned into the burgeoning heat.

Fly used a towel to blot her short curls. "You didn't answer my question."

· "You're right." Pip was warm with more than the fire's heat. It was mortifying. Looking for a distraction, she blurted, "Why'd you come with us?"

Fly sighed in exasperation and got up. "You already know the answer."

Mud was splattered on the back of Fly's jeans, kicked up from the pounding rain. Her white shirt hung loose, and a constellation of welts covered her bare arms. Pip wanted to call her back, to say she *did* know why Fly had joined them. But it felt too risky. A conversation like that would make her feel more naked than wearing nothing but a towel.

"Come on, Iris. I'm gonna look for dry clothes," Fly said.

Iris struggled out of her chair with a grumble and yanked a second knitted blanket off the back of the couch. She picked up the flashlight and followed Fly into the rear of the house.

The fire burned strong, gobbling through enough wood that Pip added more. Setting two logs onto the blaze, she left the doors open wide and inched closer. Heat baked her wounds, making the already bruised skin on her face pulse in time with her heartbeat.

She imagined Granville's fist coming at her out of the flames and flinched. Granville had changed the rules, flipped Thistle Hill Orchard upside down. He'd made fighting for things that were right into something dangerous. Veronica hadn't wanted to believe. Even Iris had taken convincing. But Fly—she'd walked into the Granville confrontation ready to fight.

She took my side. Just say it. Spit it out. You want her here; you needed her to see you. You've been seen. Why can't you trust yourself?

A rustling came from the kitchen. Pots clanged and cupboards slammed. "Iris?"

Iris peeked around the corner. "Yeah?"

"Are you chewing something?"

"Toaster pastry."

Saliva flooded Pip's mouth. "Oh God. *Tell me* there are more."

Iris dangled a crinkly silver package just out of reach.

"I hate you," Pip joked.

Iris snorted. "You'll have to get dressed before I eat the last one."

"Little monster."

"I'm opening the last bag," Iris teased.

Pip shook her head, wincing when pain flared from a cut in her eyebrow. Gingerly touching her forehead, she went to the bathroom and used the mirror over the sink to inspect the damage. She frowned when her tongue discovered a molar knocked loose by Granville. Her entire face was puffy from his fists and the hail. She leaned on the bathroom counter and gathered her accumulated aches like a dragon hoarding treasure. Each hurt meant she was alive.

Fly walked past the bathroom and clapped after each word as she entered the kitchen. "Tell me that's strawberry flavor."

Pip carried her smirk into the nearest bedroom. The room was a disaster. Fly had left the dresser drawers hanging open. Pip dug into the husband's side of the dresser, pulling on the first T-shirt that looked like it would fit. She searched the walk-in closet for a pair of pants and whooped; resting in the corner was a double-barreled shotgun. She set the heavy weapon on the bed. This was the kind of protection they needed.

Fly ran into the bedroom and noticed the shotgun. "You okay?"

In a move that surprised them both, Pip threw herself into Fly. Their breasts and hip bones banged against each other from the force of Pip's headlong rush. The muscles in Fly's back bunched under Pip's hands as she nuzzled into Pip's neck. Their hug increased in pressure, becoming almost too tight for either of them to breathe. Pip didn't mind one bit. They held together, exhilarated by the feeling of not being lost and alone.

"I'm glad you're here," Pip murmured.

"I know."

Pip snorted and squeezed tighter, soaking every bit of comfort out of their hug before relaxing her grip.

Fly still held on like they were joined at the hip. "I caught Iris sneaking out of Heather's room. While we ran through the orchard, she told me everything—about Granville grooming the girls. What she said, it fit. I'd seen him meeting a teenager over by the goat barn."

"He threatened Iris too."

"I figured." Fly let go and sat on the bed next to the shotgun. "Are there shells?"

"I haven't looked yet.

Fly checked the top shelf of the closet and pulled a full box of ammunition out from under a pile of sweaters, then set it on the bed. She cracked the barrels on the shotgun and blew down the empty tubes. A dead spider fell out onto the carpet. "Iris told me about your high school."

"Oh." Pip felt the burn of the ancient rage and anger she'd stored up for years. *That was my story to tell. But if Iris hadn't said anything, maybe Fly wouldn't have come.*

Iris danced into the bedroom and held up the last package of pastry. "I'm eating this!"

Fly grabbed for the pastry, and Pip used her pent-up anger to knock Fly out of the way. They collided, bouncing off the walls, tussling down the narrow hallway to the living room. Everyone burst out laughing when Iris tripped and thumped harmlessly down onto the muddy carpet.

Pip snagged the shiny silver package from Iris's outstretched hand. She ripped open the bag and took a huge bite. The thin glaze of frosting cracked pleasantly between her front teeth, and the sweetness of the stale treat made Pip groan with delight. She broke the pastry in half and held it out to Fly. There was so much they needed to say. But this wasn't the time.

Fly took the broken half of pastry with a nod. She understood. "Let's raid the cupboards."

"I already did that," Iris said.

"Did you? Really?" Clasping her hands and rubbing them together like a carnival barker eager for an easy mark, Pip led the way into the kitchen and opened the first door.

"Step right up, ladies and gents, and take a gander at the lovely items we have for you today." She looked at the shelves and screeched.

CHAPTER 26

The rat seemed unperturbed by the noise. Its eyes—opaque as a slick of oil—held Pip's gaze. Its whiskers twitched as it stared her down. Shuddering in revulsion, Pip slammed the door. The surprised skittering in the cupboard sounded like frantic skeletal fingers scratching on the inside of a coffin's lid.

"I hate rats." Iris backed out of the kitchen.

Pip opened the cupboard a fraction, then closed the door. "Well, he's in the walls now. Bet we won't see him again."

Iris crossed her arms. "I'm not going in there."

Instead of arguing, Pip inspected the rest of the kitchen. Fly sat at the table cleaning the shotgun while Pip picked around brown nuggets of rat poop. It didn't matter if every cupboard was filled to the brim with rat shit—she'd searched them all. They needed water bottles.

Ditching her pack at Thistle Hill had left them at a huge disadvantage. Iris's backpack had only one bottle and it was almost empty. Pip's knuckles rapped against something hard when she dug deeper into Iris's pack. She nudged aside a rolled-up T-shirt and burst out laughing. Most of the extra-large pack was filled with the violin case.

"You stole the fiddle?" Pip asked.

"It was mine in the first place." Iris tugged the case out of the pack and set it down on the table. She flicked the latches, and the lid's hinges creaked like they were in dire need of grease. Written in black marker on the inside of the lid were the words, *For Iris, the girl in the snow.*

It was Whistler's spidery handwriting.

"I saw it when I played at the wedding." Iris rubbed her name with her thumb.

Pip was staggered.

"Are you okay?" Fly asked.

Things he'd seen on the roof that night were coming true. He'd seen Iris in the orchard. Forget coincidence—*he'd known.* Pip reached for Utah's collar before she remembered she'd given it to Iris. She pressed her hands against her eyes and could hear Clare reciting her directions. *Go north, always north.* Whistler had told her to do the same, to help the girl who wouldn't be helped. She opened her eyes to a blur. It was crazy. Unexplainable. First the orchard, and now his words written in the violin case. It was too remarkable to be believed.

"*You okay?*" Fly repeated.

"Yeah." Pip closed the violin case with a thump, locking away the confusion she felt over the writing inside. "We need camping supplies and water bottles. We should search the garage."

"What're you not telling us?"

"We should check the garage for supplies."

Fly tsked. "Fine."

The house was neat. The garage was full to the brim. Piles of boxes were stacked to the ceiling, stuffing the two-car space. Traversing the narrow paths through the hoarded mess was a precarious adventure. Iris pushed her way down the first aisle, the *thock-thock* of a tennis ball bouncing on the concrete floor making it easy to track where she was.

Growling with agitation every time the jagged corner of a box jammed into her skin, Pip searched for anything useful. She discovered a camp stove but put it back when she couldn't locate fuel. A partially used box of water-purifying tablets, a sleeping bag, and a foil-wrapped MRE dinner spilled out of the next box she rummaged through. Tucking it all under her arm, she shoved a mangy beanbag out of the way, then shouted when she saw the handlebars of two bicycles.

"Are you okay?" Iris hollered.

"Abso-frickin'-lutely! I found us some rides. Get over here and help me dig them out."

Unable to believe their good fortune, Pip knocked for luck on the wooden coffee table in the living room while admiring the two granny bikes they'd unearthed from their garage tomb. Pip packed the saddlebags with a spare backpack, the sleeping bag, and the single MRE. Fly stuffed a little kid's school pack with a few empty water bottles and a few odds and ends from the kitchen. They'd had no luck getting water out of the water heater—the release valve was rusted shut. There really wasn't much else in the house; the family had cleaned it out before they left.

Pip contemplated where to store the shotgun.

"Strap it to the handlebars," Iris said with enthusiasm.

It took some fiddling and several plastic ties, but the final result wasn't half bad.

They wheeled the bikes through the living room and went outside. With the storm gone, the smell of wet earth and damp vegetation cleared their senses. Fly took a deep breath and exhaled slowly before bumping her bike down the few steps to the front yard.

It took some experimentation, but they ended up with Iris sitting on the seat of the bike while Pip stood on the pedals. Wobbling through the muck, the pair almost decked before figuring out the delicate balance of two people using the same bicycle. Fly waited farther up the road.

They rolled to a stop next to her. Pip got her feet off the pedals quickly, catching them before the bike tipped. "What is it?"

"I thought I saw a dog. Maybe it was a coyote." Fly pointed. "Over there."

They were surrounded by rolling hills dotted with small stands of trees. Fences in disrepair from a winter without farmers broke the landscape into strange geometric shapes.

Pip felt the tires sinking into the mud. "We should keep going."

They reached the Dusty Gulch crossroad in less than fifteen minutes. Pip brought them to a halt by a stop sign and carefully checked in all directions. Fly lurched off her bike and filled their water bottles from a stream running in the ditch alongside the road. She dropped a water-purifying tablet into each bottle and gave them a shake. It would take thirty minutes for the water to be drinkable. Pip licked her dry lips. Iris sat in the shade next to Fly while Pip dragged their bike to the side of the road. The sound of the tires shredding against the pavement startled a covey of quail into flight. The birds whirled through the air and crashed into the branches of pine trees.

Unlike the potholed mess of a dirt road they'd been rolling along, Dusty Gulch was paved with a slick river of fairly new asphalt. Returning to pavement would mean easier pedaling, but noticing an approaching car would be almost impossible without a telltale dust plume. If the Thistle Hill Orchard farm truck came after them, they'd be easy prey. Pip tapped a tooth and squinted when she noticed Iris mimicking her thoughtful habit.

The possibility of Granville searching them out was chilling. He might roll up in his truck before they got the bikes out of sight. What if he brought his men and their guns?

"Are you thinking about the girls?" Fly asked.

"Huh?"

"The girls at Thistle Hill. We should go back and do something."

"What can we do? It's his word against ours, and—"

"I told Heather," Iris said.

"You...what?"

"I left a note in her room. I said Granville is after Jessica and some of the other girls and that we left to protect me."

Fly held up her hand for a high five. Iris gave it a resounding smack.

"She'll believe me."

"So we go back," Fly said.

Pip got up. "No way. I'm not risking Iris."

"Hey, don't I get a say—" Iris started.

"NO!" Fly and Pip said at the same time.

"We go to Clare's—"

"Make sure you're safe, then go back." Fly finished the thought.

"Fine," Iris grumbled as she offered Pip a water bottle. "Which way is it?"

Pip took a swig and spit, rinsing out her mouth. She pointed. "Go north, always north. Right on Dusty Gulch, left on Day. Right on Cedar. Left on Bickett. You should memorize it in case we get separated."

"Not gonna happen."

"Iris..."

Flipping the bottle closed, Iris ignored Pip's tone. "Which way?"

"We go right," Pip huffed. "If we hear a car, get off the road, pronto."

They rode for another half an hour, squinting against the bright late-afternoon sunshine. Pausing in the shade of some trees, Pip eased off her bike with a groan and helped Iris down.

"Why are we stopping?" Fly asked.

Pip pointed at a rusting mountain of cars and trucks in the distance. Not much farther down the road was a sprawling auto graveyard. Granville had taken her there while hunting for a new distributor cap for the tractor. She didn't want to chance riding past if someone was there scrounging. The fewer eyes on them, the better.

"Is someone there?" Iris worried at the hem of her T-shirt.

"Probably not."

"So...just in case?"

"Absolutely." Pip kept her voice light.

Fly dug around in her pack and pulled out a package of beef jerky. She opened it, took a piece, and handed the bag to Pip.

"That smells like dog food," Iris said.

"Tasty, tasty dog food." Pip chewed a particularly tough chunk of jerky on the side without the loose tooth and studied the distant auto yard. A tree farm ran thick and green to a rusted makeshift fence. Inside the fence, the property was a maze of broken vehicles bordered on the far side by forest.

They were leaving the flat plain behind. For the last twenty minutes of the ride they'd climbed a gradual slope, winding out of farmland into the wooded foothills of Mt. Spokane. Given the change in terrain, Pip surmised that Clare's ranch must be somewhere deep in the forest surrounding the mountain. When she'd furtively drawn the map to her home, Clare said the way was over twenty miles. Pip dabbed at the abrasions Jessica had left on the back of her neck, figuring they'd come at least ten of those twenty miles already. They'd need another day to get there. She didn't like being on the open road. Every extra hour of exposure meant one more chance of being discovered.

On the far side of the auto yard, raucous cawing heralded an unkindness of ravens. The flock circled in a noisy swoop over rusted cars as they crowed in gravelly voices. Pip shaded her eyes, wondering where the airborne birds would land. Several dipped with a flash of ebony feathers into the auto property while the rest continued to circle.

A bass animal call, powerful as an avalanche, rose from the forest. More ravens startled from trees in a swirling murder of birds as the deep growl echoed around them.

"What the hell was that?" Fly asked.

Pip stood on her toes, leaning into the sun while listening to the unfamiliar animal call. The sound was something like a lion, but different from anything she'd heard before. The cry was guttural and raw, and she imagined the jaws of a predator open wide, yellowed teeth flashing as whiskers flared to deliver the agitated call. Goosebumps freckled her arms and back, chilling the hot day. She could only guess how far from the auto dump the animal was, but from the ominous swirling of disturbed birds, it appeared to be moving away.

Pip wished she'd paid more attention in biology when they talked about animal behavior. Were the ravens following the mysterious beast or fleeing? Was she willing to bet their lives on an assumption?

"Makes an ass out of you and umption," Pip tsked. There might be people in the auto yard. Better the devil she knew than one who hunted on padded feet.

Iris's frightened brown eyes tracked Pip for a moment, then peered into the distant woods as they listened to another growl.

"When the cougars came to Thistle Hill, one of the other kids said animals had escaped from Cat Tails and were going to eat us." Iris's voice was tight with fear.

Pip remembered her afternoon of shifting mutilated sheep

carcasses from the back of Clare's wagon. They were torn apart, with their lacerated sides dripping blood. Most likely a tiger had killed Clare's sheep. Pip kept that thought to herself.

"If it's from the cat place, he probably likes people."

Another roar rolled out of the trees, ending with a snarling growl. Iris was on her feet and ready to ride in an instant.

"Where d'ya think it is?" Fly asked.

Pip observed the ravens. Those that were still in the sky had moved quite a distance from the road. Crossing her fingers over her hunch, she hoped they were following the beast into the woods for a chance at stealing a meal. If she was wrong, the birds were retreating from the beast and she'd be offering up Iris and Fly as an animal's dinner.

Fly started to ride. Pushing hard on the pedals, Pip caught up and nodded for them to stay together. Their earlier pedaling had been relatively carefree, but now everyone kept silent and watched their surroundings like nervous antelope waiting for a lion to spring. Staring with apprehension at the rapidly approaching auto dump, Pip felt her guts cramp with tension.

"Truck!" Iris shouted.

Their bike swerved, tossed off balance by Iris shifting on the seat. Pip grabbed the brakes with both hands and brought them to a sliding stop. Fly was on the other side of the two-lane road, looking back over her shoulder with her mouth hanging open in shock.

Iris jumped off the bike and pointed. A few miles behind, a growing dot of yellow shimmered in the heat rising from the blacktop. Grabbing her bike with both hands, Pip practically threw it into the ditch. Iris ripped up grass and branches to cover the bike before they both dove into a thicket of blackberries.

Squirming deeper into the vines, Pip looked around. "Where's Fly?!"

"I think she jumped in the ditch on the other side," Iris said.

Oh God.

The sound of the truck's engine was close—there wasn't time to see if Fly had found a place to hide on the other side of the road. What had it looked like over there? Was there enough cover to conceal her and the bike?

The moving van squealed to a stop, a door opened, and Pip heard the pounding of feet on pavement. There was a scuffle in the dirt on the other side of the truck—people were struggling. Torn between protecting Iris and helping Fly, Pip unlatched her knife and cut the zip ties holding the shotgun.

A guttural snarl of anger from Fly was answered with the meaty thud of a body dropping. More punches and grunts covered the sound of Pip checking the gun. It wasn't loaded. She couldn't reach her saddlebags without being discovered.

"Never thought we'd see you again." Pip froze at the sound of Camo's voice. "We saw another bike on the road from way back there. Where're your friends?"

The silence following his question frightened Pip more than any sound she'd ever heard. She wanted Fly to answer, to prove she was alive. The sound of a hard slap made Iris flinch. She huddled next to Pip, crying silently.

"That the best you got, you crooked-nosed bastard?" Fly's words slurred but her voice was strong.

Curtis. Pip saw him standing over Whistler's body. *That fucker needs to die.*

Camo laughed. "Granville'll be thrilled to see you. Put her in the back."

The truck pulled away in a spray of gravel that pattered on the blackberry leaves.

"No, no, no!" Pounding the ground, Pip blackened her knuckles with dirt. She scrambled out of the blackberries and crawled up the bank. Keeping low, she rejoiced to see the truck pull into the auto yard. There was still a chance she could help Fly.

Sliding down the bank on her butt, Pip rifled through the bike's saddlebags and ripped open the box of shotgun shells. Hands shaking, she loaded it the way Fly had shown her and clicked the barrels home. Pip rested the shotgun across her lap. Choking on unstoppable sobs, she let herself cry. Iris scrambled out of the blackberry vines and sat next to Pip, tentatively putting an arm around her heaving shoulders.

"What are we—"

"You," Pip interrupted. "You are staying here."

She pulled herself together, wiping her nose on her shirt. Handing the shotgun to Iris, she stuffed her pockets with shotgun shells, then gestured for the weapon. "Stay here until I call for you."

Iris handed over the shotgun and crouched next to the silver-and-black pin-striped bicycle. Cuts from the blackberry thorns painted her with bloody welts.

Iris's teeth chattered as she asked, "What's going to happen?"

"I'm getting Fly."

CHAPTER 27

A decrepit guard shack stood at the end of the auto yard's driveway. Pip sank into tall grass and caught her breath. She'd taken the long way to the auto yard, running through the tree farm out of sight of the road. There'd been the rumble of an engine and she'd hidden. She hadn't been able to see anything through the regimented rows of evergreen trees.

Where's the moving van?

She couldn't get a clear view of the auto yard. Knocked-over blocks of crushed cars made a maze of decay almost two stories high.

She pushed through the grass, staying off the road. When she was less than sixty feet from the guard shack, she saw a person standing inside. Pip studied the silhouette. The window was made of yellowed Plexiglas—she knew because the last time she'd been here Granville had tried to shoot it out. They'd both been surprised when the bullet bounced off the weathered material like a trampoline.

"Shit."

Seating the butt of the shotgun tight against her shoulder, she moved cat-quiet toward the shack's motionless figure. *With my luck,* Pip thought, *it's a tacky cardboard cutout of some chick with big boobs.* She was only a few feet from the driveway when the head of the silhouette turned, and a hand pressed against the glass.

Her heart was already beating at a hummingbird clip. Pip thought it might burst. Gasping for air, she rushed forward. Recognition hit them both at the same time.

"Fly."

Her face was almost unrecognizable. Bruising mottled her cheeks.

"Get me out! Get me out! Get me out!" Fly yelled. Her fists pounded against the window, splitting the knuckles and leaving bloody prints.

Terror paralyzed Pip for a fraction of a second. *What if they hear Fly's screams and come running?* Turning on her heel, Pip ran for cover, diving into the dry grass next to the auto yard's fence.

Fly's screams followed her.

Not far from where she crouched, a ragged tear made a rusty hole in the corrugated fence. Pip bent the metal back, widening the gap. She climbed through, taking care to make as little sound as possible. Wiping nervous sweat from her slippery palms, she dried her hands one at a time on her pants and scanned the auto yard, quarter by quarter. Not wanting to be ambushed by her own haste, she took a deep breath and listened. Gauging by the calm chirping of birds on the property, she hoped Camo and his cronies had left.

"I told them you were farther up the road, that we'd gotten separated!" Fly yelled. "They took the truck!"

Pip jogged to the rear of the shed. Mismatched wood crisscrossed the warped door, and a hefty padlock held it shut. She was reaching for the padlock when the door bucked, pinching her fingers.

"Ow! Fuck. Calm down."

"Get me out!" Fly threw herself against the door. Dust and splinters flew at Pip's face. Each shouted word was drier than the last, cracked from heat and fear. Fly's deep voice took on the frantic screech of a trapped animal. "I don't know when they'll come back. Get me the fuck out of here."

Garages at the rear of the property had tools. Turning her back on the shed, Pip sighted down the shotgun, checking each open bay. If someone was on guard, they'd come running. Pip kicked the shed door like a mule. "Stop! You have to be quiet!"

A quiet sob pierced her heart. Pip tugged at the padlock in the vain hope it wasn't locked. Pointless. Grabbing her knife, she attacked the screws holding the latch in place. Hands shaking, she nearly cut herself a dozen times using the honed edge of the blade as a screwdriver.

The last screw stuck. Pip hocked and spit on the head, working saliva around with a mucky finger. A few minutes had passed since she'd heard a peep from inside the shed.

"I've almost got it." Pip shoved with all her might and felt the screw loosen. "One screw to go."

She lost her grip and fumbled the blade, swearing at her cramping hands. "Damn it." Her forearms burned from the tiny moves she'd performed to loosen the screws. Sweat ran into her eyes. Pip wiped her face and bent to retrieve the knife.

There was a tremendous crack, and the door gave. The top hinge tore from the wood, peeling the latch free of its last screw with a terrific squeal. Pip caught the door and hauled it out of the way. Fly burst out of the shed, took two steps, and crashed face-first into the dirt.

Setting down the shotgun, Pip dragged Fly into the long finger of shade cast by the shed. Nothing about her wasn't damaged. A grotesque wing of dried blood lined the rim of her left eye. Pip lightly touched the swollen lid—the skin was water-balloon tight and shockingly hot.

The sound of cautious footsteps sifting through grit on the side of the road brought Pip to her feet. Snatching the shotgun, she hugged the wall of the shed and quickly peeked around the corner. With a shout of dismay, she crossed the distance to Iris and shook her. Water bottles and snack bars tumbled out of Iris's pack.

"I told you to hide!" Like an angry dog, Pip gave her one last shake and let go. Iris plopped on her butt and burst into tears.

"I heard yelling," she hiccuped. "I thought you were hu-hu-urt."

Pip exhaled. *Too rough. Go easy.* "I'm...sorry."

"'S'okay." Iris crawled to the nearest snack bar and dusted it off. She placed it in the bag and reached for another.

"Iris, I—" Pip held out a hand. "I shouldn't have yelled. I was afraid."

Iris stuffed a water bottle in the pack along with the bars. Pip had never been so aware of someone avoiding looking at her. "I know."

"Water," Fly rasped.

Iris's head snapped up—she hadn't noticed Fly slumped against the shed. Iris elbowed Pip out of the way. Stepping cautiously to the boundary between the sunlight and the shade where Fly sat, Iris studied her injuries with a frown.

Water," Fly hissed.

Iris dropped her pack and had the lid off a water bottle before it cleared the mouth of the bag. Fly clawed at the plastic, greedy for a drink. Iris helped hold the bottle steady. Fly's throat worked rapidly as she drained the entire bottle. Worried she might throw it right back up again, Pip pulled Iris a short distance away, scooting the backpack out of the blast radius.

Fly stifled a belch, thumping her breastbone with satisfaction.

"I'm not gonna blow." She wiped her lips with two fingers, softly skimming where they'd cracked and bled. "Help me up."

"Are you sure—"

"Just do it."

Sharp intakes of breath accompanied Fly getting to her feet. Her shoulders hunched against the ache of standing straight. She touched a welt on Pip's cheek. "Looking at you, I don't need a mirror. You look just how I feel."

"*You* look like you lost a fight with a lawn mower."

"Screw you," Fly said with a smirk. She worked her tongue around her mouth. Pip knew she was searching for loose teeth.

"I think I hear something," Iris said.

A jittery shot of adrenaline pulsed through Pip's body, bringing the world into tight focus. Pip gestured for them to follow her away from the guard shack. She pushed Iris farther into the auto yard, out of sight. They crunched through broken glass, taking a worn path through the piles of broken vehicles. Pip jogged at an awkward crouch through the maze of cars, moving around broken-down vehicles. As the rumble of engines got closer, all she could think of was trying to get to the fence on the far side of the auto yard. Fly followed in the rear of their little group. She dodged around a rusty hulk on its side in a pile of loose gravel and stumbled when Iris slipped and fell.

Dust billowed around the three of them, making them cough.

Iris covered her mouth against the grit as Pip handed the shotgun to Fly and hauled Iris to her feet.

"I'm scared," Iris whispered.

"So am I."

Fly's face filled with murderous intent. She gazed predatorily at the shotgun and then nodded with satisfaction. "The two of us can give 'em a fight. They won't be expecting an attack."

"No."

Fly continued as if Pip hadn't spoken. "Give me the shotgun shells."

When Pip didn't move, Fly finally looked up. "We're running out of time."

The "we" was a gold coin dropping into her heart—Pip cradled the joy of being part of this fierce woman's attention, then steeled herself against feeling anything else. She'd made Iris a promise, and she meant to keep it.

Instead of answering, Pip handed Fly the shells.

"What are you doing?" Fly seized Pip's upper arm.

"I'm getting Iris out of here. What if one of us is wounded? If we fight, we risk Iris's life. I won't let that happen."

Fly let go. Frustration raged across her face. "Look, it's two on three. Only the crooked-nosed bastard is armed."

"You don't know that."

"What about all the other people they're gonna try to snatch off the street? What happens to them?"

Pip took Iris by the arm and pulled her closer to the fence. Iris resisted, dragging them to a stop. Dust from the road wove between their legs, filling Pip with the urge to run.

"Iris."

"We're not leaving Fly behind."

A cry went up from the guard shack. They'd noticed Fly had broken out.

Fly checked the shotgun was loaded and snapped it closed with a dull pop. She looked to Pip. "Someone has to stop them."

The tinted car window next to Fly burst, showering them with safety glass. A second later a bullet smacked into a truck next to Iris.

Cocking both barrels of the shotgun, Fly rounded on Curtis, catching him mid reload on his six-shooter. Her gun boomed. She missed and he dropped to the ground with a surprised yell. Buckshot ricocheted off the cars around them. Iris squealed in pain as a bloody furrow cut across one cheek.

Pip grabbed Iris by the top strap on her backpack and dragged her the last few feet to the fence. A wall of old car hoods and buckling sheet metal had been welded together to make this part of the fence. She picked an already rusted-out gap near the ground and kicked a large hole in it. Pip's breath came in heaves as she fought for some semblance of control. Hate and fear mingled hot in her mouth, gagging her with indecision.

Run or fight.

She heard an echo of Whistler ordering her to take Iris and run. She wasn't doing that again. Blood pounding hard in her temples, Pip grabbed Iris and pushed her at the fence.

"Go!"

Iris tried to fight but couldn't match Pip's terrified strength. The shotgun boomed over by the garages at the rear of the auto yard. A volley of shots answered it.

Pip heard herself chanting a mantra she hadn't the power to stop. "Not again, not again."

Iris clutched at Pip's clothes, pleading for her not to go. Peeling Iris off her abdomen, Pip gripped her bloodless fingers. "If I don't come back, promise me you'll go east, then north. Day, Cedar, Bickett."

Iris's cheeks were wet. "No!"

"Say it!"

"Day, Cedar, Bickett."

"I'll come back for you," Pip said.

She unlatched her knife and ran after Fly.

CHAPTER 28

High-pitched shots cracked from the barrel of a handgun. Climbing over a pile of car doors, Pip grabbed the dangling wires of a headlight and threw it in the direction of the gunfire. It whistled through the air, and Curtis's head came up, mouth gaping as he lurched out of the way.

Fly stood up from behind a cube of crushed cars and unloaded at Curtis from thirty feet away. A black peppering of buckshot hit him in the chest. Dropping the gun, he clutched at the wounds, trying to put himself back together. Bloody froth bubbled on his lips. He dropped to one knee and fell on his back.

Empty twin shells bounced to the ground. Fly reloaded the shotgun. Snapping it shut, she looked over her shoulder at Pip. "They went into the garages. Get his gun."

Pip ran and slid to a stop next to Curtis. His legs moved in jerks, pedaling the dirt in frantic circles. His lips were turning blue and he couldn't breathe. Ignoring the fear in his eyes, she picked up his six-shooter and opened the cylinder—there were four bullets left.

Fly was already at the door of the first garage when Granville's pickup blew into the auto yard. It slid to a stop right behind the yellow moving truck. Pip screamed for Fly to run. Taking aim at a man jumping out of the back of the pickup, Pip thumbed the hammer and fired at his head. The gun kicked in her hands. The man sprawled flat on his face in the gravel next to the truck.

The horn honked as Granville threw himself from behind the steering wheel. He yelled for the other man in the car to shoot and dove out of sight.

Pip thumbed the hammer again and shot just as the passenger-side door of the truck opened. The bullet twanged off the door, pinging into another car. The man dropped to the ground, scooting on his butt underneath the truck. He rolled onto his stomach, staying prone to take aim with a menacing black rifle. Pip launched herself behind a pile of wheel rims, hiding from the rapid bangs of semiautomatic fire. Flecks of rusty metal hazed the air as the entire pile of rims jolted from the bullet impacts.

The barrage stopped and the man swore. There was a ratcheting sound, like he was trying to clear a jammed bullet. This was her chance. She stood up, slapped the hammer down on her gun, and fired. She shot one-handed, and the gun recoiled high above her head, snapping out of her grip. The man under the truck slumped over his rifle, dead.

Booms from the shotgun and the crack of smaller weapons echoed inside the second garage bay. Fly was in trouble. Pip dropped to the ground, frantically reaching under a car to retrieve Curtis's gun.

As her fingers brushed the hot barrel of the gun, boots crunched behind her.

"Ah, ah, ah." Granville waggled a finger in reprimand from several feet away. "Caught ya, didn't I?"

He took a step closer and worked the rifle's bolt action. A brass shell ejected from the chamber, tumbling through the air like an unlucky coin. It winked through a sunbeam to land in a puff of dirt.

A short magazine thrust from the bottom of the rifle—it was impossible to know how many rounds were left. She had to assume the gun was loaded with more than enough bullets to kill. She stared at the dead black eye of the muzzle and reached for the reassurance of Utah's collar.

It wasn't around her neck. She felt naked without it.

The possibility of being shot filled Pip with an overwhelming urge to live. She gathered herself, preparing to charge off the ground, to overwhelm Granville with surprise.

"Hold up. I see what you're doing...don't even think about it." He shifted into a sturdier position. "Toss me the gun."

Pip leaned on the hip where she'd buckled the pearl-handled knife. Instead of relieving the pressure and exposing the weapon, she carefully drew Curtis's gun out from under the car.

Granville moved closer, a bead of sweat tracing down his neck. Pip transferred the gun to her left hand and held it out.

"Toss it here."

"Fuck you." Pip hauled back and chucked the gun right at his face.

Granville fired his rifle—the shot went wide, and she closed the gap between them. At the last second, Pip drew her knife and dove at him, hurling herself at his torso. Granville toppled backward; Pip rode him to the ground.

Stabbing wildly, she felt Granville's body buck in pain underneath her. She swung again, and her arm jarred when she struck dirt instead of flesh. Granville growled and wrenched himself violently, twisting his body to flip her on her back. Pip kicked hard, landing ferocious blows even as he pulled himself on top of her.

She swung her arm with all her might and felt the knife dig into something soft. Blood spurted hot and coppery onto her chest.

Granville shouted a high-pitched yip, like coyotes howling. He caught her wrist and forced the knife to the ground.

"I was gonna make it easy," he wheezed against her cheek. "But not anymore."

He elbowed her in the face. Stars sparkled in her vision, and then the world turned black for a fraction of a second. Terrified of passing out, Pip bucked, trying to break free.

They wrestled for control of the knife. Pip started biting. Her teeth met something meaty; she clamped down on Granville's shoulder. Deafening howls buzzed in her ears. He forgot the knife and punched her face, smashing her nose and cheeks.

Suddenly Granville arched in an electric bow of startled agony. His pupils shrank to tiny dots, his eyes wider than Pip would have thought possible. The bloodshot whites of his eyes swallowed his entire face. His lips drew back in a sneering rictus of pain before he slumped forward, crumpling to his side.

Pip rolled Granville's body off of her, and Iris's terrified face slipped into view.

"What?" Pip croaked and spit blood.

Iris curled in on herself. Her hair curtained her face. Pip rolled unsteadily onto her knees. It took her adrenaline-befuddled brain a moment to understand. Her knife was thrust between Granville's shoulder blades.

Iris had killed Granville.

The grating sound of another shotgun blast boomed off the metal piled around them. Someone bellowed in pain. The agonizing yell dwindled to a keening that sounded like no noise a human could make. A shot ended the suffering with a crack of finality that goosed Pip's frightened brain into action.

She yanked her knife out of Granville's back, slamming it into its sheath. She picked up the rifle—the familiar action of the bolt sliding to reload felt like every hunting trip she'd ever taken with her dad. She turned her back on Granville's body and took Iris's hand, cringing at the sensation of blood between their palms.

"We have to find Fly."

Unwilling to leave Iris behind, Pip pulled her close while they crossed the wrecking yard. They skirted along the edge of the wide parking lot—avoiding the two dead guards from Thistle Hill lying next to the truck—and crossed to the first garage in careful lockstep. Pip waved Iris behind the corner of the garage. Leaning ever so slowly into the open door, she looked inside.

A wet splash of blood covered a tool rack, glossing it with gore. The silence was killing her.

"Fly?" her whisper was loud in the empty space.

A low moan came from an oil-change bay. Pip dropped to her knees, gesturing for Iris to stay. Stealing herself for what she might find at the bottom, she crawled the last few feet across the floor to the bay. At the rim of the bay, she laid herself flat to the floor and slid along oily concrete to the metal stairs. She peeked down the stairwell and saw Navvy bent backward over a bulky piece of equipment. Her chest heaved once and stopped.

Pip pushed back from the bay, climbed to her feet, and reeled. Light-headed with shock, she collapsed, tucking her head between her knees.

"Fly!" Pip's voice cracked with urgency.

"Here!" The shout came from the next garage.

Pip reached out for Iris, and the two of them supported each other while Pip held the rifle at the ready. The second garage reeked of gunpowder—a smoky haze hung in the air, swirling around Fly's head. She had a bloody graze along her left arm. A messy wound on her scalp wept blood down her neck, soaking her shirt.

Not far from where she stood, Camo lay on the floor almost split in half. Shiny loops of guts spilled onto the floor behind him. Pip gagged, and Iris covered her eyes with both hands as Pip led her out of the garage.

"I'm okay." Iris sank onto the twisted remains of a mashed-up car and gestured for Pip to go back inside.

"Yell if you see anything."

"Okay."

Pip threw the rifle's shoulder strap across her chest and stowed her emotions, shoving them deep. She could feel them pushing against her like water against a crumbling dam. *You do not have the time to lose your shit right now.* She made herself go into the garage and take the shotgun out of Fly's trembling hands.

"Navvy's dead."

"Who?" Fly couldn't see anything but Camo's body.

"The woman."

"Oh."

Wrapping her arm around Fly's shoulders, Pip steered her outside, away from the carnage.

"Is he dead?" Iris asked.

She wasn't asking about Camo's body in the garage. She'd meant Granville.

Over by a rusted-out station wagon, Granville's cowboy boots splayed in a limp V shape. A ball of turbulent regret formed in Pip's stomach, filling her guts with a sour cramp. She'd set out to protect Iris and failed. Pip wiped her eyes with bloody hands, hating that she wasn't more.

Fly mumbled something under her breath.

"What?"

"We need to leave." Fly cleared her throat. "They have more than one truck."

Pip felt an electrifying burst of fear course through her veins. "Are you kidding?"

"No." Fly motioned with her head for them to go and winced. "Bitch shot me in the head."

Iris set her backpack on the ground and pulled out a maxi pad. The yellow wrapping crinkled as she opened the tidy package and handed it over. Fly gingerly blotted the peanut-shaped pad against her wound.

The buzzy feeling of fight or flight gave Pip the shakes. "I can't think."

"We shouldn't use the road." Fly said as she started to walk away.

"Where're you going?" Pip dragged Iris along behind her, following Fly into the graveyard of cars.

Making a detour around Curtis, Fly led them to the hole Pip had kicked in the corrugated fence. They let Iris go first, then Fly ducked through and flopped into the pine duff on the other side. Pip crouched by the hole, inhaling the clean scent of crushed pine needles.

Six dead. She couldn't fathom what they'd done.

"Pip...Pip..."

Her name seemed so far away.

Fly reached through the hole and tugged her pant leg.

"When they caught you and Iris at the grocery store, they had two moving vans with them. I was loading supplies into the other truck when they dragged you out of the store on your back. You looked like a chewed-up piece of meat. That crooked-nosed guy had you by the ankles and the other one had Iris." Fly shuddered, voice shaking with the memory. "They had two trucks. One for us and one for the supplies. They put their injured girl in the second truck and left. *They had two trucks.* We have to leave. We have to run!"

Her whole body convulsed as she gagged and threw up. Vomit spattered the pine needles at her feet.

Pip ducked through the rusty hole in the fence and rested a hand on the tense muscles of Fly's back. Iris didn't seem to notice Fly's distress. Reaching out to her, Pip took Iris's shock-chilled hand and gave it a squeeze. Iris came back to the surface with a shuddering gasp.

The threat of a second truck forced them to face the problem ahead instead of the carnage they'd left behind. Pip studied the terrain. The forest was thin enough for a glimpse of the road. The ribbon of pavement resembled a river winking between the trees.

Dusty Gulch was a main road. If she remembered correctly, it traveled almost exactly east-west to the base of Mt. Spokane. After Dusty Gulch, the next turn in the sequence she'd memorized was Day Road. The map Clare drew showed Day Road running directly north. If they followed the general track of Dusty Gulch through the woods, it would only be a matter of time before they crossed Day.

Pip helped Fly stand. Between them they had a shotgun, a rifle, Iris's backpack with two water bottles, and one sleeping bag. Pip couldn't remember how much food they'd put in the pack along with the violin case.

"Should we go back for our backpacks?"

"I have six shells left," Fly said in a monotone. "How many bullets do you have in that clip? About the same?"

"Probably."

"We won't survive another attack."

Pip nodded. "Okay. Let's go."

CHAPTER 29

Fly took point while Pip kept a hand on Iris's shoulder and steered her through the wilderness. They moved through the underbrush, making as little noise as possible. Pip backtracked occasionally, diligently checking that their passage through sparse underbrush wasn't leaving an obvious trail.

Shade from spindly pines did nothing to cool the throat-parching heat, and they all suffered the itch of sweat trickling along their backs and down their legs. Intermittently slapping at midges—attracted to the moisture on her face—Iris gulped water from a bottle, then handed the warm drink to Pip.

They had come at least three or four miles, and Pip couldn't see the road anymore. It was somewhere off her right shoulder. She'd been keeping track of the sun like her dad had taught her. It hadn't changed position; they were still going in the right direction.

Not far ahead, a small gully ran across their chosen path. The terrain was changing—clusters of rock interrupted the forest. A cliff loomed in the distance. Black basalt columns sprouted from the dirt like an irregular forest of dead trees, blocking any thought of passage. They'd left any part of Green Bluff that Pip was familiar with. It might be that Day Road was on the other side of all the rock. Or worse, she'd somehow missed it. She scratched her sweaty head in thought—it was time to find a road.

She believed the route they'd taken was the long side of a slim triangle and hoped the road wasn't far. They climbed a slope in what she hoped was the correct direction. When pavement didn't come into view, she was surprised and uneasy. Perhaps Dusty

Gulch wasn't as straight as she'd first thought. Unable to recall any specifics about the road, she could do nothing but shrug and keep going.

Wind hissed gently through the pines, ushering along the scent of a well-used woodstove. The acrid taste of ash coated their tongues despite no obvious sign of burning. A clearing in the trees beckoned and Fly hurried forward.

"The road!"

Pip stepped out of the trees, boots crunching in the burnt stubble of weeds. Jagged black streaks like the shadows of lightning crisscrossed the road where flaming logs must have fallen and burned. Blackened skeletons of trees swam in acres of soot, their scorched roots exposed to the sun. The ground felt cool when she touched it, and there wasn't any smoke. She guessed the fire hadn't been recent.

Kicking through random piles of ash, Iris climbed onto a giant log that had crashed across the road and smashed a metal barrier flat. She sat astride the charred tree, and Fly rested against its trunk, sipping water. She held it out to Pip like a gift. When their fingers touched, Pip resisted the urge to sob.

A powerful longing to be held and forgiven for the elation she felt every time she thought of Curtis gasping his last breath could hardly be contained. She wanted to scream joy and hated herself for the destruction they'd caused. She saw a reflection of those jumbled emotions in Fly's tight-lipped expression. Fly brushed her pinky over Pip's fingers and let go of the water bottle. Pip swallowed the strange agony threatening to consume her with what was left of the water.

Large trees crossed the road for miles in both directions— blocking it with accidental precision. Pip wasn't surprised by the sly wisdom Clare had revealed by instructing them to come this way. Using the road without the pressure of being surprised by a vehicle was a gift. Tracing Iris's blurry footsteps through the ash gave Pip a fierce sense of satisfaction. They might leave a trail, but no one could follow them easily.

One grueling hour later, they emerged from the burnt area and collapsed near the bank of a trickling stream. Tramping over acres of charcoaled logs covered with the broken ends of branches that yearned to poke out an eye had drained all of them past the point of caring.

Pip blinked gritty airborne ash from her eyes and spotted a green street sign peeking from the trees. She couldn't muster the energy to get close enough to read it. Sagging into the brush along the side of the road, she picked at the gritty crust in the corner of one eye. She was willing to bet they'd found their crossroad but was too exhausted to feel any sort of victory.

Iris was dirtier than when Pip had first encountered her on the bridge in Spokane. Fly sprawled flat on her back on the side of the road and closed her eyes. None of them had spoken much since they left the auto yard. Every time Pip opened her mouth to speak, nothing but a wail or lunatic laughter wanted to come out.

"I feel like the world's biggest fireplace," Iris moaned. She rolled herself into the shade of a tree and immediately fell asleep.

During the trek through the remains of the forest fire, Pip had trod on a stick that broke with a particularly loud crack. They'd all jumped, and Pip's heart had pounded painfully. No one mentioned how much the wooden snap sounded like a distant gunshot. Iris had surveyed the burnt woods with fearful eyes and kept walking.

Restless in her sleep, Iris rolled over. The dog collar slipped out of her shirt. A flicker of light reflecting off the tags was a haunting reminder of the terrible cost of her promise. Resisting the urge to submit to despair, Pip packed her feelings down deep and forced herself to stand. She washed her hands in the stream before refilling their water bottles with tepid water. Her throat ached as she plunked the last of their purifying tablets into each bottle. She licked her chapped lips and waited. The tabs would give every sip a hateful, flat, metallic taste.

She counted to sixty thirty times before taking a cautious drink. Warm water rinsed her parched insides, leaving her feeling stronger. She gently shook Iris awake. Iris responded to gentle prodding with a bleary stare and a hostile grunt of displeasure.

"Sorry, kiddo, we have to get moving."

Iris wet her lips and croaked, "Don't call me kiddo."

Fly coughed and sat up. She peeled the pad off her head. The blood there was rusty; the bleeding had stopped. One eye was swollen completely shut from the beating she'd gotten from Curtis. She looked spent.

"We need to keep moving." Pip limped on sore feet to the intersection of the two roads and read the street sign. "Day Road."

Fly groaned her way to standing and helped Iris up.

Shadows gathered as they made their way north. The sun dipped behind the tallest of trees and painted the sky tangerine and dusty purple. A nighthawk hovered over the road and chirruped an alarm for all to find a place for the evening. This stretch of road was desolate—there weren't any safe places to rest.

Sleeping on the road felt like the worst possible idea. Even if the western part of Dusty Gulch was blocked by the fire, Clare and her wagon had managed to find other ways to Thistle Hill. Someone could come from the east and catch them asleep. Pip didn't relish the thought of being ambushed. Eyes adjusting to the gradual twilight, she gave up on searching for a house and scanned the forest, hunting for a protected area to camp.

Pip was weighing the pros and cons of following a well-used game trail into the woods when a savage roar ripped through the trees.

Iris gasped. "Was that a mountain lion?"

"No. Mountain lions scream. Other big cats roar."

Another call rumbled into an emphatic growl. Spinning around on the lonely road, Pip searched for hungry shadows. There was no way to guess how close the big cat was. This had to be Clare's tiger. Another screech sounded dangerously close. They needed a sturdy tree.

Not far from the road loomed an ancient pine whose lowest branches were bigger around than Pip's thighs. Serenaded with intermittent growls, Pip stripped off Iris's backpack and shoved her into the tree. Fly went to the other side and climbed in tandem, whispering words of encouragement to Iris as they worked their way into the higher branches.

Imaginary claws tore at Pip while she took off the rifle and pulled on the backpack. Strapping the rifle over the pack, she grabbed a low branch and dragged herself into the canopy. Pushing through the tangle, she climbed with blind urgency. It wasn't long before she caught up to Iris. Pip let go of a branch and shoved Iris farther up the trunk, nearly catching a sneaker to the temple.

Surrounded by broken branches and the unexpected scent of freshly cut Christmas trees, they stopped climbing about twenty-five feet up the trunk. Years before, the young tree had bent, leaving a hollow just the right size for two butts. Fly clambered a little higher and sat on the other side of the bend, facing the tree, wrapping her legs around the trunk.

Iris squished herself into one side of the hollow, tucking herself into a shivering ball. Crashing around like a bald eagle landing in a tree, Pip awkwardly took off the rifle and the backpack. She hooked them over the splintery ends of broken branches and squeezed in next to Iris. They settled into the cool embrace of the tree. Pip inhaled all the way to her toes and tried to relax.

"Does it climb trees?" Iris breathed

"Nah."

Fly reached around the tree to pat Iris on the shoulder with a pitchy hand. "We're too dirty to eat."

The whites of Iris's eyes shone in what little light was left. "I'm cold."

The sleeping bag was tied to the outside of Iris's pack. Unhooking it should have been simple, but fighting against the tangle of branches made Pip frustrated enough to scream. Forcing herself to work with patience through the tree's obstructions took time. Iris was shivering when Pip finally managed to tuck her into their sleeping bag. Concerned the slippery fabric would cause a frictionless slide off the branch and to the ground, Pip looped her belt around Iris's waist and buckled her to the tree.

"It stopped roaring," Fly said.

She'd been so intent on getting Iris settled, Pip hadn't noticed the quiet. Unsure of whether a silent cat was better, Pip settled into the tree and crossed her arms against the night's chill. She'd have to stay awake or risk falling. As the night wore on, Pip's eyelids drooped, and she dozed until the full moon rose, fat and yellow in the night sky.

Blinded by the moon's unexpected light cutting through pine

needles, she recoiled and slipped off the limb. Instinctively throwing her arms starfish wide, she wrapped herself around a thick branch. Air woofed out of her lungs. She slipped again, folding herself upside down over a limb.

Pip gasped for air and groaned into the white-hot cramp radiating from her guts. Dangling like an ornament, she watched shadows move like liquid through the trees and swallowed incipient fear.

"What was that?" Fly said.

"I fell," Pip grunted, forcing her pulled muscles to move. Undeterred by pain, she got herself back onto the limb next to Iris.

"Were you asleep?"

"Yeah."

"Every time I close my eyes all I see is blood."

Pip reached up and rested her hand on Fly's calf. "I know."

"How many were in the other truck?"

"Maybe four."

"Do you think they'll try to follow us?"

Granville and Camo are dead. Without their leaders...

"I don't think so."

Cheeks and arms stinging from a myriad of tiny scratches, Pip folded in on herself. Better to be cold than fall again. Bleary eyed from exhaustion, she blinked slowly as if a heavy weight pulled at her eyelids. With a growl, she viciously pinched herself and snapped awake.

Random cracklings and rustles filled the woods as night-shift animals went about their business. She studied the forest floor. A porcupine, hunched under protective quills, snuffled around a nearby tree and dug in the dirt. It ate something with meaty crunches that made her stomach gurgle.

"Care to share?" Pip asked the porcupine. It skittered away at the sound of her voice. Once it was a few steps from the base of her tree, one ear seemed to point in her direction like it was considering her request. It whuffed softly and resumed munching along the forest floor.

Cheered by the timid animal, Pip dug into a pocket for their last protein bar. It had long passed the expiration date. The chalky texture didn't stop her from enjoying the sweet vanilla taste of every bite. It was almost impossible to save half, but Pip passed the bar to Fly and listened to the sound of her chewing.

Hunger barely mollified, she rested her head against the tree's rough bark. The night's chill seeped into her tired joints and curled there like metal filings. Finding a comfortable position was impossible. Faced with waiting out the rest of the night, her mind wandered into darker territory. Pip imagined blood staining the ground in gloopy splashes. The sound of the tortured wails in the auto yard haunted her.

"Did we murder them?" Pip asked

The wrapper crinkled. "With Granville dead, we've saved every single girl at Thistle Hill."

"But—"

"I feel dirty to the bottom of my soul. But I'm telling you, what we did wasn't wrong."

CHAPTER 30

As dawn filtered through the woods, every fiber of Pip's being complained. It felt like she'd spent the night being beaten with sticks. She brushed at long scabs on her face, managing a weary smile. She *had* been beaten by sticks. Next to her, Iris snored.

Branches snapped in the clearing. Pip spun around to see Fly squatting on the ground, gathering sticks into a pile. She must've foraged while waiting for them to wake. Sliding down the trunk, Pip nodded good morning, then went to relieve herself behind a leafy shrub.

She knelt in the dirt and rolled up her shirt, checking the gunshot wound. A web of purple-green bruising wrapped around her ribs. The entire side of her body ached, but it looked to be healing. She didn't dare touch the thick scab crusting it—her hands were filthy. Settling her shirt back into place, she scrubbed her palms with fine, sand-like dirt.

Her eyes were sore from lack of sleep. Pip squeezed them shut tight and sighed with pleasure when sunlight broke through the canopy to warm her little hideaway. *Had it really been only one day since they'd left Thistle Hill?*

Her thoughts skirted around the details of the auto yard, counting hours and bodies since they'd started their journey. She remembered Granville toppling after Iris stabbed him. Pip traced the handle of her knife and unsnapped the leather guard holding it in place. The snap was louder than she'd expected. Pip flinched at the sharp metallic click like it was a stray bullet. Fly came through the bushes, a thick branch held high, ready to strike.

"What was that?"

"My knife." Pip drew the blade and held it gingerly, remembering the feel of pulling it out of Granville's back—the thick resistance, almost a sucking sensation. Forcing herself into practicality, she gave the knife a once-over with a handful of dirt. The handle was gritty when she finished, but the blade gleamed dangerously.

"You'll have to wash the holder."

"Yeah." The blade was clean enough. She put it back in the sheath.

In the clearing, Pip knelt on the opposite side of a protective ring of stones and watched Fly stack a log cabin of sticks in preparation for a fire. There was so much to say; Pip didn't know where to start.

Fly struck a match and the flame wound along the thin wooden handle. At the last moment, she tossed it onto some dry lichen. Fire jumped with a hungry whoosh, licking at the kindling, surrounding them in a whirl of smoke.

"Do we have any water left?" Fly asked.

Pip went to retrieve the pack, and Iris lowered it and the rifle into her hands. Back at the fire, Fly took the plastic bottle, gripping it tight. "When they jumped me out of the ditch yesterday, I thought I was dead."

Pip rubbed at the scratches on her knuckles. They were swollen from punching the dirt when they'd grabbed Fly. "I was..."

"What?"

"I was so scared I wouldn't find you."

Bruising mottled Fly's face. Her eye was swollen, and the gash along the side of her head formed a crust in her hair. She was a disaster. They both were.

"I didn't want them to catch you," Fly said.

"What we did," Pip said, poking at the fire, "killing those people..."

A vision of Granville's shocked face warped in the orange gold of the flames.

"When I was little, my paw-paw made me raise a pig for 4-H," Fly said. "Every damn weekend of my summer went into that pig. Buckets of half-rotten leftovers, making me want to puke, dumped in his pig trough. I shoveled piles of muck into a wheelbarrow. Paw-Paw always left a week's worth of shit for me to clean up. I hated it. Hated Paw-Paw. D'you know pigs' eyes sink into their faces, they get so fat?" She pointed to her swollen eye. "It was like this, only nastier. We took that damn thing to the fair, and after it won second place, I thought, that's it. I'm done."

But she wasn't done.

"Next weekend, my dad drives me up to Paw-Paw's, and there's a fuckin' witch cauldron in the middle of the front yard. Fire underneath, boiling. And he's got my pig staked to a tree. He made me shoot it. Right between its bloated eyes. It hadn't stopped thrashing when Paw-Paw cut it ear to ear."

Fly shuddered, her breathing ragged. Frowning, she closed her eyes, and tears poured from the good one. "Until yesterday, I'd never seen so much blood."

"Fly—" Pip wanted to stop her.

"That man in the garage, he shot at me. I didn't know he had a gun. I didn't even think, I just pulled the trigger. We were only a few feet apart. He screamed. And the smell—oh God—the smell of him dying. I couldn't reload the gun. I tasted gore on the air. I..."

Iris slid out of the tree in a shower of bark and moved toward Fly's shaking body like a bird cautiously checking a branch before landing. She rested a hand on the back of Fly's neck.

Fly looked up, shocked out of her memory.

"Iris," she gasped.

Sinking into the hollow made by Fly's crossed legs, Iris turned sideways and curled herself against Fly's chest. Instead of protesting the unexpected affection, Fly crumbled like a sandcastle before an oncoming tide. Iris formed a tidy bundle—a young girl tucked into the lap of a fierce woman, protecting her from the shadow of guilt over decisions she'd been forced to make.

When Fly's sobs trailed off, Iris dabbed her face with a sleeve. A contemplative expression aged Iris's face. She took a deep breath and confided, "I killed Granville."

Fly's mouth dropped open in surprise.

Iris chewed a dirty fingernail and looked to Pip.

"I couldn't tell you yesterday." Pip tasted guilt on her tongue. "I couldn't tell you what happened. He tackled me to the ground. It was a fight to the death. Iris saved me."

Iris looked pure love at Pip, then dropped her eyes to the ground. "I stabbed Granville in the back."

In a move of tenderness Pip would never have expected, Fly kissed Iris on the forehead. "That was the right thing to do."

"I know," Iris whispered. Extracting herself from Fly's lap, Iris came around the fire to sit against Pip's side. Sparks popped, launching embers into the air. Red-orange coals floated and flared out, sinking under the weight of fragile ash. "You did the right thing, too."

Pip's stomach grumbled, burbling hunger at maximum volume. Iris snorted at the rude noises coming from Pip's midsection, breaking the mournful spell of sadness that had settled over them like wet wool.

"Anybody *else* hungry?" Pip finally asked.

Iris nodded, and Fly managed a lopsided smile.

Pip poured half a bottle of water into their MRE bag of stew. Giving it a stir with their only spoon, she handed it to Iris. They passed the bag around, taking turns scooping out bites of cold stew. It was thick and gross. Pip bit into a dried piece of potato that crunched against her teeth.

"This sucks, sucks," Iris said.

Pip laughed. Just like the awful spaghetti they'd had in the music store—spaghetti, spaghetti. It felt like a million years ago. She thought of the porcupine from the night before, wandering in the forest searching for food. It made her wonder what had happened to Kitty. Pip hoped she was somewhere sitting on Whistler's shoulder, keeping him safe.

Pip caught Fly watching her over the fire, but for once she didn't feel the need to look away. Prolonged eye contact wasn't something she'd ever been comfortable with—there was always a danger the person would guess something about her was different and hate her for it.

Pip broke the intensity of their connection with a nervous laugh. Iris glanced between them with a confused look. Instead of inquiring, she scooped the last of the stew out of the foil bag. The random chirps and whistles of foraging birds were the only conversation for the rest of the meal.

When they finished eating, Fly smothered the flames by kicking dirt onto the fire. Heavy gray smoke oozed through the blanket of dirt. Fly reached through a particularly thick cloud and offered her hand to Pip. She let Fly pull her to her feet.

"Can I talk to you alone for a minute?" Fly asked.

Pip shrugged. "Sure." She tipped her head at Iris holding the dirty spoon. "Give that a rub with dirt to clean it and put it back in the pack."

"'Kay." Iris clearly wanted to join them but didn't protest.

Fly wandered into the trees. Pip tried to judge by the set of her shoulders what the problem was; it was like guessing the weather by staring at a mountain. When they'd walked a fair distance from Iris, Fly paused and sucked in a breath, making air chirp through the gap in her teeth.

"I don't care how cool she is—Clare is only expecting two people." She looked relaxed but her tone was wary.

"That's true."

"Three is a lot more than two."

"Clare is a tough bird—she takes in strays. That's why she offered for Iris and me to come."

"This isn't another Thistle Hill, is it?"

Unspoken accusations in Fly's tone riled Pip's dander right up. "You worked with her. What do you think?"

Fly cracked her knuckles with a pained wince. "I guess what I'm asking is, should we trust her?"

Pip thought of the wedding speech. It felt like Clare had spoken to her—"find your other half, what makes you complete." She'd seen through the binder, had seen her crush on Fly. Nothing fazed her.

"She won't let us down."

They watched Iris stick the cleaned spoon into the backpack. Utah's collar swung loose around her neck. Contemplating Fly, Pip realized that she couldn't live with the thought of her not coming with them.

"I've only spoken to Clare a few times, but she saw through the binder and my masculine bluff. She saw *me* and knew I needed a way out. Look, Clare will be honest about how she feels and what she wants. We'll just have to ask and see what she says."

"Are we going?" Iris shouted.

Pip held her breath.

Fly picked up a loose rock and tossed it into the trees. She walked back toward Iris. "We'll never know if we don't go, will we?"

"Right on Cedar, left on Bickett," Iris recited. "Then, find her driveway…"

Fly retrieved the shotgun from where she'd left it at the base of their tree. As they hiked through morning rays of sun slanting through the trees, Pip passed in and out of the bright light, marveling at how much Fly's presence changed Iris. She didn't complain about her feet being tired or how much farther they had to go—she kept pace with their longer strides and sometimes even held Fly's hand.

The three of them together, almost like a family. It should have been weird, but it wasn't.

CHAPTER 31

They turned right on Cedar less than half an hour later. Broken pavement interspersed with rocky potholes told the story of a road rarely maintained. They were on a journey into a wilder part of the forest.

Sprinkled along the roadside were shrubby vine maples covered with white and crimson flowers wilting in the late spring heat. The dry pine forest surrounding the road gradually gave way to wetter woods in the shadow of Mount Spokane. Lichens hung from trees like delicate shawls, and mushrooms dotted the ground. The unexpected shush of water rushing over rocks hurried them along. Pip was relieved—even being conservative, they'd drained the last water bottle.

Slicks of dried mud crossed the road like spilled hot chocolate. The river must have flooded in early spring. The herby scent of cottonwoods and riverbank welcomed them to the end of the road. Pip stopped, jammed her hands on her hips, and swore. The bridge was gone. Chunks of concrete and twisted rebar thrust out, pointing at the remains of the bridge on the other side.

"Great."

Iris ignored Pip's sarcastic tone and slid down the embankment to the river's rocky beach.

"Be careful!" Pip admonished.

Fly studied the road and followed a trail beaten into the brush in the opposite direction.

Pip threw up her hands in exasperation. "Where is everybody going?"

Iris scrambled up the bank, her shirt and mouth wet from drinking out of the river. A shadow of concern crossed Pip's mind, but yelling at Iris for slaking her thirst would be pointless. Besides, the water was running fast and clear—hopefully it was clean enough to drink. Pip shrugged. They were out of purifying tablets anyway and would have to fill their bottles from the river.

"Pip! Iris! I've found a way across!" Fly yelled.

The trail Fly took into the brush wound across a slope to a wide beach a few hundred yards upstream of the ruined bridge. Thrusting halfway across the river was a sandy spit covered with puddling butterflies. Dry-topped rocks crossed the rest of the channel. They wouldn't have to risk wading against the swift remnants of spring runoff.

"How'd you—"

"Deer!" Fly interrupted.

"Deer?" Pip laughed. "What are you talking about?"

Fly crossed loose rocks like a dancer and pointed at Pip's feet. The double-diamond prints of several deer traced a dainty trail in the river's sand.

"There were prints in the old mud on the road." Fly pointed at the tracks and the beach like her solution was elementary.

Iris hooted from the other side of the river. She cupped hands around her mouth and shouted. "Slowpokes!"

Pip shoved Fly, attempting to give herself a head start. Pushing against Fly's muscular arm was like trying to shift granite. Fly guffawed and nudged Pip with an elbow, knocking her over. Pip climbed out of the bushes and growled happily, breaking into a run.

Dodging frightened butterflies, Pip hit the river an instant before Fly. She jumped lightly from rock to exposed rock, her lungs stinging with the effort, but she beat Fly to the other side.

Chest heaving, Fly set down the shotgun up the beach, then ran back to splash a handful of water at Iris. She hooted at Iris's wet-cat shriek of indignation.

Pip peeled a large rock out of the riverbed and lobbed it just as Fly turned. A cascade of water splashed over her head. Iris raised her arms in victory when Fly yelped at the cold. Rivulets of water ran over Fly's wide smile. Stumbling over loose stones and howling with laughter, she gave up and sat on the sunny bank.

"Good thing it's hot," Fly said when Pip sat.

Fly was soaked. Pip cringed. "I might have overdone it."

Fly pretended to brush water off her clothes. "Don't worry, I'm gonna kill you in your sleep tonight."

Pip imagined curling up next to Fly under the stars and her stomach did a slow flip.

She cooled her blushing cheeks with her water-chilled hands and handed Fly a plastic bottle to fill. The three of them went upstream for undisturbed water. Two checkerboard-patterned butterflies twirled up from wet sand at the river's edge, flying around each other like a colorful whirlwind. Pip held up a hand to stop Iris from crossing the beach and disturbing their dance.

"What?" Iris asked.

The pair of butterflies fluttered up the bank into the forest. Pip gave Iris and Fly a wistful smile. "Would you believe I was thinking of a crazy old man and something he saw that can't be possible?"

Now it was Fly's turn to be confused. "What do you mean?"

"My friend Whistler had seizures—they started after he recovered from the One Mile Cough." Unsure of why it felt right to tell, Pip found herself unable to stop explaining. "Not long before we were captured, I'd found him convulsing. When he could talk, he described a girl with snowflakes trapped in her black hair. I told him it was a dream. He always saw unexplainable things right after his seizures, visions of stuff that wasn't there or hadn't happened." Pip lowered her voice like she was talking to herself and looked at Iris. "The snow he saw was white flower petals. I don't know how, but Whistler saw you."

Iris gasped.

"Coincidence," Fly snorted.

Pip refused her explanation. "He saw orange-and-black butterflies too." She waved in the direction the checkered butterflies had flown in. "They made me think of him. After one of his seizures, we sat on a roof in Spokane and he described thousands of wings, swarming around our heads as the sun went down."

Fly fumbled her water bottle, dropping it into the river with a clunk. The current snatched it, racing to carry the bottle away before it filled and sank.

"Clumsy," Iris chided, racing after it.

"Monarchs?" Fly whispered.

Pip snapped her fingers. "That's it! I couldn't remember the name he'd called them."

Fly sat down. She looked like she might faint.

"Are you okay?"

A checkerboard-patterned butterfly glided out of the trees, landing on the sand not far from Fly's boot with a contented flutter. She flinched and shooed it away.

"Are you sure you're—"

"*I'm fine,*" Fly said sharply.

"It's just, I think what Whistler saw was real. But off-kilter, confused. What if his mistaking flower petals for snow means there's something twisted with his vision of butterflies?"

Fly took the water bottle from Iris with numb fingers. She hardly watched what she was doing while refilling the bottle and tightening the lid. She handed it back to Iris.

"Right before my mother died, she told me she saw me marrying a man," Fly sighed. "I'm gay. Why would I ever marry a guy? One Mile burned up their brains. That's all."

Pip's face grew hot, pulsing in time with a nervous heart and the possibility of what Fly's mother had seen. "You're too young to get married."

"I'm eighteen, that's not young."

"It's not old either," Pip laughed.

Fly's gaze was frank. "How old are you?"

"Seventeen."

Fly raised an interested eyebrow.

Chest tight, Pip looked away. Across the river, iridescent butterflies fanned themselves on the sand. So many visions—could they *really* believe all of them? Did she even have a choice? One of Whistler's seizure dreams had proven true: he'd told her that the dark-haired girl wouldn't want to go and that safety lay in the north—away from Thistle Hill Orchard and Granville and danger.

And here they were, going north, always north.

It was Whistler's mistaking flowers for snow that had her feeling uneasy. She couldn't help but wonder what version of Whistler's orange-and-black-striped fantasy was still in their future.

"Whistler really saw me in a vision?" Iris looked charmed by the idea.

"When we fought in the orchard, you rolled your eyes at me and tossed your hair—"

Iris flushed. "No, I didn't."

"You totally did." Pip poked her in the shoulder. "And when you flipped that ever-so-cool preteen hair at me, flower petals caught in it."

"Like snow."

"Like snow," Pip agreed.

Pip knew they were both thinking of the words he'd written in the violin case: *For Iris, the girl in the snow.*

Taken with delight, Iris turned on the spot and pointed to where Fly knelt filling the last water bottle. "Did he see Fly too?"

"No," Pip and Fly said at exactly the same time.

"Jinx," Iris said, completely missing the tension sharpening the angle of Fly's shoulders.

She almost shouted the word, Pip thought. *What isn't she saying?*

Unsettled by Fly's angry refusal, Pip shook her head at what couldn't be proved or understood and knelt next to her on rounded pebbles. "What is it?"

"Did he really see monarchs?"

"Thousands of them. I wish I could've seen what he saw. They sounded beautiful."

"Monarchs don't migrate until later in the summer."

"Why are you angry?"

"I'm not. It sounds crazy."

"I know."

White fluffs of cottonwood drifted over the river like early-summer snow. The wind shifted and blew the cotton to drift in fuzzy shoals on the river. Pip wrinkled her nose. The air had taken on a sour note, like a hot dumpster.

"You smell that?"

Iris pinched her nose and pointed to the top of the bank. "It's coming from that way."

They clambered up the slope into a chorus of buzzing flies. The sound raised the hair on the back of Pip's neck. That many flies only congregated over piles of garbage—or the recently dead.

Not far from where they stood, grass and shrubs were haphazardly smashed flat. Pools of blood dried in the sand. A clod of dirt and roots dangled from a nearby tree, a sign of strange things ahead. Pip took off the rifle and stepped protectively in front of Iris. Fly saw the red splashes and cracked the shotgun. She fumbled for two shells and loaded the weapon without taking her eyes from the stain.

"Wha—"

Pip silenced Iris's question with a curt gesture. Hand still raised, she pointed to the road and mimed walking. Fly nodded. They moved in a tight formation to the pavement. A shiny black-and-green fly landed on Pip's rifle sight and cleaned its eyes. Bobbing the barrel didn't budge it.

Fly pointed to a disorganized shape in the ditch. A roiling carpet of black hummed and buzzed over a dead thing. Four legs with pointy hooves jutted at impossible angles from what had been the body of a deer. Pip gagged at the fetid scent of sun-warmed meat, pulling Iris close.

Pip's terrified exhale caught Fly's attention, and she shrugged. They were both wondering where the rest of the dead animal had gone when a rolling chuff froze them in place.

CHAPTER 32

The tall grass rustled, and Pip saw a flash of bright white through dried stems. An electric growl trailed into a breathy inhale. She was unable to comprehend the tumble of orange and black in the ditch until the growling animal's outline shifted with the shadows, and Pip understood. They were within mauling distance of a tiger.

It roared. Light-headed with fright, Pip pressed against Fly, shielding Iris from the cat.

The tiger grumbled, flumping on its side. Watching orange stripes weaving into the long grass, Pip took a cautious step. One golden eye opened. The pupil widened, tracking her movement. Certain that each next second would send the tiger rushing forward, she lived a thousand terrified lifetimes waiting for it to pounce. She whimpered deep in her throat.

Fly slid a hand onto Pip's wrist and squeezed. Moving her head the smallest fraction of an inch, Pip saw nothing but determination on Fly's face. Her damaged eye had opened to the barest slit as she stared down the tiger with a growl of her own. Fly's cheeks were ashen from tension, but the hand on Pip's arm was steady. Cocking the shotgun, Fly took a deep breath and slowly moved.

Pushed along by Fly's determination, Pip followed her lead and racked the bolt on her rifle. Iris clutched anxious handfuls of Pip's shirt and belt, sticking to her side like a tick. With every crunch of grit under their boots, the tiger's thick tail lashed in irritation.

They moved haltingly, freezing each time it shifted. Fly gradually rotated, keeping a watchful eye on the restless cat. She held the shotgun tight to her shoulder and walked backward, trusting Pip to take the lead.

Blood whined in Pip's ears like a ghastly case of tinnitus—an undulating, high pitched note singing in tune with her fear. She rode the sound, putting one foot in front of the other.

A cloud of flies swarmed into the air as the tiger rose to a crouch, shoulders bunched high. Staying perfectly still, it watched them with palpable intensity. The force of its gaze built in her head, making her hands shake—holding the rifle steady was impossible.

Fly paused and planted her feet. Taking her lead, Pip sighted down the rifle, placing the bead dead center on one golden eye. A great roar assaulted her ears, pressing against her skin. The tiger jumped, blurring into motion. Bounding through the grass, it was a juggernaut of orange in the green. Gravel pattered on the road when it slid to a stop at the edge of the grass and huffed. All Pip saw were yellowed canines and a lolling tongue.

Rank breath, pungent with the smell of long-dead meat, fogged the summer air. A low growl rumbled in the tiger's chest as it took a soft step forward. The toes of its paw spread, threatening without a sound.

Pip placed an unsteady finger on the trigger. Fly did the same. They stood hip to hip, weapons pointed at the tiger's beautiful head. Dried blood covered the fur on its neck and crusted into the white on its chest. The tiger panted in the sun, belly swinging low, full of deer.

It won't make any difference. It's too big.

The attack came between heartbeats. Fly fired the shotgun. Two bangs almost on top of each other. Buckshot caught the tiger in the face, and it stumbled, screeching at the lash of pellets. Rearing up on hind legs, it towered over them, paws spread wide, claws extended, ready to rip and tear.

Pip shot at the cat and missed. Its claws raked the air, knocking against the rifle. It moved so fast, she couldn't reload. Reversing her grip, Pip shoved Fly out of the way and struck the cat in the face with the wooden stock.

Hot saliva and blood splattered the pavement as the cat bit the rifle. The stock gave with a mighty crack, showering them both with splinters.

Seizing a fallen branch thick as her arm, Pip pointed the jagged end at the tiger. Its golden eyes met hers as it paced. Blood oozed from buckshot wounds—one ear had a quarter-sized hole torn straight through it. The tiger shook its head, dislodging flies and a spray of blood. It pawed its own face and growled.

Their shotgun shells littered the road. They'd fallen out of Fly's pockets during the fight. The four red tubes mocked them. They'd have to get close to the tiger to collect them. Pip inched to the nearest shotgun shell. Reaching out with her toe, she dragged it close and reached to pick it up while keeping her eyes on the pacing cat.

Her fingers brushed the shell and it slipped away. Pip clenched her fingers into a fist, willing them to stop shaking. She picked up the shell between her pointer and middle finger, holding it in place with pressure. Straightening up, she threw the stick at the tiger like a javelin. It shied away with a roar that tore her ears.

Sweat stung Pip's eyes, jumbling the tiger into silky waves of black and orange. She couldn't breathe; fear clenched her chest tight. Forcing herself to move, she reached a hand behind her and Fly placed the solid weight of the shotgun into Pip's open palm.

The tiger snarled. A bead of moisture rolled down its nose, falling when its nostrils flared, scenting them. It lunged forward, swiping the air, growling on the exhale.

Pip cracked open the barrels. Shoving the shell into place, she answered the tiger's roar with one of her own. Fly and Iris's voices joined hers, screaming defiance. The tiger jumped. Pip dropped to one knee, brought up the weapon, and fired.

A gaping hole exploded high on its shoulder. Dropping to the pavement with a scream, the tiger crashed into Pip, knocking her flat. Rough fur filled her nose and mouth. Muscles thrummed under the skin as the cat scrabbled for footing, trying to escape Fly pounding against its head with a stick.

Pip was steamrolled by the weight. Her world was orange and black—she was covered with it. The peppery stink of cat pressed into her nose, smothering her with fear. Arms pinned at her sides, she twisted against the pressure, lacerating her arm against rough pavement. The bright shock of pain cleared her head. The knife was still on her hip. Snapping off the guard, she fought to draw the blade. Pinned under the shifting weight of the tiger, she couldn't thrust with any force.

"Pip!" Fly screamed.

The tiger lurched to its feet, swiping at Fly. Pip jabbed the knife hard against the tiger's side, hooking the blade under its ribs.

The tiger flinched, jumping back faster than she'd thought an animal could move. Frantic to dislodge the blade, the cat snapped at the pearl handle, but couldn't reach it. With the knife buried deep in its side, the tiger flashed its teeth—all show and no fight. It limped into the woods on the far side of the road. Grass whispered in the breeze, covering the fading rustle of the injured tiger moving through the woods.

Fly wasted no time reloading the shotgun. Iris dropped to her knees and crawled across the blacktop, tucking the last shell into a pocket.

"Let's go!"

Pip didn't have the energy to respond. Her ribs burned with fire; they felt loose, torn from her sternum. The pain was intense, but she gathered Iris to her side.

"Hold my belt. It won't catch us off guard again," Fly said.

Their shuffled steps were nearly silent as they moved together, huddled for an entire muscle-cramping mile. Pip wheezed shallow breaths. The aching pain in her chest flared with each inhale. It wasn't until Iris hiss-whispered she saw a road sign hidden in the trees that their formation cautiously drifted apart. Relief brought hot tears to Pip's eyes when she read the name on the sign.

They'd found Bickett Street. A deep cramp trembled the muscles in her chest as she glanced down Cedar, sure she'd see the tiger striding with feral confidence just behind. Nothing was there. Only leaves blew on the abandoned road.

CHAPTER 33

They rounded the corner onto Bickett and Pip hugged Iris, inhaling the tangy smell of her sweaty head with relief. Fly tugged at the straps of Iris's pack and handed Pip a water bottle. Most of Pip's drink spilled down her front; she couldn't keep herself from shaking. Taking the water bottle, Fly steadied the back of Pip's head and helped her drink.

The tenderness of Fly's hand felt like a new kind of promise. They'd faced down the tiger together, neither of them breaking.

Iris stood in the shade, holding the shotgun. She watched them with traumatized eyes. "We didn't die?"

"Not today," Fly said.

Determined to leave the tiger far behind, Pip ignored the deep agony of her ribs and pushed herself into a jog. Fly stayed to the rear of their threesome, alternating between running hard and stopping to watch the forest for signs of the tiger. They exchanged the water bottle as they ran, taking drinks on the run, soaking their shirts with water spills and sweat.

Staggered by the mounting pain in her chest, Pip finally stopped and caught her breath.

Iris peeled her sweaty shirt away from her chest and flapped it. "Are you okay?"

Every breath was a knife in her lungs. Pip wheezed and lowered herself into the shade. "It's like I got hit by a car."

"A car with teeth," Fly grunted. She flopped next to Pip onto the shady roadside.

Digging into her pack, Iris found a one-use aid kit. It fit in the palm of her hand. She sat next to Pip. "I've got bandages."

Pip pressed hard against the pain in her ribs. A wet snap and the feeling of something tearing made her gasp. It felt like her chest was a knuckle that needed to crack. Sliding her hands along her ribs until she found a painfully irregular spot, Pip shoved against the lump. One of her ribs popped into place with a hollow thump. The pressure eased and she took a full breath. "He squashed me, but I didn't get cut."

"You're bleeding."

Blood seeped from the road rash she'd given herself when the tiger cheese-grated her against the pavement. Iris opened a small metallic package of antibiotic ointment and held it out.

"Thanks." Picking gravel out of the wound, Pip got most of the grit before smearing on the goo.

Iris took back the almost empty container and offered a granola bar in its place. Sticking the bar in her sweat-soaked jeans pocket, Pip stood on unsteady legs, scanning the edges of the forest, looking for the way forward. She couldn't find the brush-covered opening to Clare's.

When she'd drawn the map at Thistle Hill Orchard, Clare had described the brush cunningly piled to hide an old trail to her farm. Pip wiped her sweaty face and looked back the way they'd come. Their tiger-panicked run might have hurried them right past the hidden road. Hopefully the path they needed was somewhere ahead. She didn't fancy getting any closer to the wounded cat.

Pip was too tired to think. "Let's keep moving."

They hadn't walked far when Iris stopped and pointed a grimy finger at the right side of the road.

"What's that?"

Sprawled across most of the right lane were the skeletons of at least two people ripped from their clothes and scattered by scavengers. Deep furrows rent the bones—these people had died fighting. A few steps from Pip's feet, an arm held together with dry tendons curled around the delicate skull of an infant. A promise had been made to that child on the day it was born. A promise of love and protection. Pip forced herself to look at Iris and gagged on her ridiculous promise to protect the girl. What made her think she could ever save anyone? People died every day.

One more piece of Pip broke, crumbling the edges of the person she thought she was. She was so tired. "I don't want to see any more."

"Hey," Fly breathed.

Pip slid her numb hands into her pants pockets, looking from the tiny skull back to Iris. Fly was speaking into Iris's ear, walking her along, angling their path to the other side of the road.

"C'mon, Pip."

That woman—that mother—was dead on the road.

"Stop dicking around." Fly didn't pause in ushering Iris past the skeletons. She looked over her shoulder and shouted, "Hey! Get your ass moving, you fucking coward."

Pip grabbed the lifeline of Fly's insults and let them pull her along.

Heads together, Fly and Iris spoke in indistinct whispers while Pip lagged behind. The road wound deeper into the forest. When a bend in the road finally hid the carnage, Fly let Iris walk alone.

"I'd bet that's theirs." Fly pointed.

A pickup truck had plowed into a stand of trees nearby, snapping the hitch and flipping a compact camping trailer on its side. Doors on both sides of the truck were open. Leaves had blown into the cab, partially covering what remained of the driver.

Pip's knees felt weak; she couldn't take a deep breath. Lightheaded, she sank into pained confusion. Without adrenaline to keep her moving, she faltered.

"Pip?" Fly asked from far away. "You alright?"

She took a step, felt her ankle turn, and collapsed.

CHAPTER 34

She opened her eyes to an *Alice in Wonderland* view. A table thrust from the middle of a wall. Curtains hung from the ceiling bordering windows filled with blue sky. Fly and Iris sat on a wall that had become the floor, eating from single-serving boxes of fruity cereal. Neither of them looked in Pip's direction, and both were talking about the sideways stove halfway up the other wall.

Try as she might, Pip couldn't figure out where she was or how she'd gotten there. Her insides felt empty. Except for her chest. *That* was full of fire burning on ice.

Their whispering had woken her.

"Is she okay?" Iris's voice was soft on her ears.

"Shhh," Fly admonished. "She got squashed and couldn't get enough air. She fainted. Get back over here."

Pip rocked as Iris stood and moved farther away.

"Will she wake up?"

"When she's ready."

"But—"

"God. Do you ever stop talking?" A package crinkled. "How can you be hungry again? We just finished that cereal."

"Fly, can I ask you a question?"

Fly grunted. A heavy sigh blew through Pip's hair, tickling her scalp. "What?"

"What's your real name?"

"Fly *is* my real name."

"Come on. It has to be a nickname."

That tone, Pip thought. *I can hear Iris rolling her eyes from here.*

She watched the pair, squinting through her lashes. Iris rested against the wall. Fly perched on the end of an upturned bench.

"Your mother *did not* name you Fly," Iris argued.

"My mama," Fly said, "had a PhD. She was the smartest woman you'd ever meet. She was an entomologist. Know what that means?"

Iris shrugged.

"She studied bugs."

"Yuck."

Fly huffed a laugh. She played with her gold nose ring, twisting the thin band through the piercing. She'd lost her train of thought.

"Your mama..." Iris prompted.

"Named my big brother Cruz. After Santa Cruz, California. It's where she studied butterflies in graduate school."

Pip opened her eyes all the way and watched Fly nibble at one of her fingernails. She spit the nail out a broken window and looked pleased at Iris's disgusted expression.

"Big bro called me Butterfly. It stuck. Over the years the nickname kept getting shorter and shorter."

"Butterfly?" Iris clapped hands over her mouth, eyes crinkling with glee.

"You call me that again, and I'll..." Slashing the back of her thumb across her neck, Fly turned and noticed Pip watching.

Pip cleared her throat and coughed. "Where—"

"Inside the trailer." Iris gestured at the open door in what was now the ceiling. "We carried you in—"

"You know the part where I told you to shut up when she woke up?" Fly nudged Iris with her boot. "Now's that time."

This time Pip got to see the preteen eye roll—Iris *was* getting better at it.

Fly hopped down from her perch and sat on the floor. She touched Pip's forehead with the back of a cool hand. "You want some water?"

"Nah." Pip sat up. "How long was I out?"

"A while." Fly rolled her head around her neck, grunting at each pop and crackle. "Long enough for me to bandage your arm."

A neat bandage of white gauze wrapped around her arm from

the wrist to slightly below the elbow. She flexed her arm—the road rash made it stiff, but it didn't hurt. Pip leaned close enough that they could've kissed. Nose to nose with Fly, she breathed her unique dry-clay scent.

"Thanks."

Fly's gaze bounced from Pip's eyes to her lips and back. "Don't worry 'bout it."

Iris gave Pip two painkillers they'd found in the sideways bathroom. She swallowed them while testing her weight on her twisted ankle. It was sore, but strong. She could walk.

Iris and Fly repacked their bag with all the goodies they'd scrounged from the trailer. The two of them worked as a team. *Well, Iris is on the team,* Pip thought. Fly was more like the soccer coach who treated you like an idiot, but who you loved anyway.

Everyone was being careful with each other. The tiger had changed things, forged them into something new. Pip would die for either of them, and they knew it.

"Thank you for helping me."

"You would've done the same for us."

Fly put on Iris's loaded pack and reached for the open door in the ceiling. Grabbing the lip, she jumped, kicking her feet while pulling up. She disappeared for a moment, then lay down and held a hand out to Iris. "Let's go, kiddo."

Pip smiled. "Don't call her kiddo."

The worry on Iris's face melted. She took Fly's hand.

Back on the road, they walked with caution, keeping watch for the pile of brush at the end of Clare's road.

"Guys!" Iris shouted.

"Here we go again." Fly groaned.

Iris did a little dance of victory, pointing with jazz hands in the direction of a huge pile of brush. The ditch was crumbled and uneven, like someone had been in an accident and had run their car off the road. Pip fancied she saw hoofprints in the dry soil. Piles of branches woven into a gigantic maze of foliage completely hid a subtle track on the other side. They'd found the way to Clare's farm.

The hidden path had never been heavily traveled, and it wound a maddeningly random trail through the trees. Iris pointed each time Pip limped along the trail instead of cutting corners. She felt ridiculous weaving around trees like a dog weaving between agility poles. Regardless, she stayed on the track instead of cutting a more direct route. Her gut said if she strayed from the track, they'd lose the trail and never find their way.

Fly held up a hand; she'd taken the lead. On the side of the rough road, a circle with rusty spikes stuck out of the leaves. A sheep's head was staked in the middle.

"That's terrifying," Pip said. "Where the hell are we going?"

Fly wiped sweat off her forehead. She waved for Iris to make a wide path around the trap. "We should be careful, there could be more. How far from the road did she say the farm was?"

"She didn't." Pip unwrapped Iris's granola bar and ate it in four angry bites. "She said the whole journey was over twenty miles. That's it."

A dog barked in the distance. Barks cracked off trees twice more, echoing through the woods. Afraid to hope, Pip waved them onward.

Anticipation lent speed to their steps as Pip broke into a painful jog. At the edge of the woods, a road began. Iris stepped out of the trees onto a crushed-gravel drive. Fenced pastures on both sides were topped with shiny new barbed wire. Rolling fields dotted with flocks of sheep filled a clearing larger than several football fields.

The land sloped uphill with the road ending in a large barn and a house. Fly held her shotgun at the ready as they eased out of the wood's cover. Another bark caught their attention as a massive white dog burst from a nearby herd of grass-cropping sheep.

Pip grabbed a handful of rocks and Fly pushed Iris behind her as the dog cleared the fence in one easy jump. A cloud of dust flew into the air when it landed, kicking dirt into their eyes. The dog's red tongue lolled in the heat, and its barks hit like automatic gunfire. Answering yaps echoed from other fields as more dogs raced from the panicking herds of sheep. A piercing whistle quieted the dogs mid-bark.

Heart racing, Pip was stunned when the dog wheeled and ran up the road toward the house.

"Who whistled?" Fly panted.

In the confusion, she'd fumbled the shotgun. It lay at her feet in the dust. Pip thanked whatever gods were watching over them that it hadn't gone off.

The rest of the dogs melted into their flocks. Pip didn't really care where they went as long as Iris was safe from all the sharp teeth. "I don't think my heart can take any more scares today. You?"

Fly gestured in the direction of the house and started walking. Climbing the gentle grade, Iris paused to work a piece of wool out of the barbed-wire fence. After the day they'd had, seeing her so calm filled Pip with worry. She searched the grounds with empty eyes. Did the farm even belong to Clare? They might be in the wrong place—somewhere even more dangerous than Thistle Hill.

Speed walking toward the house and whatever answer waited there, Pip recognized the two mules with rabbity ears curiously pointing in their direction. She dropped to her knees in the middle of the road.

"Pip! Are you okay?" Iris rushed to her side.

Unable to halt the flood of emotion that washed tears from her eyes and blurred the approaching figure of a woman in overalls, Pip covered her face and sobbed. Iris's thin arms wrapped around her shoulders, holding her tight.

"Pip!" Clare called.

Pip stumbled into the older woman's arms. Dashing away relieved tears and trying on a sloppy, wet smile, she gasped, "You forgot to mention it was a thousand miles to get here!"

Wrinkles creased the corners of Clare's eyes as she guffawed. "I might have misjudged the distance a bit." Clare patted Iris's shoulder, pulling her into their hug. Looking over Iris's head, she reached a welcoming hand out to Fly.

Pip rushed to explain. "Fly couldn't stay at the farm—"

"Pip rescued me," Fly interrupted.

"She's saved our lives so many times," Pip said. "I couldn't leave her."

Clare sized up the fierce young woman who held a shotgun like a security blanket. Pip searched Clare's face for some sign of what she was thinking. Asking her to take on three people was an enormous burden. Trying to survive was hard enough without extra mouths depleting her stores. Even so, running a farm of this size had to require an enormous amount of work. Pip hoped uninvited help would be welcome help.

Clare's thoughtful silence dragged on. Fly patiently met Clare's gaze and waited. It felt like they were both taking a test.

"I wouldn't've been able to leave her behind either." Clare winked. She gestured at a neat farmhouse with solar panels covering the roof. "Come on up to the house."

Every window had a flower box overflowing with herbs and colorful flowers. Waving for them to follow, Clare turned toward the house. Fly fell into step beside her.

Pip doubled over as a cramp lanced her ribs. While her hands were on her knees, something flipped around her neck and buckled there with a metallic click. Dog tags jingled as she turned to face Iris. Pip brushed at the nubby fabric of Utah's collar.

"I gave it to you."

"You gave me a promise." Iris rolled the wool she'd collected between her hands into a thick strand of yarn. Her eyes were solemn until she grinned. "I don't need it anymore."

Pip felt like she was breaking inside and found she didn't mind.

Iris's expression was serious. "You can ruffle my hair if you want."

"Nah," Pip said playfully. "Maybe another time."

They linked arms and walked to the home's open door. The downstairs was one big room—part kitchen, part workroom—filled with piles of things left mid-project. Grease covered a card table holding a torn-apart engine. A few squashy-looking chairs and plastic flats filled with sprouting plants took up a corner near the windows. The rest of the room was filled with a pine table. A chorus of chicks peeped from a box nestled against a ticking woodstove, and the floor was covered with tracked-in dirt.

"Welcome to the farm." Clare handed Pip a slice of bread smeared with seedy jam.

Iris cooed over the chicks and plopped down next to the box. Pip lowered herself into a chair and took a nibble of the bread. It hurt to swallow, but she still moaned at the taste of sugary black-berries and fresh bread.

Clare poured a glass of water from a pitcher and pushed it across the table at Pip. "You three look like you've seen better days."

They glanced at each other; Fly pursed her lips. "We met your tiger."

"Pip protected us." Pride made Iris's face glow despite the dirt. "Its stomach was full of deer. That's the only reason we didn't die."

Fly snorted and pantomimed the three of them walking in lock-step from the full-to-bursting tiger. Sitting around the table and mocking the dreadful fear they'd shared filled Pip with a sense of belonging she'd never experienced before. She wanted the mo-ment to last forever.

When Fly excused herself from the table with directions to the outhouse, Clare waited until she was gone and scooted closer to Pip. Shooting a cautious look at Iris, she asked cryptically, "What happened?"

It was clear Clare knew something she didn't. Unwilling to ruin the peaceful moment, Pip mulled over how to explain their exit from Thistle Hill. In the uncomfortably silent room, Iris held up a protesting fluffy ball of feathers. The chick struggled wildly for a second, calming when Iris stroked the yellow fuzz on its head. Reaching across the space between them, Pip slid her fingers into Iris's hair and ruffled the top into a crazy blackbird's nest.

"They have no idea where we are." Pip dodged Iris's miffed slap at her knees over the hair mussing, and then she sobered. She would always carry the memory of the auto yard and what they'd done. "Anyone who might've followed us, can't."

"Hmm." Clare looked thoughtful. She relaxed into her chair and buttered another slice of bread.

The oddly comforting reek of domestic animals wafted in as Fly returned to the kitchen.

"Fucking roosters," she announced, displaying a wrist covered with fresh lacerations.

Clare grumbled and picked up a hatchet from where it leaned next to the woodstove. "Not for long."

"What's the ax for?" Iris asked.

"Can't have people getting flogged by roosters," Clare said as she and Fly left the kitchen.

The screen door banged against the frame and stuck open. A rough-looking barn cat slithered inside. Eyes on the cardboard box full of chicks, it hugged the wall and stalked toward the stove. Pip watched the drooling cat. She'd seen this dance before. Eat or be eaten, attack or defend. Even on a good day, there were gonna be battles. Untying a boot and sliding it loose, she winced at the tightness of her swollen ankle and waited for the cat to come closer.

Iris hadn't noticed the cat; she still wanted an answer. "Pip. What's the ax for?"

At the sound of her voice, the cat froze, slitting its eyes in agitation at the human curled next to its prey. Pip flicked the boot and cheered when it bounced off the cat's side. Claws scrabbling for traction and tail fluffed into a frightened bottle brush, the tomcat crashed onto the porch and streaked for the barn.

Iris clucked her tongue at the retreating cat and picked up another chick. "The ax?"

Hopping across the kitchen to keep her sock off the dirt-strewn floor, Pip slid her foot back into the boot.

"The ax is for the roosters who ripped up Fly's arm. And I'd bet we're having them for dinner."

Iris's mouth dropped open in surprise. She shot a guilty look at the chicks cheeping for her attention. "I'm a monster."

"Ha!" Pip laughed. "What do you mean?"

"I've always wanted to try fried chicken."

CHAPTER 35

It wasn't long before Clare returned holding two headless roosters by limp feet. Iris set down the chick she was cuddling and offered to help Clare pluck.

"Pluck?" Fly looked green at the prospect of watching Iris tug all the feathers out of a carcass. "I've had enough of dead things to last me a lifetime."

"Lucky for you, this young lady has already volunteered." Clare handed a dead rooster to Iris and gestured for her to go out the back door.

She nodded at Pip. "Why don't you two take a walk?"

Pip followed Fly out the front door into the late-afternoon sunshine, stopped to pick a sprig of parsley from a nearby flower box, and paused in surprise. She hadn't noticed the thirty or so raised beds on the southern side of the house. Every single one was full of growing vegetables. Pip marveled at the bounty of food to come and found herself smiling.

"There's more in the back," Fly said. "At least a hundred chickens too. Clare said her husband saw the end coming and prepped everything."

"She isn't worried about four of us surviving here."

Fly dabbed at the bloody scratches on her wrist. "Not at all."

"We should go back in and clean those."

"Let's give 'em a minute," Fly muttered.

They walked along the top end of one of the sheep pastures. This time the dogs only watched and didn't bark. Pip found herself wanting to take Fly by the hand, to feel the rough skin of her palm against her own. She didn't dare. Did she?

Fly paused by a steel water trough and tossed in a pebble. "Make a wish." Her eyes bounced to Pip's lips for a fraction of a second.

Does she want to kiss me? Pip's heart soared and crashed at the thought. Her insides were a roller coaster. Pip watched Fly toss a few more tiny rocks into the trough and considered the strong line of muscle from Fly's neck to where it disappeared into her shirt. It felt like she was on the verge of something. Something a little like love.

Fly hopped up on the railing.

"It wasn't the tiger." Fly sounded grim, like she expected Pip to argue.

"What do you mean?"

Fly inhaled and held her breath for a long moment. Her words finally came out in a rush. "What your guy saw. I think it was me."

"Whistler," Pip said. "His name was Whistler."

She studied the lovely lines of Fly's cheekbones for a moment and had to look away. "Thousands of butterflies. He said they collect in groves together for the winter, hanging from trees like strange leaves."

"I know."

"So you think Whistler saw you just because your brother called you Butterfly? That's—"

"Heard that, did you?"

The snark was back. Pip held up her hands in truce. Fly caught one of Pip's hands and rubbed the palm with her rough thumb. It felt like an apology.

"My mother named me after her favorite butterfly," Fly snapped. "Look at me, do I look like a fuckin' butterfly to you?"

"You swear too much." Pip grinned.

Fly flipped Pip off with her free hand. "You aren't funny."

They were getting off track, and Pip felt a little drunk on the smell of Fly's skin. She took a step, closing the distance between them. "What about the tiger? It *was* black and orange."

"Nope. That's not it at all." Fly reached to pull Pip close, wrapping her legs tight around her hips and resting her head on Pip's shoulder. Pip thought her heart would burst. It was like being hugged by a lightning bolt. She sank into the feeling and hoped it wouldn't end.

Fly spoke softly, keeping her words between them. "That's what I've been trying to tell you. It's me. It's *my* name—I'm Monarch."

"We're done!" Iris shouted from the covered front porch. She set a sagging plastic bag on the top step and went back inside.

Fly dropped her legs, resting them against Pip's sides. The pressure hurt her ribs, but she didn't ask her to move. They stared at each other.

"Your name is Monarch?" Pip couldn't believe her luck. Whistler *had* seen everything. She wanted to sink into Fly and never leave.

"*Come on!* You're taking forever!" Iris shouted from the porch.

"We should—"

"Clean my arm," Fly finished.

They walked back to the house holding hands.

The bag on the porch was filled with a gross blend of feathers and what looked like guts. Pip went inside wondering why Clare hadn't just thrown them away.

"Did you see the tiger bait?" Iris asked. Her sleeves were rolled up and she was rubbing a mix of flour and spices into chicken pieces.

"Tiger what now?" Fly asked. She sat at the kitchen table next to a small pile of first aid supplies Clare had put out.

"Didn't you see my traps walking in here?" Clare said.

"Actually, we did." The thought of the sheep's head made Pip's stomach turn. The dead eyes watching them. *Gross.*

"Be careful, they're all around the property. If your shotgun wounds don't kill him, the next time that stripy bugger comes looking for an easy sheep meal"—she clapped her hands together—"we'll get him."

Fly caught the sad look on Pip's face and poked her in the arm. "Don't you go feelin' sorry for that beast. He could've eaten us today."

Clare placed the first piece of chicken into the hot oil, and the savory sound of crackling filled the room. Pip took over Fly's attempt to clean the rooster scratches and bent to the job of getting every speck of grit out of the lacerations. Fly was sweating by the time she was done. Pip placed the last bit of tape on the clean bandage and Fly caught her hand.

Clare cleared her throat. "Iris, would you mind going upstairs and making the beds?"

Iris angrily surveyed the kitchen. "You just want to talk without me. Again."

"Beat it." Fly smiled.

Clare waited until the sound of Iris's feet pounding on the stairs faded, and then she set down the fork she'd been using to turn the chicken. "I visited Thistle Hill yesterday."

Pip was instantly cold.

"Granville and two of his men took the truck. The whole place was in an uproar. Heather used the opportunity to throw out the rest of his men. They didn't want to go. It looks like a war zone. What did you do?"

The children, was all Pip could think. She saw little Stella dropping her clothespins in the grass and felt sick.

"Granville tracked us down after we left. We killed him," Fly said.

Clare took her time sitting down in a chair.

"Is Heather—are the kids—" Pip was almost too afraid to ask.

"Ben rallied the others when Granville's men fought back. Jack stole a few of their guns. And Ben's bride—"

"Alison," Pip interrupted.

"Alison's been shooting targets since she was a tot. Turns out men aren't much different."

"Lord," Fly breathed.

Clare pursed her lips and got up to flip the chicken pieces over. "You did them a favor by getting rid of Granville. That man was cancer."

"She's not wrong," Fly said.

Pip flinched and felt the hot reek of Granville's breath on her face. She closed her eyes and saw him falling on his side. "But Iris—"

Iris slipped into the kitchen with a sigh. "You told her I killed Granville?"

Pain and guilt lanced Pip from all sides. "She did it to protect me."

Stillness filled the kitchen as each of them reckoned with the consequences. It was Clare that finally placed a warm hand on Pip's shoulder. "Of course she did. That's what family does."

Family. Pip reached out and Iris ran into her arms. Resting her chin on the top of Iris's head, Pip caught the wide smile on Fly's face and answered it with one of her own. It felt impossibly good.

Clare set them to work picking early lettuce and pumping water from the well to drink. It wasn't long before Fly and Pip were grinning at Iris complaining she was so hungry she thought she might die. Clare dished up plates of food and sent them out to the porch to eat.

Four sets of teeth crunching through crispy, fried layers of flour and chicken skin sounded like heaven to Pip. Sitting on a porch rail, she crouched over a metal camp plate and held the steaming ends of a slightly stringy drumstick. Taking another bite, she chomped with pleasure.

Fly bent over her plate with the same eagerness. A few stray chicken feathers were stuck in the curly tangle of her short hair and flopped with every bite. Iris must have put them there when Fly wasn't looking. Pip opened her mouth to say something, but Iris shook her head and smothered a grin. Fly slitted her eyes playfully; she knew something was up.

Clare belched with meaty satisfaction and surreptitiously loosened her belt. "'Scuse me."

The feathers on top of Fly's head fluttered like a small bird. Everyone chuckled.

"What?" she grunted.

Pip set down her empty plate, wiping her greasy hands along the sides of her pants before getting up. Placing a hand on Fly's muscular shoulder, she carefully picked out each feather, then blew them off her palm.

"Pip!" Iris groaned.

Fly snorted at the tiny storm of feathers and covered Pip's hand with her own. Heat from their joined hands traveled up Pip's arm. She froze, locked in place with affection. Clare held up her glass, toasting them. A pleased smile wreathed Iris's face as she took her plate and went inside.

Pip studied Fly's gold nose ring and the clever gap between her two front teeth. The grotesque swelling of her injured eye had faded a bit too. A maroon bruise tinged with green highlights covered almost the entire side of her face. It must have hurt terribly.

Iris burst out the screen door with a slam. She held the violin case. She opened it on the table and looked triumphant.

"It isn't broken." She plucked a string, wincing at the sour note. "Needs tuning."

Holding the violin under her chin, Iris plucked the strings with two fingers while deftly adjusting tuning knobs. Finding correct pitches by ear, she gradually settled the instrument into a sweeter sound. She laid the violin back in the case and tightened the bow string.

"Where'd you find that?" Clare asked.

Tucking the chin rest tight to her neck, Iris answered while making final adjustments. "I grabbed it when I went back for my things. Heather had it in her room."

"Crafty," Clare said with approval.

The bow flicked over strings in a sliding scale of notes that ended with a flourish. Iris twisted one knob a fraction, then rested the bow on the strings with a bold smile.

"What should I play?"

Pip's heart skipped at the memory of Iris huddled over the violin case in the music store. It was Whistler who'd managed to draw her out. Seeing Iris standing proud and strong made Pip miss the old man even more. He'd never have the chance to see Iris bloom.

"I hate classical music," Fly griped.

"Bah," Pip sighed. She tucked sadness away for another time and sat on the porch railing with her back to the setting sun. "Play that train-sounding song like you did before."

Iris looked confused. "Train song?"

"Yeah, the one you played in the music store. Only this time, kiddo, play it as loud as you like."

"Don't call me kiddo," Iris said with a shy grin.

Two plucks on a metal string and Iris was off, chasing the rapid tempo of a fiddle tune. Clare jumped to her feet, clapped her hands, and snatched Fly right out of her chair. They spun around the table, square-dancing the length of the porch. Fly took charge, swinging Clare around by the waist, twirling the older woman a few times before dipping her.

Iris performed a run over the strings of her fiddle, ending the song with a flourish.

Pip sank into the porch swing and gestured for Iris to join her. Iris sat on the cushioned seat, tucked her feet under her, and rested the fiddle on her lap.

"That was spectacular."

A fleeting smile disappeared under the weight of a frown. "D'ya think Whistler would've liked it?"

Pip felt his dog tag resting safe against her chest. "He would've loved it."

Iris leaned her head on Pip's shoulder. The weight put pressure on her injured ribs. It hurt, but Pip didn't mind at all. Fly sat on her other side, taking her hand and holding it in her lap. Settled in the warmth between them, Pip relaxed against the puffy seat cushion with a sigh.

"What's wrong?" Iris asked.

"Nothing."

"You sure?"

Sheep bleated in the fields, their white fleece shining in the twilight. The farm was still, waiting for night. Pip plucked a fiddle string and placed her fingers against the side of the instrument. The clear note vibrated the thin wood.

"I've never been better." Not even the dark could hide Pip's wide smile.

She'd kept her promise.

AUTHOR'S NOTE

I began the journey of researching and writing *The Names We Take* because I saw in my youngest child a yearning to be seen in YA fiction. As they explored their own identity, I thought that this story might help them understand that I could accept, love, and celebrate them.

As a bisexual, cisgender woman, my hope in forming a character like Pip was to capture some of the experience of being both bisexual and intersex. I also wanted to give readers the opportunity to explore a character who didn't need to be rescued, but instead had knowledge of their own power.

Each person's journey of identity is different and never ending. I've spent years exploring my own gender identity and sexual orientation. I welcome the possibility of criticism and frank discussions about the book because we cannot do better until we know better, and there is always so much more to know.

While the manuscript has gone through several authenticity reads, I am aware that no community, gender identity, or sexual orientation is a monolith. Pip's story is fictional and will never reflect everyone's experiences. What is most important to me is the possibility that this book could be a positive contribution to conversations about how we represent individuals like Pip who embody multiple identities.

I'm delighted that you found this story, and I hope with all my heart that you discover some of yourself in Pip's adventures.

RESOURCES

Teen Health Source: Identifying as Lesbian, Gay, Bisexual, or Queer.
http://teenhealthsource.com/giso/i-think-im-lesbian-gay-or-bi/

RAINN: National Sexual Assault Hotline.
Safe and confidential 800.656.HOPE (4673)

ACKNOWLEDGMENTS

This journey started with my parents' bookshelf. Nothing was off limits, and I devoured all the words. Mom and Dad, I'm sorry for all the family trips where the only thing you saw was the top of my head as I turned pages. Words can't express how grateful I am for all your encouragement and support. The two of you started me on the journey to becoming the writer, reader, and person that I am today.

A giant bear hug for my intrepid first readers. Suzie Henning, you found the threads that didn't fit and helped me clip them away, shaping that horrible draft. Lani Caraway, this story would be nowhere without you calling bullshit every time I tried to cut corners. And last, but never least, thank you to Charles R. Kerr, my father-in-law and punctuation wrangler. You three have my solemn promise: call anytime, day or night, and I'll be there.

A pile of thanks goes to the Ooligan publisher, Abbey Gaterud, and the entire team at Ooligan Press. To the unstoppable acquisitions teams who ran the show when I submitted to Ooligan— Alyssa Schaffer, Joanna Szabo, Taylor Thompson, and Ari Mathae— thank you for picking me up out of the slush pile and insisting somebody had to die. I couldn't say no to that.

The Names We Take would be nowhere without its two project managers, Kelly Hogan and Hazel Wright. I owe you both for handling every late-night—or ridiculously early—panicked email with grace.

The Ooligan managing editors, Madison Schultz and Melinda Crouchley, and their teams are the only reason this book isn't full of dangling participles, misplaced commas, and ass-backward sentences. Thank you all for polishing this manuscript.

Des Hewson, the cover is beautiful. You saw inside the story and plucked out the perfect image.

Meagan Macvie, thank you for picking up the phone to talk me off a ledge. Your mentorship is golden.

To all my writing friends in the Summer Fantasy Writers Group—Thom Caraway, Ben Cartwright, Jeremy TeGrotenhuis, Caitlin Wheeler, Cail Magnum, Joseph Edwin Haeger, and Zach Caraway—you came along at the end of this journey, but I'm so grateful for each and every one of you.

I would be nothing without my cheer squad. You sent encouraging texts that made me cry (I'm looking at you, Amy Barton). Nicole Davis and Kathleen Moore graciously listened to me ramble about my writing journey way too much. When I said, "Screw progress, everything is hard," you both sweetly told me to suck it up. My coffee and dinner buddies—Lisa Jonckers, Theresa Bolin-Jones, and Gabi Eckley—you gals always ask the right questions. Y'all are my six voices of reason, and I love you for that so, so much.

To my favorite eldest child, Anson: you gave me the soundtrack for this book—the music that made me feel all the feels. You've also earned a lifetime supply of homemade mac and cheese for helping me keep my weapons and ammunition straight. Hashing out a fight scene with you is way more fun than it should be. Thanks for making me watch way too much YouTube.

To my favorite youngest child, Dane: you read and reread my terrible early drafts and fought valiantly for the best lines and the most honest prose. You are the reason I started writing this story.

Chas. Without you, none of this is possible. Thank you from the bottom of my writerly soul for my room with a view.

ABOUT THE AUTHOR

Trace Kerr is a lifelong Pacific Northwesterner who never uses an umbrella when it rains. When she's not prowling the shelves of indie bookstores in Spokane, she co-hosts the Brain Junk podcast and writes books about undaunted queer teens and magic. *The Names We Take* is her first novel.

Follow her on Twitter at @teakerr or online at: www.TraceKerr.com.

OOLIGAN PRESS

Ooligan Press is a student-run publishing house rooted in the rich literary culture of the Pacific Northwest. Founded in 2001 as part of Portland State University's Department of English, Ooligan is dedicated to the art and craft of publishing. Students pursuing master's degrees in book publishing staff the press in an apprenticeship program under the guidance of a core faculty of publishing professionals.

Project Managers
Kelly Hogan
Hazel Wright

Acquisitions
Des Hewson
Ari Mathae
Taylor Thompson
Kimberly Scofield

Design
Denise
  Morales Soto

Marketing
Sydney Kiest
Sydnee Chesley

Digital
Megan Crayne

Social Media
Faith Muñoz

Editing
Melinda Crouchley
Madison Schultz
Olivia Rollins

Book Production
Callie Brown
Andre Cole
Kendra Ferguson
Anastacia Ferry
Selena Harris
Tia Hilts

Stephen Hyde
Elle Klock
Chris Leal
Jennifer Ladwig
Alix Martinez
Bayley McComb
Laura Mills
Vivian Ngyuen
Ruth Robertson
Corey Talbot
Siri Vegulla
Monique Vieu
Gina Walter
Xian Wang
Desiree Wilson
Emma Wolf
Erica Wright
Courtney Young

COLOPHON

The Names We Take is set in Chaparral Pro and Oswald. Designed by Carol Twombly for Adobe, Chaparral Pro is a hybrid slab serif that is accessible, open, and light. Oswald, designed by Vernon Adams for Google, is a condensed sans serif originally designed to better fit the pixel grids of digital screens.